The
Bridesmaid's
Dilemma

Karen King

Published by Accent Press Ltd 2018

ISBN 9781786150967
eISBN 9781786150707

Accent Press Ltd
Octavo House
West Bute Street
Cardiff
CF10 5JL

Printed and bound in Great Britain by Clays Ltd, Elcograf S.p.A.

For my daughters, Julie, Michelle, Lucie and Naomi.
I am so proud of you all.

Chapter One

Jess stretched out on the sunbed, factor fifteen and the parasol protecting her already golden skin from the heat of the afternoon sun. It was lovely to finally have the chance to relax by the pool. As usual, the morning had been full-on. She and Libby – lounging on the sunbed next to her – were in charge of the Fitness Classes and had spent two hours jumping, bending, stretching, and jogging on the spot with a group of holidaymakers. Being a holiday rep with *Time of Your Life Holidays* was fun but exhausting.

'This is heaven. I could lie here all day.'

'Me too. This week's been so hectic. It's going to be non-stop now the schools have broken up.' Libby sighed. 'Lucky you, having next weekend off. I wouldn't mind flying back home for a few days.'

'I'd like it a lot more if I didn't have to be chief bridesmaid at Charlotte's wedding,' Jess replied. 'That's going to be a barrel of fun – *not*.'

Her first reaction when her cousin Charlotte had asked her to be chief bridesmaid was astonishment – she and Charlotte had never got on and usually tried to avoid each other.

Her second reaction had been panic. She didn't do weddings, or frothy dresses, and she knew that Charlotte, with her obsession for perfection, would be the bridezilla from hell. She couldn't refuse though, not when she knew how much it meant to her mum. And so, Jess had reluctantly agreed, even though she suspected that she'd only been asked because Charlotte had no sisters and precious few friends – even the other two bridesmaids were sisters of her fiancé, Russell.

'It might not be that bad. And I bet the best man is a hunk. You know what they say about the chief bridesmaid and best man,' Libby teased. 'It's compulsory for them to have a dance together and a few kisses – at the very least.' She grinned at Jess and cocked her head to one side. 'What's her fella like?'

'No idea, never met him. I haven't seen Charlotte for years. All I know is that his name's Russell and his work involves something to do with exports.'

'I can't believe your cousin doesn't have a Facebook page. We could have a nose then, see what this Russell is like.'

'Charlotte "doesn't approve of society's obsession with social media."' Jess made finger quotes as she said the words. It would have been a lot easier to keep in touch with Charlotte if she was on Facebook – and if she was

2

less of a nightmare person – but as it was, wedding-related messages were coming solely through email.

'She sounds a right barrel of laughs. So, you've no idea who the best man is?'

'Mum said he's an old school friend of Russell's. I expect he'll be very staid and boring. Russell will be, too. Charlotte's boyfriends always are.' She'd met a couple of Charlotte's previous boyfriends and hadn't been impressed. One of them, a sleaze-ball called Simon, had taken a shine to Jess and become a bit of a stalker. 'Which reminds me, I've still got some stuff to get before I leave, new shoes for a start. I won't have time to buy any when I land.'

'Isn't your cousin providing the shoes?' Libby asked her. 'I thought she had everything planned.'

'She's got my bridesmaid's shoes – they're quite pretty, not the sort of thing I'd normally wear, though. Look…' Jess fished in the beach bag beside her sunbed, took out her phone and slid to photos. Selecting the wedding folder she'd created, she zoomed in on the picture of the shoes Charlotte had sent over to her. Gold, strappy, high-heeled sandals decorated with tiny crystals.

'They're gorge. But yeah, not your usual style,' Libby agreed. 'Let's take a look at your dress again.'

Jess swiped to the picture of the bridesmaid's dress; whimsical, strapless, lemon chiffon with a floaty skirt that

3

draped up above her knees at the front, but trailed delicately down the backs of her legs, brushing behind her ankles. Pretty and elegantly simple.

'It's gorgeous. What an unusual colour, it'll suit you. Are all the bridesmaids' dresses this colour?' Libby leaned over to get a closer look at the photo.

'Yes, we're all wearing the same dress. Charlotte said she thought pastel colours were kinder for "older" bridesmaids.' Jess wrinkled her nose. Although Charlotte was only two years younger than her she took a delight in pointing out that, at almost thirty, Jess was the eldest of the three bridesmaids. 'It is a lovely dress, isn't it? I hope it fits.' She'd been relieved Charlotte had gone for such a beautifully cut, classic style. Knowing how over-the-top her snooty cousin could be, she'd been dreading having to wear a princess gown of frills and lace.

'Pity you couldn't fly over for a fitting,' Libby said.

'No chance of that. You know what Ziggy's like. It's a wonder he's given me time off to go to the wedding, Charlotte didn't give me much notice.' Charlotte had only emailed asking her to be chief bridesmaid a couple of months ago, having got Jess's email address off her mum, and it had taken all Jess's powers of persuasion to talk Ziggy into allowing her four days off in the middle of the holiday season so that she could attend the wedding. She didn't dare ask him for an additional weekend beforehand to fly over for a dress fitting and wedding rehearsal. He'd have had a mega-fit. Not that she minded not being able to go. The flights would have cost her a few hundred pounds this time of year, and the less time she spent with Charlotte, the better. So, she'd sent her dress and shoe size and left her cousin to get whatever she thought was best – crossing her fingers she wouldn't choose anything too ghastly.

'You're going to look totally stunning in that dress and those shoes.'

'I hope so. Not too stunning, of course, can't outshine the bride!' Jess fingered a lock of her long red hair. 'Do you know Charlotte and Aunt Jean actually wanted me to dye my hair brown or black so it,' she made quote marks with her fingers again '"wouldn't dominate the photographs."'

Libby shot her an amused look. 'What a cheek. Yeah, your hair is a bit... bright... but it suits you. I can't imagine it any other colour.'

Neither could Jess. She'd always been confident and – as her mother often said – stubborn – so her reaction to the High School playground teasing of her naturally ginger hair was to dye it traffic light red one afternoon when her mother was out. It got her grounded for a week, but the bullies soon shut up, in fact some of them even tried to imitate her, much to Jess's delight. She had kept it red ever since, sometimes alternating the shades - tomato bright for the summer, more of a berry colour in the winter. She loved her hair and had no intention of dying it a boring black, especially for her spoilt cousin's wedding.

'I wish I could see you all dolled up as a bridesmaid,' Libby said. 'Make sure you take plenty of pictures.'

'I wish you could come with me. I'm dreading it. Aunt Jean and Charlotte will have everything planned down to the last detail, I'll be terrified of saying or doing the wrong thing. And of course, it'll be totally boring.'

Libby grinned. 'I can't imagine you being terrified of anyone! You don't give a damn what anyone thinks!'

'*I* don't, but Mum does. She'll be devastated if I do anything to upset them. She's made up that I've been asked to be chief bridesmaid, so I'll have to be on my best behaviour.' Jess returned her attention to her phone and swiped onto the next photo. 'Anyway, here's Charlotte's wedding dress, she sent it to me last night.' A frothy white creation of lace, satin, and net filled her screen. Charlotte's madly expensive designer dress was a big secret and not to be revealed until her wedding day, but as Jess was chief bridesmaid – and more to the point, Charlotte couldn't resist boasting – she'd agreed to send her a photo, swearing her to secrecy first. Jess had never seen a dress like it. It was so *Big Fat Gypsy Wedding*.

6

'Wow! Talk about a meringue!' Libby exclaimed. She leaned over and panned out the photo with her fingers. 'That must have cost a fortune.'

'Only the best for precious Charlotte,' Jess said lightly. She'd decided long ago not to let Charlotte or Aunt Jean get to her. The only child of doting parents who thought they would never get their dream of a family of their own, Charlotte was cossetted and spoilt. Anything she wanted, she got. Whereas Jess and her two older brothers, Ned and Jake, had learnt early on that life didn't revolve around them and they had to make do. Their father had walked out when Jess was only a toddler, leaving behind a trail of debts and a falling-down house. Jess's mum had worked all the hours she could, both as a child-minder and at the local supermarket, to pay off the debts, do up the house and feed them all, and as soon as they were old enough, Jess and her brothers had got jobs, too. Jess was loved, but there was no time or money for spoiling.

'Never mind, it'll all be over with next week. And it'll be lovely for you to see your family again,' Libby told her, leaning back on the sun lounger. 'What type of shoes are you looking for?'

'Something dressy to wear over the weekend. Charlotte's booked me in at the hotel overnight and the other two bridesmaids are staying there too, so we'll be having a few drinks.' Jess shoved her phone in her beach bag, got up, and slung it over her shoulder. 'I'd better be off now. See you later.' She paused. 'I don't suppose you fancy coming?' It'd be good to have some company, although, knowing Libby, she'd try to persuade her to buy something outrageous.

'Do you mind if I don't? I just fancy lying here and sunbathing for a bit. I'm feeling lazy.'

'No probs. See you later.'

Jess changed into a pair of frayed denim shorts and a yellow T-shirt, smoothed on some more sun cream, slipped on her sunglasses and a pair of flip flops, and headed off to the main area of town where the bigger shops were. It was teeming with holidaymakers as usual. She recognised a couple of hotel guests and waved at them. This was the first time she'd worked in Majorca, and she was loving it. It was a pretty island, and thankfully she was working at a hotel on the quieter side. Libby had complained, preferring to work over in the livelier resort of Magaluf, but Jess didn't share her younger friend's enthusiasm for such a wild social life. She'd gone through all that 'dancing until dawn, grabbing two hours sleep then getting up and working again' thing, and now liked to be in bed by one at the latest if she was working the next day. The reps were a great bunch and

Ziggy wasn't a bad boss, although he could be a bit of a slave driver.

'Ah, Jessica!' Damián said, coming out of the jewellers where he worked. 'How are you?'

They chatted for a while. Damián and his wife, Marta, were good friends to Jess. She had already told him about the wedding, so now she showed him the photo of her bridesmaid's dress.

'You'll look *maravilloso,*' he said. 'I bet the best man won't be able to keep his eyes off you.'

'You're as bad as Libby! I've told her, the best man will probably be a total bore and I'll spend the entire day trying to avoid him.'

Damián leaned over and kissed her on both cheeks.

'Enjoy your shopping. Maybe we will see you and Libby later, at Aquarius? *Si?*'

Aquarius was the local night club, a favourite of the reps who often dropped in for an hour or so after finishing work, especially if they weren't on early morning duty. Jess and Libby were part of the evening animation team, so were off duty until two tomorrow afternoon – but then it was non-stop until midnight.

'I'll be there,' she said. '*Hasta luego!*'

She waved and set off on her way.

It didn't take Jess long to find the shoes she wanted in her favourite shoe boutique in the middle of the town.

Royal blue suede with skyscraper heels, they were perfect and would look good with either jeans or a dress. True, they were a bit more than she had wanted to pay, but she couldn't resist them. She picked up the other couple of odds and ends she needed then set off back home, taking the beachfront route so she could paddle barefoot along the sea shore.

What a glorious day.

She wished she could spend the afternoon sunbathing on the beach like the scores of holidaymakers. Still, she had the whole day off on Sunday and could enjoy the sunshine then.

Libby was still lounging by the pool, and had been joined by Kurt and Charlie, two other reps, when Jess returned.

'Did you get your shoes?' she asked.

Jess opened the bag and took them out.

'What do think?' she replied, holding them up.

Whistles of appreciation greeted her.

'Sexy!' Kurt said appreciatively.

'They're fantastic,' Libby told her. 'They look just like Louboutins.' She picked up her phone and jabbed at a couple of keys. 'Look.' She held up the screen so Jess could see. She'd got up the Louboutin website and there were a pair of blue shoes almost identical to the ones Jess had just bought – except for the trademark red soles.

'I wish! I can just imagine Charlotte's face if I turned up in a pair of Loubs,' Jess said.

Libby grinned mischievously. 'Why don't you paint the soles red? They'll look just like Loubs then. Nail varnish will do the trick,' she added, as if she'd tried it. Knowing Libby, she probably had.

'Classic. I think I will,' said Jess. 'If I don't let Charlotte get too close a look at them even she might be fooled.' She chuckled at the thought of her snooty cousin's reaction if she turned up in a pair of Louboutins.

She stood chatting for a while, then left to put her things away. As she walked through reception she saw Manuel remonstrating with a group of men, all dressed identically in jeans and black T-shirts. She paused and looked over as a fair-haired man in the group raised his voice.

'We're booked in. You can't send us away,' the man said angrily. 'This is my stag do.'

'Exactly, and this is a family hotel. We don't allow stag parties to stay here. It is against our policy. It's written quite clearly on our website.'

'That's ridiculous,' the man protested. 'If there was a problem you should have told my fiancée when she booked the room.'

'A junior member of our staff dealt with the booking and didn't realise it was for a stag party. As I said, it's stated quite clearly on our website that we don't accept bookings for hen or stag parties.' Manuel swung the screen around to show them the homepage where Jess knew the policy was written. She guessed it was Elena who had taken the booking, she was the newest member of staff.

'You mean we've paid to stay here but you're not going to let us?' another of the group demanded.

'Rules are rules,' Manuel said. 'We will refund your money, of course, so you can book in somewhere else. This is a family hotel. We can't have groups of drunken men coming home late from nightclubs disturbing everyone.'

'Charming...!' One of the other men joined in but Manuel cut him short.

'Sir, you are over here on a stag party so I presume you don't intend to spend the entire weekend lounging by the pool and watching the hotel entertainment? In fact, it is quite obvious that you have all had a few drinks during the flight over here.'

Jess couldn't help feeling sorry for the guys but knew that there was no way Manuel would let them all stay here. The hotel prided itself on its reputation for providing for families. She carried on over to the lift.

'Surely there eez something you can do? We will be no trouble. And we need somewhere to stay.' At the sound of the French accent Jess turned back and looked over. The man had his back to her, but there was something about that unruly dark hair that curled at the back of his neck and the deep, sexy voice that made her walk over to the desk to see if she could help.

Chapter Two

'Look, I know it's disappointing, guys, but Manuel is right, it is hotel policy not to allow stag or hen party groups to stay, so he's only doing his job,' Jess said as she joined them. 'I'm one of the reps here - let's see if we can sort something out, after all, you made the booking in good faith.' She turned to Manuel. 'Perhaps two of them can stay at our sister hotel next door and the other two over the road, Manuel? Could you arrange that? Do they both have a room spare?'

Manuel frowned. 'It's very irregular, Jess.'

'What? Stay at different hotels?' The groom-to-be turned towards her and she noticed the name Ross printed in white on the front of his T-shirt in typical stag do tradition. 'This is my stag do. We're all meant to be holidaying together.'

'I know, but I'm afraid that it's a policy of all three local hotels not to accept a booking for single sex groups,' Jess explained. 'Not that they're likely to have three empty rooms at this time of year anyway. You'll find that most of the hotels will only have the odd room spare – if any at all.'

'Some stag do *this* will be,' Ross grumbled.

'You won't be that far from each other, you can use all three of the hotels' facilities and can easily meet up,' Jess told him. 'I know it isn't perfect but it's not too bad, surely? If you're anything like the stag parties I've seen, you'll only be in your rooms to crash out.'

She could feel the French guy's eyes on her so flashed him a smile hoping to get him on side. He smiled back. Nice.

'That sounds a veree good idea. Doesn't it, Ross?' Good, she'd convinced – she looked at the name on his T-shirt – Eddie – not a very French sounding name, but it suited him. Let's hope he could persuade the others. She was pretty sure Manuel would agree. The hotel was partly at fault, after all, for not checking although Manuel would hate the fact that she was the one who suggested an alternative, not him.

Ross didn't look too happy. 'We are all booked to stay here. It won't be as much fun if we're split up,' he protested.

'Well that is out of the question. I've told you it's against our hotel policy.' Manuel crossed his arms firmly.

'Come on mate, it'll be fine. The other hotels are minutes away,' said another man – Tony, according to his T-shirt.

15

'Yeah, like the lass said, we only need our rooms to crash out.' This was from Matt who spoke in a strong Northern accent.

Manuel didn't look convinced. Jess knew he was a stickler for regulations and upholding the good name of the hotel. Whilst he didn't mind guests enjoying themselves, he was very aware that it was a family hotel with children staying, so wouldn't allow any kind of rowdy behaviour. A stag party was probably his worst nightmare. Still, she felt sorry for the guys, they seemed a decent bunch. Most people would be angry at arriving at the hotel they'd booked into only to be told they couldn't stay and would probably become quite aggressive.

'That'll be okay won't it, Manuel? They're here now and we can't turn them all out onto the street,' Jess pointed out.

'I can guarantee you that we will be no problem,' Eddie assured him.

Manuel reluctantly relented. 'All right, I'll check to see if the other two hotels have spare rooms.' He clicked on the computer and studied the screen. After a few minutes of tapping away on the keyboard and sighing to himself, he continued speaking. 'Yes, luckily they do. I'll book you in, but I must *insist* that you don't all gather in one of the rooms after midnight holding wild parties.' He looked at each of the men in turn. 'And no inappropriate attire.'

16

'Inappropriate attire?' Ross gaped at him. 'What do you mean?'

'No strutting around in little tutus or women's underwear. I have heard about you Englees when you are on your stag nights.' Manuel replied. 'We will have no nakedness either.'

Jess burst out laughing and caught Eddie's eyes. He was grinning, too, his dark brown eyes twinkling.

I wouldn't mind seeing you naked, Jess thought.

He was quite something. Sooty black hair that she longed to run her fingers through, a cute moustache and even cuter goatee beard, smiling eyes the colour of rich dark chocolate, a silver hoop ring through one ear and a silver dog-tag hanging from a chain over his compulsory stag-do T-shirt. Forget hot, this guy was sizzling.

Ross looked offended. 'We've no intention of wearing tutus or strutting around naked,' he said. Then a wary look crossed his face and he shot a worried glance at the other five men. 'You haven't got anything like that planned, have you? Because if you have, forget it. Carly will go ballistic if I get into any scrapes over here.'

'Chill, mate. We're not about to cross Carly.' Greg said, giving a mock-shudder. The others nodded in agreement. 'Anyway,' he pointed at the French guy. 'Eddie's the one she'll hold responsible. He's the one she's entrusted to' he made little quote marks with his fingers. '"Look after you."'

They all laughed.

'As long as we're all clear on the kind of behaviour that's expected, stag party or not.' Manuel looked at each of the men in turn.

They all nodded their agreement.

'Very well.' He checked the computer screen. 'Then let's sort out your rooms.'

'Jess!'

Jess turned at the sound of her boss' voice. Ziggy was standing by the lift.

'Can I have a word with you, please?'

She guessed he probably wanted to run through the entertainment schedule for that evening. At least she hoped it was that, not something she'd done wrong. She hated to get on the wrong side of Ziggy. As bosses went he was fairly easy going but upset him and he made sure you knew it.

'Sure.' She turned back to the group. 'I'm glad that's all settled. I hope you enjoy your stay.'

'Thank you for your help,' Eddie told her, his dark brown eyes holding hers.

'No problem.' She met his gaze for a moment then rather reluctantly turned away.

'Me and Eddie will stay here,' Ross was saying. 'It's my stag party so I get first choice. They can go to the other hotels.'

Jess didn't hear Manuel's reply, but she didn't think he'd be too pleased at that. He was probably hoping to ship Ross off to one of the sister hotels. There again, it might be a good idea to have him stay here where they could keep an eye on him.

Well, this promised to be an entertaining weekend, Jess thought, as she walked over to Ziggy. Wait until she told Libby. She couldn't help feeling pleased that Eddie and Ross were staying here. With a bit of luck, she might run into them again.

Don't get too carried away, someone like Eddie is bound to have a girlfriend, she told herself. Married even. Not that it mattered, he might be a hottie but she had no interest in him long term. Or anyone for that matter. She liked to go out on a date or two, have a bit of fun, but that's as far as it went. No one had ever floated her boat enough to make her even consider getting serious. Which was great, because she was enjoying life far too much to get tied up with some guy who wanted to curtail her freedom.

'Is everything okay over there?' Ziggy asked, nodding towards the reception desk.

'Sure. Those guys are on a stag do but Elena took the booking and didn't realise. It's sorted now, though, a couple of them are staying here and Manuel's managed to get a room for another two next door and the other two over the road. I don't think they'll be any trouble.'

'If they are, I'm sure Manuel will soon mark their card.' Ziggy looked down at the notebook in his hand. 'I've got to change your shift around for tomorrow,' he said. 'Tanya's ill so I'll be needing you to take over the morning pool session with Libby again. You can have a couple of hours off in the afternoon instead.'

Jess frowned. 'But I'm doing the entertainment tonight – and tomorrow night.'

'I know, can't be helped.'

Damn, now she wouldn't be able to stay out late this evening and have a lie-in in the morning. She'd have to leave at one at the latest, just when things were livening up. Still, she could have a late night on Saturday –unless Ziggy had changed Sunday's rota, too.

'I've still got Sunday off, haven't I?' she asked.

'You can have the morning off but I'm going to need you in the afternoon.'

'But...'

Before she could protest any further Ziggy gave her one of his 'don't mess with me' glares. 'We're a member of staff down and you're away for four days next weekend.'

'Yes, because I'm chief bridesmaid at a wedding – and I booked the time off weeks ago,' Jess reminded him.

'I know you did, Jess, but it's still the middle of the holiday season when I never normally grant time off, so work with me on this. Okay?'

What the hell, at least she still had Sunday morning off. She nodded slowly. 'Okay.'

She'd been looking forward to having tomorrow morning off. Her job as part of the animation team at the hotel meant she spent most evenings entertaining the guests, having just one precious evening off a week which she liked to spend clubbing until the early hours with the other reps. She could still hit the town for a few hours, but it would have to be a Cinderella at the Ball evening if she was back on duty early in the morning.

***

Eddie had a bad feeling about this stag weekend as soon as Ross mentioned it, but he couldn't get out of it. He was the best man. He hadn't been able to get out of that, either. As Ross's oldest friend, how could he refuse? Especially after all Ross's family had done for him. So here he was, sharing a room with Ross in a family hotel of

21

all places – he was sure Carly had booked that on purpose so that they'd all have to watch what they were doing – and with the task of keeping Ross out of trouble all weekend. Like that would be easy. Especially with the other guys, Greg, Matt, Sam and Tony, in tow. They were determined to have a good time. And their idea of a good time was drinking until they couldn't stand. No doubt they had some pranks planned for Ross, too, and he was the one who would have to try and stop them. He'd be glad when this weekend was over. When the whole wedding was over. He hated weddings.

Mind you, that mix-up at the desk was probably a good thing. If they were all in different hotels then the other lads couldn't get up to so much mischief, could they? No booby-trapping Ross's room, or anything like that. It could have all gone very wrong though, and they could have found themselves without any accommodation if that rep hadn't butted in and come up with a solution.

His mind drifted back to the rep, with her 'stop the traffic' red hair. She was pretty in an unusual, quirky kind of way. She looked fun. And kind. He knew she was probably only doing her job, but even so, it had been nice of her to help them out like that. The manager had looked like he wanted to throw them out on the street. Stag parties tended to make people panic like that. Hell, they made *him* panic!

'Well this is a right bloody nuisance, I wanted us all to be together,' Ross complained. 'I'm pretty sure they can't make us split when we've all booked in together. It was their receptionist who messed up. I reckon they're legally bound to let us all stay here.'

'It does say on their website that it's a family hotel and no stag or hen parties are allowed, and we did turn up rather drunk,' Eddie pointed out. Why hadn't he checked the hotel out himself instead of leaving it to Carly? 'Anyway, it's not worth making a fuss about. We're only here a few days and won't be in our rooms much. We can still meet up and go out together.'

'Yeah, I guess. It's not the same though, being in different hotels.' He put his case beside the bed. 'You ready to hit the bars?'

Eddie stared at him. 'What, now? Don't you want to get changed and grab something to eat first?' He was dying for a shower and a strong cup of coffee.

'Nope, I'm fine how I am. Let's get cracking. I don't want to waste any time. Like you said, we're only here until Tuesday.' He took his phone out of his pocket as it started to buzz. 'It's Greg, they're all ready to go.'

'Give me five minutes,' Eddie said, heading for the bathroom.

This was going to be some weekend.

Chapter Three

It was eleven by the time Jess and Kurt, who had also been on evening entertainment duty, arrived at Aquarius. Jess had felt so exhausted she had been tempted to cancel and have an early night instead, but as soon as she stepped inside the nightclub, she felt a kick of energy. The bubble machine was going, the coloured lights flashing, and a mass of people were jiving around to the latest hits.

One of the fantastic things about being a holiday rep was the social life. That, and the sun, and all the countries she got to visit. Last season she'd been stationed in Tenerife and the season before that it had been Barcelona. It was hard work, long hours, and sometimes the rooms were pretty basic – a few times she'd had to share with another rep –but she loved the job.

Libby was dancing with Damián, Marta, and a group of holidaymakers. She waved to them and Kurt grinned.

'Go on, I can see you're itching to dance. I'll go to the bar and get the drinks.'

'Thanks. You're a star,' Jess told him, giving him a peck on the cheek then heading off to join Libby and the others. She only had a couple of hours to dance, and she intended to make the most of it.

Eddie recognised her as soon as he walked in. The bright red hair was a dead giveaway, although now it was hanging loose around her shoulders instead of tied up in a ponytail, and she was wearing a strappy silver mini-dress rather than the yellow T-shirt and faded denim shorts she'd worn this afternoon. Very sexy. There was a carefree air about her, a suggestion that she didn't conform, wasn't scared to be different. It intrigued him. Jess, that's what the hotel manager had called her.

He watched as she kissed a fair-haired guy on the cheek then went over to join a group of people dancing while the guy went up to the bar. Were they an item, he wondered. Someone as gorgeous as Jess was bound to be taken.

'I'll get the first round in,' Ross said. 'What you all having?'

'Jack Daniels for me,' said Greg.

Eddie tore his eyes away from Jess and followed Ross to the bar. When they returned with their drinks, a crowd had gathered around Jess and a woman with long dark hair, and people were cheering and clapping as they both danced in the middle of the floor. Jess tossed her long hair, shook her lithe hips and rocked it like there was no tomorrow. While the other woman was gyrating, twirling, twerking, you name it, her black satin halter-neck jumpsuit clinging to her body like a second skin, emphasising her long legs, slender frame and sun-tanned skin. She was pretty, in a conventional sort of way, but Jess was striking. And had curves to die for.

Greg followed his gaze. 'Hey, isn't that the lass who helped us sort out our rooms at the hotel? Who's that stunner with her?'

'Probably another rep. Good dancers, aren't they?'

'Cool it, mate, getting off with a couple of chicks is not what this stag weekend is all about,' Ross told him.

'You might be chained, but the rest of us aren't,' Greg said, walking over to join the group around the two dancers.

'It'd only be polite to say hello, she did help us out,' Matt said, following Greg.

Ross shrugged his shoulders. 'I guess so.'

Greg and Matt joined the circle around the two girls, clapping and stamping their feet along with the rest. Tony and Sam followed them. Ross and Eddie looked at each other, shrugged then walked over, too. When the song had finished, the crowd gave the girls resounding applause.

Eddie saw Jess glance over at him, smile and wave. Then she and her friend both walked over to the bar to get a drink.

'Let's go and talk to them,' Greg said. 'I'd like to meet the friend.'

Eddie followed him, feeling ridiculously pleased that it wasn't Jess Greg was interested in.

***

'Don't look now, but there's a group of guys coming over to us. And they're pretty fit.'

Jess turned her head slightly and saw that it was Eddie and one of the others from the stag group. She'd hoped he'd come over. All the while she was dancing she felt his eyes on her. He really was something. She wouldn't mind spending a bit of time with him.

Take it easy, he's probably got a girlfriend, she reminded herself. In her experience, guys in stag parties were always trying it on, conveniently forgetting their girlfriend/partner back at home.

Still, as a rep at the hotel he was staying at, she had to be friendly.

'That was some dance.' The other man – Greg according to his T-shirt – said, his eyes on Libby. Sandy-haired, a roguish twinkle in his blue eyes, just the right amount of stubble on his chiselled-chin, the sort of smooth operator with a 'bad lad' air that Libby always went for but had never appealed to Jess. Good job he wasn't the groom.

Libby, true to form, flashed him a megawatt smile. 'Thanks.'

'Hello again,' He nodded at Jess, but it was obvious his attention was on Libby. 'Thanks for helping us sort the rooms out.' Greg was slurring his words slightly. They'd probably been drinking all afternoon and evening, taking advantage of the cheap drinks here.

'You're welcome,' Jess replied. 'Which hotel did you get sent to?'

'The one over the road.'

'Oh, this is the stag party you told me about,' Libby said. 'Now which one of you is the stag?'

'Ross,' Greg pointed his thumb at Ross. 'Are you a rep at the hotel, too?' He pointed to the name on the front of his T-shirt. 'I'm Greg.'

'So, I see.' Libby shook the hand he offered. 'I'm Libby. And yes, I'm a rep, too. Glad you managed to get your rooms sorted out. Manuel is a stickler for obeying the rules.'

'Thanks to Jess,' Eddie joined in. 'We haven't been properly introduced, have we? Hello, Jess.' He leaned forward and kissed her on both cheeks, soft sensual lips fleetingly touching her skin, a heady waft of after-shave, warm breath enticingly close. She felt a bit dizzy. She must have drunk more than she realised.

'I am Édouard, Eddie.'

Édouard. She mentally rolled the name around on her tongue. Nice. It seemed a shame to shorten it.

'Er... hi.'

'Thank you for your help, Jess.' Every time he spoke it sent goose bumps down her spine.

'It was nothing,' she replied.

Greg was looking at Libby as if he'd never seen anyone as amazing as her before. Libby often had that effect on men.

'Let me buy you and your friend a drink to say thank you. It would have been a really difficult situation without your help.'

'Thanks, vodka and coke please,' Libby replied before Jess could decline. Not that she was about to, not with Eddie looking at her like that.

'And you?' Greg looked questioningly at Jess.

She smiled and nodded. 'A vodka and coke for me too, please.'

'I'll give you a hand,' Libby offered while the words were still forming in Jess's mouth. It was one of their rules to never let a stranger buy you a drink unless you were with them, thus making sure they didn't dope it. They'd had stuff like that drummed into them at their initial rep training and reinforced by Ziggy who was constantly reminding them all how important it was to keep themselves safe. As Ziggy said, most people are okay, but some are scum, and those are the ones you've got to watch for. Then he'd gone on to tell them a gruesome tale about one of his reps who hadn't followed his rule and got date-raped because of a drugged drink. Jess wasn't sure if he'd made it up to drive home his point, but she'd never be daft enough to take a chance, even without his warnings. She'd heard the tales herself.

As Libby walked over to the bar with Greg, Jess felt Damián's eyes upon her. She turned to smile reassuringly at him, knowing that he was checking to see if she was okay.

Kurt and some of the other reps had soon befriended a group of holidaymakers and gone off to another club with them, but Damián and Marta had remained. They both walked over.

'These are friends of yours, Jessica?'

Damián was like a surrogate big brother, always looking out for Jess and Libby when they were clubbing, especially if a group of men were hanging around.

'Not friends exactly, they're with a stag party over from England. Eddie here, and Ross, the groom-to-be, are staying at our hotel, the rest are staying next door and over the road. Manuel wouldn't let them all stay together,' she explained. 'He thought they might be disruptive.'

'A fair guess for a stag party,' Damián agreed, staring at Eddie. He was obviously waiting for Jess to introduce him.

'Eddie, this is Damián and his wife Marta, they own a jewellery shop in town.'

'Pleased to meet you,' Eddie said politely.

'Hey, are you guys coming?' Ross staggered over and slapped Eddie on the back, almost knocking him off his feet. 'We're off to Beachwaves.' His voice was slurred.

'Greg has gone to get more drinks. We'll come when we have finished them,' Eddie replied.

'Did you get me a drink?' Ross asked, swaying slightly and waving an almost empty glass in his hand. 'My glass is empty.' He tipped up the glass and slurped the contents then handed it to Eddie. 'Make it a double.'

He looked like he was about to keel over any minute, Jess realised. 'Do you think he needs to sit down?' she asked Eddie.

'Why don't we all sit down, there is a table free in the corner,' Eddie suggested.

'I don't want to sit down. I'm gonna dance,' Ross said. He pulled Jess's arm. 'Come and dance with me.'

He must be joking; the way he was staggering he'd either step all over her toes or collapse in the middle of the floor, pulling her with him. Or both. She didn't want to give a curt reply though, he might be drunk but he was a guest.

'Let me sit down for a bit and have a drink first. I'll dance with you later,' she promised.

She glanced over his shoulder and saw the other three men from the stag party making their way over to them.

'You coming, mate?'

'We'll catch you up when we've had this drink,' Eddie butted in before Ross could reply.

'Ok, see you in a bit.' They all staggered off.

'They look very drunk,' Damián said disapprovingly.

'It's a stag party,' Jess reminded him. 'That's what they do.'

'Drinks at last. There's a right queue at that bar,' Greg said as he and Libby returned with a tray loaded with booze. 'I got one for you too, Ross.'

'Come on, let's go and sit down for a bit.' Eddie put his hand on Ross's shoulder and guided him over to the empty table in the corner. Greg and Libby followed with the tray of drinks.

'I was going to dance,' Ross protested.

Jess turned back to Damián and Marta. 'I'll go and join them for a bit, best to be polite as they're staying at my hotel. See you later.'

Marta frowned. 'Be careful, Jess, they are very drunk, and you don't really know them.'

'Don't worry, we know how to look after ourselves. We have to in this job,' Jess told her.

Chapter Four

When Jess joined them, Libby and Greg were already engaged in conversation and seemed to only have eyes for each other, while Ross was downing drinks like there was no tomorrow.

'Have you been to Majorca before?' Jess asked as she sat down in the chair next to Eddie.

'No, this is my first time. How long have you been working here?' he asked in a sexy French accent. I wonder if he's taken, she thought. Probably. Guys like him usually were.

'This is my first season here and I love it. Most of the guests are great, although you do get some tricky ones.'

'Like stag parties,' Eddie said with a twinkle in his eyes.

'You bet. Especially when I was in Barcelona.' She grinned. 'You should see what some of them get up to.'

Libby turned around at that. 'Hey, do you remember that stag group who stripped the groom naked, painted him green and left him tied to a statue in the middle of the square?'

Ross jerked his head up, a horrified expression on his face. 'You'd better not try that!' He pointed his finger at Eddie and Greg. 'I've told you, no tricks.'

'Don't worry. I've assured Carly that I will take care of you and I'm a man of my word.' Eddie patted his hand. 'There will be no pranks and no dressing up.'

'Pity, I could just see you dressed up in a tutu!' Jess teased.

'I think I'd like to see you in one,' Eddie shot back.

'I've worn one a couple of times,' she said with a grin. She and Libby had joined in the fun with a few hen parties on the island, once wearing pink tutus and another time wearing angel wings – although the hens in the party had been far from angelic. It was all in good fun, though. Her thoughts drifted to Charlotte. Was she having a hen do? There had been no mention of it, but Jess wouldn't have been able to make it anyway. Not that she'd be missing out on anything, from what she could remember of Charlotte she didn't do fun. Her hen party would probably consist of them all sitting down for a meal and talking about baking!

'How did you and Ross meet?' she asked, curious.

'My father is English, an admiral in the navy, he and my mother met in Marseille when he was on leave.' Eddie curled his hand around his glass, staring down into it for a moment then raised his eyes to meet Jess's.

35

'My mother died when I was six, so my father and I went to live in England with my grand-mére. I went to High School with Ross. Then my grand-mére died, and I didn't want to change schools, so Ross's family kindly let me stay with them during term time. I spent the holidays in France with my French grandparents as my father was often away. Ross and I have kept in touch ever since. He asked me to be his best man, so here I am.'

How tragic to lose his mother and grandmother so young. She reached out and placed her hand over his in sympathy. 'I'm so sorry. You must have been devastated.'

'It was a long time ago now, but yes, it was hard as a boy.'

His eyes locked with hers and she could almost feel that young boy's pain. I wonder if he's got commitment issues, she thought. Scared to love someone in case they die. She'd heard of people being affected like that if their parents had died when they were young. Then she realised that her hand was still over his and it felt oddly intimate. Picking up her glass gave her the chance to move it. 'Do you live in France now?' she asked.

'Yes, in Marseille. I moved back after uni.' His hand went to the silver dog-tag hanging around his neck and she wondered if there was a sentimental attachment to it – his mother's or grandmother's, perhaps? Or a former girlfriend's? 'And you, where do you live?'

36

How did she answer that? Most of the time she was working in various holiday resorts around the world, so had a room in whatever hotel she was working in. On the few occasions she went home she slept in her childhood bedroom in her mum's semi-detached on the outskirts of Solihull. 'Wherever in the world I'm working,' she told him. 'I'll be here for the season, then move onto another resort for the winter. It's often really quiet around February and March, so then I usually go home and do a bit of temping work.'

She was about to ask Eddie what he did for a living when Ross stood up. 'Let's go to Beachwaves now. The other guys will be waiting.'

'Is it far?' Greg asked.

'No, only ten minutes or so. We can show them where it is, can't we, Jess?'

It was obvious that Libby wasn't only up for showing them where the club was, but joining them there, too. Which meant they'd be rolling in at five in the morning with just enough time to shower and change. She was tempted, she'd like to get to know Eddie better. He was definitely the best looking guy she'd met for ages.

Be sensible Jess, there's no way you can go out clubbing tonight when you have to work in the morning, she thought. And sexy as Eddie is, he isn't worth upsetting Ziggy over.

'Not tonight, we're both on morning duty tomorrow, remember,' she pointed out. 'And I don't know about you, but I definitely don't want to get on the wrong side of Ziggy. He'll have us down for the Kids Day Club for the rest of the season.'

Ziggy was a fair boss, but he frowned upon anyone coming in late or hungover. The guests came here to relax and have a good time, he said, so he expected the staff to be professional at all times. A stint in the Kids Club when anyone transgressed was his favourite method of keeping the team in line. Not that Jess minded looking after kids. Her mum used to be a child-minder, so she grew up in a house full of children and was quite adept at keeping them entertained. She preferred being part of the evening entertainment team, though, and knew Libby did, too.

'Being a travel rep sounds interesting, but I think it is an exhausting job, no?' Eddie asked.

'Very, but good fun,' Jess replied. She loved her job and the variety it gave her.

'Well, we're in no rush. We can finish these drinks and have a dance perhaps, before we join the others?' Eddie's eyes twinkled as he looked at Jess. 'Do you have the energy for one more dance?'

Did she? His gorgeous chocolate eyes held hers and she felt a frisson of excitement. You bet she did!

'I think I can manage that,' she said, taking a sip of her drink.

They chatted easily, Libby and Jess taking it in turns to share anecdotes of their repping experience – Libby's were grossly exaggerated, of course – and Greg and Eddie adding their holiday horror tales, too. Greg's were so outrageous that she was sure he was making them up.

'You're kidding!' Libby burst out as he relayed a story about coming back in the early hours of the morning when he was on holiday in Tenerife and crashing out on the sofa in his apartment only to be woken up a couple of hours later by a very irate husband. He was in the wrong apartment. His one was on the floor above. Evidently the wife had gone to bed early and kept the door unlocked for her husband to return when he'd finished his drink.

Greg shook his head, 'No, it's true. I had to do some fast talking to get out of that one. Not easy when you've had a few drinks. I can tell you.'

'Were you with him then?' Jess asked Eddie.

He shook his head. 'No, thank goodness, but I don't doubt that it's true. Greg is always getting into scrapes. So is Ross. That's why Carly ordered me to keep an eye on him this weekend. She doesn't trust him to stay out of trouble.'

A sudden loud snore made them all turn to look at Ross.

He was leaning back in the chair, fast asleep.

Very wise of Carly, considering the state Ross was in already. Although why would you want to marry someone you didn't trust to behave themselves on their stag night? Jess had no plans to settle down with anyone in the foreseeable future, but when she did, it certainly wasn't going to be with a guy who gave her brain ache. She had more important things to do than worry about what her guy was up to when she wasn't there. Not that she'd even got a guy. Her last serious relationship was years ago, when she was still at High School, now she was too busy enjoying herself to want another one. Life was too much fun to be saddled down. There was a whole world out there waiting to be explored, and she intended to see as much of it as she could.

'Looks like you've got your work cut out,' Jess said as Eddie tried to wake Ross up.

'Shall we leave him to snooze while we have a dance?' Greg suggested.

'Sure.' Libby stood up and followed Greg onto the dance floor.

'Honestly, I don't know where she gets her energy from,' Jess said as Libby got into her stride.

'She's a good dancer. I don't think Greg can keep up with her,' Eddie chuckled.

Greg was jiggling about on the spot, gesturing wildly, obviously thinking he was a real mover and shaker.

'Shall we join them?' Eddie asked, after a quick glance at Ross to check he was still asleep.

'Sure.'

They'd no sooner stepped onto the dance floor when the music changed to a smoochy number. Eddie immediately reached out and gently pulled Jess into his arms.

I'm glad he's not the groom, Jess thought, as one arm slid around her waist, pulling her closer whilst the other arm moved up to the base of her neck. She rested her head on his shoulder, savouring the warmth of his body, the heady musky smell of the cologne he was wearing, the effect the feel of his hand on her back through her flimsy dress was having on her senses.

Cool it, Jess.

A thud behind them brought her back to Earth.

'Ross!' Eddie gasped, releasing her.

Jess spun around to see a crowd of people gathered around Ross who had fallen off his chair and was lying face down on the floor.

'I shouldn't have left him. Carly will kill me if he's bruised his face.' Eddie rushed over.

That certainly would ruin the photos, Jess thought, but the wedding wasn't until next weekend so even if Ross had got a couple of bruises they would have cleared by then.

'He's unconscious.' Eddie was kneeling now, bending over him. Jess hurried over to join him, as did Greg and Libby.

'Ross!' Eddie shook him urgently. 'Ross. Can you hear me?'

Ross groaned and opened his eyes. 'Where am I?'

'On the floor in the middle of the night club,' Libby said, not very helpfully.

Jess groaned as Ross tried to get to his feet and fell back down again. She hoped he wasn't about to start throwing up everywhere.

'Come on, mate. You can't stay there.' Greg reached out for one of Ross's arms, and Eddie reached for the other one. Between them, they lifted him up again.

'Here comes Mick,' Libby whispered.

Jess glanced over to see a hefty bouncer walking over to them. Trust it to be Mick, he was a tough one.

'Okay everyone, let's clear this area.' Mick crossed his arms and stood over Ross who was now scrambling to his feet, helped by Eddie and Greg. 'I think you'd better call it a night, mate. Looks like you've had enough.'

Jess knew it was an order and not a request. 'They're leaving now,' she told Mick. 'They're on a stag weekend,' she added, as an explanation for Ross's behaviour.

'Well this stag needs to sleep it off,' Mick said. 'Shall I escort them out or can you girls handle it?'

Jess stood to her full height of five foot four, put her hands on her hips and levelled her gaze at him. 'We can handle it.'

'Five minutes then, and I expect these three – he nodded at Ross, Greg and then Eddie – to be outside.' Which Jess thought was unfair as Eddie and Greg hadn't been out of order at all, but before she could protest, Eddie slung his arm around Ross's shoulder to support him.

'We're on our way,' he promised, propelling Ross over to the door. 'Come on, guys.'

Grumbling, the guys all made their way to the exit. Jess and Libby followed.

Outside, Ross was swaying slightly as he remonstrated with Eddie. 'This is my bloody stag do and I want to go clubbing with the others,' he slurred.

'We should call it a night, Ross. You've drank way too much,' Eddie told him.

'Eddie's right. You should go back to the hotel,' Greg said. 'We'll take you back then carry onto the club.'

'Hic! You're not bloody going without me!' Ross told them. 'This is my... hic... stag do!'

'You've had enough already. We can go for a drink again tomorrow. We have three more days yet,' Eddie said softly, trying to placate him.

'No way.' Ross pushed Eddie's arm off his shoulder. 'I'm going to bloody Beachwaves to join Matt, Tony and Sam. I'll go on my own if you don't come.'

Eddie relented. 'Okay, but only for a couple. I promised Carly I'd look after you.' He glanced at the girls. 'I guess we'll see you around seeing as we're at the same hotel.'

'You can't miss us, we're the reps. Come and join us at the pool keep-fit session tomorrow morning if you want,' Libby replied.

Jess sighed. That was typical of Libby. She was happy to perform no matter who was watching, but Jess didn't fancy Eddie staring at her with those soulful eyes of his while she pranced about in her swimming costume. She wasn't ashamed of her body – she was shorter than Libby and not as slender, but there was nothing wrong with curves. Jess didn't give a hoot what anyone thought of her. If Eddie found her figure lacking, that was his problem. She was just bothered that his intense stare might put her off her steps. Well, she'd worry about that tomorrow. It was unlikely they'd turn up to an early pool exercise session anyway. When they finally dragged themselves out of bed they were bound to join up with

44

their mates and take a taxi over to the other side of the island.

Eddie put out his hand as a taxi came into sight. The taxi slowed down then pulled over at the side of the road. Ross staggered over to it, supported by Greg.

'It seems that Ross is intending to make the most of his last weekend of freedom,' Libby remarked.

As Eddie was about to get into the taxi he turned, glanced over at them, and waved. 'See you tomorrow,' he shouted.

Jess waved back.

'I think he's got the hots for you,' Libby told her. 'Good job he isn't the groom.'

'Funny, I thought the same about you and Greg,' Jess replied.

She had to admit, she really liked Eddie, and hopefully would see more of him over the weekend.

Chapter Five

Jess was so exhausted she fell asleep as soon as her head hit the pillow, and it seemed that it was only a few minutes later that her alarm announced it was time to get up. She reached out groggily and switched it onto snooze. If she could have just ten more minutes...

The next time the alarm went off she jumped out of bed before she could be tempted to switch it off all together and headed for the shower, adjusting the setting to lukewarm. She had to liven up, there was a morning of pool exercises ahead. As she showered, her mind drifted to Eddie, Ross, and the others. Ross had been very drunk when they left, so she guessed he'd be sleeping it off today. Greg had been slightly less so and Eddie didn't seem too bad at all. She guessed he wanted to remain relatively sober so he could keep Ross out of trouble. Well, if they followed the usual path of stag parties, they'd be out drinking again as soon as they woke up. They certainly wouldn't be taking up Libby's invitation to join them at the pool – that is if they even remembered it.

Libby, annoyingly, looked full of life when she knocked on Jess's door half an hour later, dressed in a chic blue swimsuit that moulded her slender figure, her long dark hair worn in plaits over each shoulder.

Jess had scooped her hair up in a messy ponytail that looked, well, messy, and her rainbow coloured swimsuit was more boho than chic. Not that Jess was bothered. She had long come to terms with the fact that at five feet four and with a pear-shaped figure, no matter how much exercise she did she would never have model girl looks. And she didn't hanker after them. From an early age she'd liked to be different, to tread her own path. Her mother had despaired at the vibrant mix of colours and eclectic combination of clothes that Jess had liked to wear, even as a toddler.

She wouldn't mind some of Libby's energy, though.

'You look ridiculously full of beans for someone who didn't go to bed until two o'clock,' she grumbled as she pulled the door shut behind her. 'I'm knackered.'

'I'm lucky, I don't need much sleep,' Libby said with a grin. 'Do you want me to lead?'

Jess nodded. 'Thanks, just until I liven up.'

'Okay ladies, now stretch your arms above your head.' Jess stretched her arms above her head as high as she could. 'Now swing them to the left. Then to the right.'

God, she was too exhausted for this. Thanks to staying out late with Eddie and the rest of the stag party, and then

Libby keeping her chatting for half an hour when they finally reached the hotel. There was another half hour of the 'Fitness by the Pool' lesson to go yet, followed by ball games in the pool with the kids. She'd had a couple of scoops of caffeine in her coffee this morning, but still felt like she could curl up and sleep. It was going to be a tough day.

The group of twenty or so ladies facing her, all dressed in their swimwear, copied her actions. Some of the younger ones, suntanned and slender and dressed in the skimpiest of bikinis, were stretching with gusto, obviously enjoying the admiring glances of the men on the nearby sun loungers, while the older ones were a bit slower. Jess knew how they felt. Her bed was calling her, but somehow she stuck a smile on her face and swung her arms above her head.

'On your toes now, ladies. Stretch as high as you can.'

Beside her, Libby stood on tip toe, arms straight, fingers pointing up to the sky. She looked youthful and bursting with energy, Jess thought with a flash of irritation. It amazed her how Libby could get by on such little sleep whereas if Jess didn't get at least six hours she had to drag herself through the day. And there weren't many days she managed to get six hours' sleep, not with Libby's habit of popping in and chatting until the early hours of the morning. Stop being grumpy, she scolded herself. Libby is a good friend, it's your own fault for going out clubbing last night.

Oh, but it had been worth it for that dance with Eddie.

'Okay, now let's do a bit of jogging on the spot. Ready. On the count of three.' Libby announced as she turned up the music.

Jess started jogging. 'Come on ladies one, two, three!' The younger women took it seriously, but the older ones were giggling and joking around as they jogged away.

'Now turn around still jogging on the spot.' Jess lead the way, and nearly tripped over herself when she spotted a familiar dark-haired guy with a cute goatee beard sitting at the table in front of her.

Eddie!

So he had remembered. Catching her glance, he waved.

Damn, she was out of step now. Everyone else had turned. Forget Eddie. Concentrate on what you're doing. She jogged around swiftly and joined the others. Thank goodness the session was nearly over, she felt awkward prancing about in her swimming costume with Eddie sitting there. How long had he been there?

The music finally finished. Libby clapped her hands. 'Right everyone, let's take a break for fifteen minutes then we'll do some pool aerobics.'

Jess walked over to her as the group dispersed. 'Did you see who's on the table behind us?'

'Yep. Spotted him when you nearly fell on your face.'

'I did not! I just... faltered...a little.'

'Sure you did. Shall we go over and join them for a few minutes?'

'Them? Is Ross here, too?'

'Nope but Greg is, he's at the bar. Coming?' Libby sauntered over without waiting for Jess's reply and leaving her no option but to follow. She'd look churlish if she didn't. But first Jess grabbed her sarong from the chair she'd thrown it onto before the pool exercise class and tied it around her waist. Crazy that she felt so self-conscious dressed in her perfectly respectable swimsuit in front of Eddie when she never felt at all awkward dressed like this running poolside sessions with the guests. It was the way he looked at her with those deep brown eyes, it was unnerving. Libby, of course, had no such inhibitions. Confidence oozed from her every pore as she sauntered over to the table, pulled out a chair and sat down, crossing one long leg over the other.

'Well, hello boys! How are your heads today?'

'My brain feels like it's playing ping-pong,' Greg said ruefully. He nodded towards his glass 'I'm on diet coke for a bit.'

'I'm not surprised,' Jess said as she sat down beside Libby, acutely aware that Eddie was sitting on her other side and hadn't taken his eyes off her. He sure did have an effect on her. 'You were in a bit of a state when we left you. Did you go on to the other nightclub?'

'We couldn't talk Ross out of,' Eddie told her. 'We rolled back in at four thirty this morning. Ross is still in bed, recovering. So are the other guys.'

'And you two got up early so you could join in the pool session?' Libby teased. 'Sorry guys, it's ladies only.'

'No worries, we can enjoy the view.' Greg said, his eyes resting on Libby's cleavage.

Libby wagged her finger mock-playfully at Greg. 'Wind your eyes in. What would your girlfriend say?'

'There's a vacancy for that position at the moment.' Greg told her with a cheeky grin. 'Fancy applying?'

Libby pouted mock-indignant. 'Got a queue, have you? I think I'll pass, thanks.'

'Take no notice of him, he's an impossible flirt,' Eddie told her. 'Behave yourself, Greg.'

'This *is* me behaving,' Greg replied. He winked at Libby. 'I'm much more fun when I misbehave.'

She grinned. 'I bet you are.'

'Don't worry about Libby, she'll be more than a match for Greg,' Jess said as Greg and Libby carried on bantering.

'I can see that.' Eddie's eyes rested on her, and her stomach did a peculiar flutter. 'You are both so energetic. Those exercises, they are so strenuous. Do you do this every day?'

'Pretty much, depending whether or not we're part of the evening animation team. If so, then we either have the morning off or get a few hours off after lunch as we'll be working until midnight. Like tonight.'

'You're entertaining the guests tonight?' Eddie sounded surprised.

'Yep, we're doing a show – Songs from Broadway,' Libby butted in. 'Why don't you all come and watch us?'

'That sounds fun,' Eddie said to Greg. 'Do you reckon we can persuade Ross?' He seemed enthusiastic, but Jess wasn't sure whether that was because he really did think the show sounded fun, or if he just wanted to keep Ross out of trouble and thought that spending the evening in the hotel was the best way of doing that. She didn't envy him. Ross was evidently hell bent on enjoying his last weekend of freedom. She wondered if his fiancée – Carly – was doing the same on her hen party.

'We're going out on the razz with the rest of the lads, but maybe we'll pop in for an hour before we go.' Greg took a gulp of his coke. 'If you're free this afternoon why don't you both join us all? We're going to Spike's Bar on the beachfront.'

'Thanks, but drinking in the afternoon isn't a good idea when we have to sing and dance tonight,' Jess said quickly before Libby could agree. It was obvious that there was a connection between her and Greg. 'Right, we've got the pool exercise class starting soon, so we'd better get going. Have a fun day.' She flashed a smile at them both, refusing to let her eyes linger on Eddie.

'See you later, boys.' Libby stood up, gave them both a finger wave and sauntered off.

'I reckon Greg fancies you,' Jess said as they made their way back to the pool where a crowd had already gathered. 'And he must be keen to get out of bed early and come over to the hotel just to watch the pool session. He put back quite a lot last night.'

'I reckon he does, too. He's okay, but I'm not that struck.'

'Well you could have fooled me, you were flirting like mad with him.'

'It's only a bit of fun,' Libby turned and winked. 'Now the French one… he's adorable. I wonder if he has a girlfriend.'

What, she fancied Eddie? All this flirting with Greg was a smokescreen so she could get close to Eddie? Jess hadn't thought of that. She and Libby had completely opposite tastes and had never fancied the same guy before.

Libby grinned. 'You should see your face! I knew you fancied him. Go for it, he's not the groom and he *definitely* has the hots for you.'

Did he? Down, Jess. Eddie was going home Tuesday and would probably be out drinking with the rest of the gang all weekend, so there wasn't really much chance to get to know him.

Shame.

The whistle blew for the start of the session, so she quickened her pace to the pool.

Chapter Six

'They're a pair of stunners, aren't they?' Greg said, watching Jess and Libby start their exercise routine again.

'Yes, they are pretty girls, and very friendly,' Eddie agreed. Stunning was exactly the word he'd use to describe Jess. Pretty didn't do her justice. He wasn't about to admit to Greg just how attracted he was to her, though. Didn't even want to admit it to himself. He hadn't had a serious relationship since Yvette and had no intention of committing again. Being stood up at the altar tended to make you wary of getting too involved.

He was over it now, of course. Three years had passed, and he had soon realised that he would have made a big mistake marrying Yvette, even if she hadn't decided to run off with an old school friend she reconnected with on Facebook on their supposed-to-be wedding day. Yvette was beautiful, but she knew it, and was demanding and high maintenance. He didn't know why he hadn't seen it before. He guessed he'd been too smitten to see what she was really like. Well, he wasn't about to make that mistake again, so he made sure that he never got close enough to anyone to get hurt.

There again, there wouldn't be any harm in having a bit of fun while he was here. And Jess looked fun.

***

The day, as usual, passed quickly, and after a few hours' break resting by the pool and catching up on missed sleep, it was time to get ready for the evening entertainment. It was the part of the job that Jess loved most. She enjoyed singing and acting, as did Libby. Last week was the first week of the school summer holidays which meant there were lots of children at the hotel, so one night they performed The Lion King. Jess was Nala and spent the whole performance dressed in a furry lioness costume which was hot and uncomfortable, but she still enjoyed it. Tonight was Songs from Broadway, one of her favourite shows. They got to dress up in beautiful evening dresses and sing some of the popular oldies such as 'Razzle Dazzle' from Chicago. Jess, Libby, Kurt and Charlie were the four main characters in the act, with other reps as backing singers.

'Do you think Greg and Eddie will come to see the show?' Libby asked as she stepped into a long red dress with a plunging neckline. 'They seemed interested in it.'

Jess shrugged. 'I doubt it. I think they were just being polite. They'll be on a pub crawl with their mates.' She smoothed down her emerald green gown, which she knew brought out the colour of her eyes and picked up a long white glove. 'Anyway, don't get too struck on Greg, you know what guys on a stag do are like – out for a good time and quick to forget that they've got a partner back at home.'

'Don't be such a party-pooper,' Libby replied. 'Besides, don't pretend you don't fancy Eddie and wouldn't love him to see the show.'

Jess had to admit that she'd love Eddie to see her dressed up like this, it was a big improvement on the swimsuit she wore this morning. She knew she looked good, and the show was great entertainment, but she shrugged, the guys would be off on the town and she wasn't about to waste any time bothering about that.

'They'd only be a distraction,' she told Libby, pulling on her other glove. 'Come on, we're due on stage.'

***

When Eddie, Ross, Greg and Sam walked into the lounge, Jess, Libby and two men were centre stage singing 'Give my Regards to Broadway.' The men were dressed in white jackets and black trousers whilst Jess and Libby were made up like starlets in one of the old movies. Eddie couldn't take his eyes off Jess, she looked sensational.

Her hair was cascading over her shoulders like a glorious red wave, the emerald green dress she was poured into emphasised her small waist and ample bust, whilst the scarlet lipstick defined her full lips.

'Not bad, are they?' Greg asked, his eyes fixed on Libby. Or rather the plunging neckline of her dress. He'd arrived at the hotel with Sam half an hour ago and suggested they drop in at the show on the way out. Always one with an eye for the ladies, he was obviously attracted to Libby.

'Fancy staying to watch them for a while?' Eddie suggested. 'It's still early yet.'

They'd spent the afternoon at a beach bar, drinking with the lads, then come back for a snooze and to get changed. He knew Ross was looking forward to hitting the clubs again, but he'd rather stay here and watch the show. He wished he could tell Ross to go and meet the others and he'd join them later, but he daren't. Ross was like a loose cannon when he had a drink inside him, and the others encouraged him. He wouldn't put it past them to tie him naked to a lamppost and leave him there, something the British seemed to find incredibly funny.

'Sure, but let's grab a pint first.'

The singers were bowing to the audience now and, as they stood back up, Jess spotted him. For a moment they locked eyes, then she turned and went off stage as the curtains closed behind her. Eddie followed Ross to the bar, by the time they'd got a pint and returned, the curtains had opened again to reveal Jess and Libby in figure hugging black leotards, fishnet tights and killer heels, each holding a cigarette holder.

The scene was from Chicago. Eddie watched, mesmerised, as Jess and Libby sprung into a rendition of 'Razzle Dazzle'.

Greg whistled. 'Hey they can sing. And they look…'

'Amazing,' Eddie added. 'How about we grab a seat and watch for a while? We can catch up with the other guys later.'

'You stay if you want, I'm carrying on to the club,' Sam said. 'You coming, Ross?'

'You bet I am. I haven't come away to watch a cabaret show.'

Eddie hesitated. He should go with Ross, really.

'Look, I can keep an eye on Ross. We're going to be in the same club we went to last night. Watch the show then come and join us,' Sam suggested. 'I can see you two have the hots for those lasses.'

Eddie shrugged. 'We haven't got the hots for them at all. It's a good show. Nice to have some entertainment.'

'You speak for yourself,' Greg said. 'I deffo have the hots for Libby. She's gorgeous.' He raised a hand to Ross and Sam. 'See you later, fellas.'

'We won't be long,' Ed promised. He'd just stay to watch Jess perform one song, he decided, as he followed Greg over to an empty table.

Another costume change then they sang 'All that Jazz', followed by 'Cabaret', '42nd Street', 'There's No Business Like Show Business' and, finally, 'Broadway Baby'. It was such a slick performance, so professional. Jess sung and danced like a pro. Eddie watched as the man she was partnered with, the fair-haired guy she'd come into the club with last night, swung her round, then rested her head back onto his arm and gazed into her eyes as he sung to her.

Eddie felt an irrational stab of jealously. Were they an item? They certainly looked close. The guy snaked his arm around Jess's waist then swung her around again.

Well, what did he expect? Someone like Jess was unlikely to be single. What did it matter to him anyway? He would never trust a woman again, not after Yvette. He'd built a wall around his heart and it was staying there.

Jess stepped forward and sang a solo. Her voice was exquisite. Soft, yet filled with such strength. As Eddie listened to her, he felt the wall start to crumble.

Chapter Seven

Jess could feel Eddie's eyes on her as she sang, and she tried not to meet his gaze, to concentrate on her performance, but she was so aware of him it was as if her nerves were standing to attention. The show had been half way through before Eddie, Greg, Sam and Ross had walked into the lounge, and she'd only expected them to stay for one song and all head off for the clubs once they went backstage for a costume change – but Eddie and Greg were still there when they came back, and remained there throughout the show, clapping enthusiastically after every song. When the show was finally over, and she and Libby had changed into their going out clothes ready to hit the clubs, the two men were still sitting there.

Greg rose and beckoned them both over. 'You were both fantastic,' he said as Jess and Libby joined them.

'Yes, you are very talented,' Eddie agreed. 'The show, it was so professional.'

'Thank you,' Libby replied with a wide smile.

'Glad you enjoyed the show.' Jess glanced around. There was no sign of Ross. 'I thought you'd have gone with Ross and the others out on the town.'

'We wanted to see the end of the show. But, yes, we'd better go and join them. I don't trust Matt, Tony and Sam not to get up to something,' Eddie said, smiling.

'Why don't you girls come with us?' Greg suggested eagerly, his gaze fixed on Libby.

'Sure!' she turned to Jess. 'We're both off tomorrow morning. No early alarm for once.'

'You're on afternoons tomorrow?' Eddie asked, getting to his feet.

'I am, Libby has the whole day off and I should have too, but one of the reps is ill so Ziggy's changed the rota,' Jess told him. 'That's why I had to work this morning.'

'That's a shame.' He sounded like he meant it.

'Oh, I don't mind, I'm away for a few days on Friday and, I've still got the morning off, so I can stop out late tonight.'

'So yes, we'd love to join you. We were off clubbing anyway, so we might as well come with you and make sure you don't get into any trouble,' Libby added mischievously.

'If you're sure we're not intruding?' Jess asked. 'I thought a stag night was for men only. Won't your friends object?'

'Nah, they won't be bothered,' Greg replied before Eddie could. 'You ready to go? We could share a taxi.'

***

'Mon Dieu!' Eddie exclaimed as soon as they walked into the nightclub. Ross, Matt, Tony and Sam, all dressed in naughty nurse outfits, complete with stocking and suspenders and curly blonde wigs were dancing in the middle of the floor surrounded by a large crowd, who were stamping their feet and clapping. The guys must have taken an outfit for Ross to change into. He knew they were up to something!

Jess giggled. 'Don't stress, it's pretty mild for a Saturday stag night. You should see some of the things other stag parties get up to.'

'It's not so much the outfit they've got him dressed up in as what they're planning next,' Eddie groaned.

'You take your best man duties seriously, don't you?' Libby asked.

'You don't know Carly.' Greg made a throat slitting motion with his finger. 'If anything happens to Ross that messes up their wedding day, she'll hold Eddie personally responsible.'

'I hope they've put Ross's clothes somewhere safe,' Jess remarked. 'Manuel's on duty tonight and I don't think he'll let him back into the hotel dressed like that.'

A look of panic crossed Eddie's face and he dashed over to the other men. Jess watched them talking for a while then Eddie went over to a table and came back with a carrier bag. 'It's okay, Ross's clothes are in here.'

'I'll have them put in the locker to make sure they don't get lost,' Jess told him. 'We can collect them at the end of the night.' She took the bag from Eddie and handed it to Suzie at the cloakroom, who promised to take good care of it.

***

It was a fantastic night. The other guys in the stag party, Matt, Tony and Sam were a really nice bunch: fun, friendly – and taken. All except Eddie and Greg, Jess learnt from Tony. Apparently, Eddie had been jilted at the altar by his fiancée three years ago and hadn't had a long-term girlfriend since. She felt for him. That must have been an awful experience. She was surprised anyone would want to dump a hunk like Eddie. Had his fiancée decided she didn't love him after all? Was she in love with someone else? Or had Eddie cheated on her? She wanted to ask Tony what had happened, but it felt like prying, so she let the subject drop and jigged away amongst the bubbles pouring out from the bubble machine.

They drank, danced, and drank some more, but it was all in good spirits. The social life was one of the things

Jess loved about being a rep. She met lots of different people who, as they were on holiday, were usually in a good mood, just looking for a bit of fun.

It wasn't until they were piling out of the night club that Jess realised quite how much she'd drunk. As soon as the fresh air hit her she felt light-headed. Whoops, maybe she should have cut back on the drinks a little bit. It had been such a good night though, the best she'd had for ages. Eddie and the lads had been fantastic company.

Greg was the worse for wear, as was Libby. They were both holding each other up as they walked along, Libby giggling as she tottered along on her high heels, and Greg swaying everywhere. They'd certainly hit it off and had been inseparable for most of the night.

Ross broke into a loud, out of tune, dubious sounding song. He danced on ahead, swaying and singing at the top of his voice. That's when Jess noticed that, like the other lads, he was still wearing his naughty nurse attire. But unlike them he had to walk through reception with Manuel on duty, and there was no way that would end well.

'Ross won't be allowed into the hotel in that state. We need to sober him up a bit and get him to change back into his normal clothes,' she whispered to Eddie. 'Did you remember to collect the bag from the cloakroom?'

'Yes.' Eddie held out the carrier bag holding Ross's clothes. 'I've been trying to get him to change but he refuses.'

'Let's walk back,' Greg suggested, his words slurred. 'It's only twenty minutes or so.'

Sam, Tony and Matt agreed so Matt and Tony linked arms with Ross, then Sam linked arms with Tony and they all walked on ahead singing 'Dancing in the Street' at the top of their voices, breaking into a crazy dance every now and again.

'I'd better catch them up,' said Eddie. 'There's no telling what they'll do. You girls get a taxi.'

Libby and Greg were still wrapped around each other. 'I don't mind a walk, it's a lovely night,' Libby said.

Jess agreed. 'As reps of the hotel you're staying in, we really should make sure you get back in one piece.'

So they walked back along the now almost deserted street. The lads – even Eddie – were all singing 'he's getting married in the morning' at the top of their voices. It was an entertaining walk home, and Ross managed to stay on his feet and not puke, much to everyone's relief.

'Okay, mate, see you at lunch time tomorrow,' Tony said when they reached the hotel he and Matt were staying at. But as they released Ross he stumbled and fell forward.

'Where you gone, guys?' he stammered.

'Merde!' Eddie cursed, sprinting to grab Ross, as did Sam.

Jess smiled, *merde* – the French word for 'shit' was one she'd soon picked up when she did a stint on the French Riviera.

'Oooh, I nearly fell there,' Ross slurred. 'Good job you guys caught me.' Then he broke into 'I'm getting married in the morning...' again in a loud, slurry voice.

'Shh, mate. You'll wake everyone up.' Eddie told him.

'Good luck with him. I reckon that manager did us a favour putting us in a different hotel,' Sam said with a grin. 'I don't fancy your chances getting Ross into his room.'

'Or getting him changed back into his clothes – thanks you two,' Eddie said.

Greg, Sam, Matt and Tony all gave a mock salute and staggered off to their respective hotels. They were lucky, the staff at both their hotels were fairly easy going and would look on their naughty nurse attire in amusement. Whereas Manuel would have a fit if he saw Ross like this and was sure to bar him.

'It's the shots,' Eddie explained to Jess. 'He got into a drinking competition with one of the guys at the nightclub.' He shook his head. 'I dread to think what state he's going to be in by the time we go back on Tuesday. Thank goodness our flight isn't until the afternoon, so he'll have time to sober up from Monday night. I bet he'll be out until the crack of dawn then.'

Libby was watching Ross warily. 'He looks a bit green. I hope he doesn't puke.'

'I hope so, too.' Eddie tugged at Ross's arm. 'Come on, Ross. We're almost there. You must put your trousers and shirt on. You can't go in like that.' He pointed to the wall running alongside the hotel gates. 'Quick, duck behind that wall and change.'

'I'm gonna be sick!' Ross groaned then promptly brought up the contents of the night out and slid to the floor.

Chapter Eight

'*La vache!*' Eddie muttered, bending down and shaking Ross. 'Get up. You can't stay here.' He tried to lift him up, but Ross simply lay back down again and stretched out on the ground.

'Looks like he's comatose,' Jess said. 'Want some help to lift him?'

'Don't expect me to help, I'm keeping my distance,' Libby said with a shudder. 'I don't want to get covered in vomit!'

Jess's brothers, Ned and Jake, had come home drunk now and again, and she'd often helped her mum take them up the stairs. Rule number one was keep them facing away from you – just in case they puked. Rule number two was to keep calm, and be reassuring, and avoid conflict at all costs.

'Let's put his clothes on over this outfit while he's out for the count. It'll be easier,' she said. She opened her handbag and took out a pack of travel wipes. 'You might want to clean him up a bit first. Luckily, I've always got a pack of these on me, you never know when you might need them.'

'*Merci.*' Eddie wiped Ross's face. Between them he and Jess managed to pull Ross's jeans over his stockings and suspenders, tuck his naughty nurse outfit into the waistband and pull his T-shirt over it. Libby took off the hat and curly blonde wig and shoved them into the carrier bag, along with the wipes. Ross didn't stir.

'Wake up, Ross.' Eddie shook Ross's arm. 'Come on, we need to get you inside.'

Ross muttered something but didn't open his eyes.

'Let's lift him up. If we can get him moving he might come round,' Jess suggested. She looked over her shoulder at Libby who'd been cautiously keeping her distance. 'We need you to give us a hand too, Lib.'

'Okay but I'm staying at the back,' she replied.

'Sure, just slip your hands under both his armpits as Eddie and I lift.'

Jess bent down and slipped her hand under Ross's left arm. Eddie did the same with Ross's right arm. She felt Libby hands slide beneath his armpits to support him.

'Ready?' Eddie asked.

'Ready.' Jess and Libby said together.

'All together now. Heave!'

They all lifted at the same time, pulling Ross to his feet. Wobbling unsteadily but standing upright, he had one arm slung over Jess's shoulder and the other one slung over Eddie's.

'My head hurts,' Ross groaned. 'I need to sleep.'

'And so you can, mate, as soon as we get you back to the hotel,' Eddie told him. 'Come on, you need to walk a bit. We'll help you.'

'I need to sleep,' Ross mumbled and promptly closed his eyes, refusing to open them again no matter how much Eddie urged him.

'Sorry to ask this, Jess, but can you help me into the hotel with him?' Eddie asked. 'If we can just get him into the lift I can take it from there.'

'Sure,' Jess nodded. She glanced over her shoulder. 'Lib can you check who's on the reception desk? With a bit of luck Manuel might have finished his shift, or gone for a break, then we can sneak Ross in.'

'Sure.' Libby tottered off up the drive to the hotel entrance. Jess and Eddie followed at snail pace, practically dragging Ross along with them.

Suddenly Ross opened his eyes. 'Wot's appenin'?' he slurred.

'We're taking you back to the hotel room,' Eddie muttered. 'Do you think you can help us along by actually walking a few steps?'

Ross obliged, carefully putting one foot in front of the other. Then he stopped and turned to Jess. 'You're pretty. Want to come 'ome with me?'

'Behave yourself, mate. Jess is helping get you back into our room.' Eddie sounded annoyed. He shot Jess an apologetic glance and mouthed sorry.

'It's fine,' she mouthed back. An amorous drunk she could cope with. It was the aggressive ones that were the real problem.

Libby was heading down the path towards them now. 'Manuel's on Reception,' she said at the top of her voice.

'Shh!' Jess put her finger to her lips warningly. Damn. They couldn't take Ross through Reception like this, Manuel would kick him out.

'What do we do?' Eddie said. 'Perhaps we can walk him around a bit until he sobers up.'

There was no way she could do that. She hadn't got the energy. Ross was too heavy. 'We'll have to take him through the back entrance and hope no one sees us.'

Only the staff were allowed in the back entrance, and Jess knew they'd be in mega-trouble if Ziggy caught them sneaking a drunken guest in that way. Well, what choice did they have? She couldn't stand by and let the two men be kicked out into the street. Where would they go? They were in no state to be looking around for another hotel. The staff entrance was the only way.

'You go ahead, make sure the coast is clear,' she told Libby, 'and you,' she turned to Ross who had started to break into song, 'be quiet!'

'I'm happy,' Ross slurred. 'Don't you want me to be happy?' He wagged a finger right under her nose. 'You're too pretty to be so miserable. You need to lighten up.'

'And you need to be quiet,' Eddie said sternly.

'Miserable, the lot of you,' Ross muttered under his breath then promptly slumped in their arms.

'Oh no, he's zonked out again,' Eddie groaned.

'Probably for the best,' Jess told him. 'We'd have trouble sneaking him in singing like that.'

Libby pushed open the door to the staff entrance, poked her head through then popped back out again. 'All clear,' she whispered.

Ross's head had now dropped onto his chin and he was snoring softly. He was quite a weight. Dragging him between them, Jess and Eddie made their way along the corridor.

'What room are you in?' Jess whispered as they walked past Jess's room towards Libby's.

'One six one,' Eddie told her. 'We're sharing…unfortunately.'

That was on the third floor and there was no way Ross could do the stairs, so they'd have to get him to the lift and hope no one else was in it. If they were discovered in the staff quarters with guests – and male guests at that – there would be hell to pay.

Suddenly Libby stopped. 'Someone's coming!'

There was nowhere to hide. Unless... Jess looked over her shoulder and made a quick calculation. They were a few metres away from Libby's room. 'Quick, Libby! We'll have to hide in your room!'

Libby raced to her room, rummaging in her bag for her key, opening the door just as Jess heard the door open at the end of the corridor. 'Get in! Quick!' she shoved Ross through the door Libby had just opened and Eddie dived in after him.

'Hi you two! You just got back from clubbing?' Chloe, another rep, stepped into the corridor.

Jess nodded as Libby spun around, pulling the door to behind her. 'Yep. You?' she asked.

'Yeah, been to Beachwaves, met up with Kurt and the others. What a night.' Chloe giggled and waved to them both. 'See you in the morning... oh, it is morning!' She giggled again and tottered off up the corridor.

'Thank goodness it wasn't Ziggy,' Libby said. 'Now let's get those guys out of my room before someone else comes along.'

She opened the door, stepped inside and groaned. 'Oh no! Bloody Ross has zonked out on my sofa.'

Zonked was a good description. Ross's body covered the full length of the sofa, flat on his back, arms above his head, legs apart, one on the arm of the sofa, the other on the floor, eyes closed, mouth open wide, snoring. On the coffee table in front of him was a half-empty glass of water.

'Look at him!' Libby scowled. 'And where's Eddie?'

The chain flushed and Eddie came out of the bathroom. He glanced over at Ross and cursed. 'Sorree, Libby.' He strode over to the sofa and shook Ross's arm. 'Come on, mate.'

Ross replied with an extra loud snore.

Libby and Jess joined in, shaking Ross, calling him, trying to rouse him to his feet, but to no avail. He couldn't be budged.

'We're going to have to leave him to sleep it off,' Jess said flatly.

'What? Leave him to sleep in my room? On my sofa?' Libby sounded outraged.

'What else can we do? He's out for the count.' Jess pointed out.

'I really am sorree but I think Jess is right.' Eddie looked worried. 'Do you want me to stay and keep an eye on him?'

'No I don't! I don't want either of you here. Ziggy will go ape if he finds out I've had a couple of guys stay in my room overnight – especially guests. I could get the sack for this.'

Jess didn't blame Libby for freaking out. She wouldn't want a drunken bloke who she'd only just met falling asleep on her sofa for the night either. Mind you, she could guarantee Libby would be a bit more accommodating if it was Greg! But she was right, inviting a guest back to your room in the staff quarters was a dismissible offence, although they were so short staffed she doubted if Ziggy would take such drastic action in the middle of the summer season. The punishment would more likely be Kids Club duties for a month.

Ross snored loudly, mouth open wide. He looked like he was settled for the night. They had to wake him up. A jug of cold water always worked with her brothers, but Jess thought she'd try the more gentle approach first. She leaned over and pinched Ross's cheek. 'Ross! Wake up!'

Ross opened one eye and looked at her, then opened the other one. A smile lit up his face as he reached up, wrapped his arms around Jess's neck, pulled her down on top of him, and started snogging her.

Chapter Nine

Ross's arms were clasped around Jess so tight she could hardly breathe, and his lips were locked on hers. She tried frantically to wriggle free, but Ross tightened his grip and kissed her more passionately.

'Ross, stop it!' she heard Eddie shout. Then she felt Eddie's arms around her waist, tugging her away from Ross. Suddenly yanked backwards, she landed on the floor, on top of Eddie, his arm still wrapped around her.

Jess lay there for a moment, too stunned to move. She could hear Eddie's ragged breathing, feel his breath on her neck, his arm around her waist. Then realised to her horror that his right hand was cupping her right breast.

And it felt good. *Too good.*

'Move your hand!' she yelled, trying to wriggle out of his grasp.

'So sorreee,' Eddie stammered and quickly released his grip on her.

Jess rolled off him, staggered to her feet, stormed over to the sofa and furiously whacked Ross across the face. 'How bloody dare you!'

The slap seemed to bring Ross to his senses. He sat up, rubbed his bright red cheek and groaned. 'What's up?' He peered at her through slitty, out-of-focus eyes. 'Carly?'

'I am *not* Carly! And what's up is that you have just grabbed me and given me a yukky slobbery kiss.' She wiped her mouth. 'You're *disgusting*!'

Ross blinked, confused. 'Jess?' He peered at her again. 'Oh fuck! I'm sorry. I thought you were Carly. Honest I did.' His eyes were glazed but there was definitely a contrite look on his face.

'Really? And Carly has bright red hair and looks just like me, does she?' Jess retorted.

'Well, not exactly...You have the same cute nose, though...'

Eddie stood up and brushed himself down. 'It was a mistake, Jess,' he assured her. 'Ross loves Carly, he wouldn't cheat on her. He's drunk...'

'I know he's bloody drunk! I had a close up of his foul breath when he wrapped me in a bear hug and snogged me!' Jess folded her arms to stop herself from lashing out at both of them. She was furious. 'And as for you, pulling me over like that and ... manhandling me! I ought to report you both and get you thrown out of the hotel.'

Except that would get her and Libby into trouble for allowing Ross and Eddie into Libby's room in the first place.

Ross was sitting up now, his head in his hands. 'Carly will kill me,' he muttered over and over again. Jess's anger thawed a bit. Maybe in his drunken state he had genuinely thought she was his fiancée.

'Are you okay, Jess?' Libby put her arm around her shoulder. 'You took quite a tumble, as well as a horrible drunken kiss.' She glared at Eddie and Ross. 'I think you'd both better go.'

'Yes, we will,' Eddie took hold of Ross's arm. 'Come on, you've done enough damage for one night.' His dark eyes looked troubled as they rested on Jess. 'I am so sorree, Jess. I hope I didn't hurt you. I was trying to get you away from Ross. I didn't mean to…'

'It's fine.' She waved her hand dismissively. 'Just get Ross out of here and get him to his room before he causes any more trouble.'

'Come on, Ross, let's go.' Eddie pulled him up.

Ross staggered to his feet, leaning on Eddie for support. 'I feel sick,' he slurred.

'Oh God, get him to the bathroom quick!' Libby said in a panic.

'This way, Ross.' Eddie had his hand around Ross's waist as he led him to the bathroom, opening the door with one hand then guiding him in.

'I wouldn't fancy being Eddie right now!' Libby said. She glanced at Jess. 'You sure you're okay, you took a tumble then.'

'I'm fine.' Jess frowned as a loud crash came from the bathroom. 'What the…'

'Oh no, what have they broken?' Libby groaned.

A few minutes later both men came out, Ross looked decidedly green and Eddie not much better. I guess holding the groom's head over the loo while he was being sick wasn't one of the nicest best man duties, Jess thought.

'He knocked some toiletries over, but nothing's broken,' Eddie explained apologetically. 'I'll get him out of here now. Sorree for…' he quickly glanced at Jess and she felt her cheeks flush, 'the trouble.' His arm around Ross's shoulder, Eddie guided him towards the door.

'Hang on! I'd better check the coast is clear.' Libby dashed ahead of them, opened the door and peered out. 'Okay,' she beckoned them. 'Follow me and for God's sake keep quiet! If anyone sees you here – you'll be kicked out and we'll be in mega trouble.'

Jess sank down onto the sofa as they all piled out of the room. She was so shaken up she was trembling. *Don't be ridiculous, it was a stupid drunken kiss.* But she knew it wasn't Ross's kiss that had shaken her. It was the feel of

Eddie's body against hers, of his hand on her breast, and the emotions they'd stirred within her.

It was because she wished it was *Eddie* who had kissed her.

Pull yourself together, Jess.

She got up and switched the kettle on – giving it a shake to check there was enough water in it first. What she needed now was a strong black coffee. She opened the top cupboard, took out two mugs and spooned coffee into them, guessing that Libby would want one, too. She was pouring boiling water into the first mug when Libby came back.

'Right, they're in the lift on the way to their floor, so it's out of our hands now.' She looked at Jess. 'Are you sure you're okay? I know Eddie broke your fall but I bet you've got a couple of bruises. It must have been awful.'

'Too bloody true, his breath was rank. I hope you don't mind, I've made us both a coffee.' Jess took a slow sip of the scalding liquid and tried to stop her hand from shaking. She wasn't going to admit to Libby that she was more shook up because of the effect Eddie's touch had on her, than Ross's drunken kiss. 'I feel sorry for his fiancée if that's how he acts when he's not with her.'

Libby picked up her mug and cupped it in her hands. 'I know. Fellas! But I do think it was a genuine mistake.'

Jess shrugged. 'I guess there's no real harm done.' She checked her watch. 'Gosh, it's almost four o'clock. We'd better get some sleep. Mind if I take the coffee with me and finish it off while I get ready for bed?'

'No problem hun. See you later.'

***

Eddie groaned. His brain was mush, his head felt like it had been used as a football. Heavy drinking didn't agree with him. Not that he drunk that much, not compared to the rest of the guys. He'd been too busy keeping an eye on Ross, who seemed hell bent on getting legless all weekend. Anyone would think he didn't want to get married.

And he wouldn't be if Carly found out about him kissing Jess.

Eddie rubbed his eyes and put his hands behind his head, linking his fingers as he thought about the recent events. He couldn't believe that Ross had lunged at Jess like that, pulling her on top of him and kissing her. And as if that wasn't bad enough, he'd gone and made the situation worse himself by manhandling her. Okay he hadn't meant to. He was trying to help. To pull her off Ross before he could get any more amorous. Instead he pulled her on top of him and groped her.

82

Mon Dieu. He still felt embarrassed at the way his hand had cupped her breast. Yes, it was an accident. He hadn't meant to slip his hand from her waist to her breast, it had happened during all the confusion of falling back onto the floor. But he should have let go as soon as he realised instead of lying there, holding her, revelling in the feel of her.

He closed his eyes as he remembered the feel of her breast. Soft, round, and just the right size to cup in his palm. In those brief moments while Jess had lain on top of him, her back against his chest, he'd noted the fragrant smell of her hair, her perfume, heady and strong, her slim waist that his left hand was still wrapped around. He could have stayed there forever, taking in the smell and feel of her, and for a moment she was still, too, as if she hadn't realised what had happened, but then he'd heard her gasp, felt her wriggle, and had quickly let her go. She'd jumped to her feet, angry and flustered. And who could blame her?

She had taken it well, he had to admit that. Apart from slapping Ross across the face, Jess hadn't caused a scene, and she definitely could have. He guessed that she and Libby encountered lots of drunks in their job as travel reps, they were used to handling them.

He had to find her and apologise in the morning. And make Ross apologise, too. Jess and Libby had both been kind to them, allowing them to go through the staff quarters instead of chancing it at the reception desk and probably being thrown out. And how had they repaid them? It was humiliating to remember it.

He could hear Ross snoring and glanced over to see him flat out on his back on the bed, dressed in last night's clothes over his naughty nurse outfit. He'd leave him to sleep it off. The longer he slept, the less he could drink. He'd go and find Jess himself and get Ross to apologise later.

First, though, he needed to sleep. He closed his eyes and drifted off, memories of the feel of Jess's body against his floating across his mind.

Chapter Ten

It was gone ten before Jess managed to drag herself out of bed. Between the amount she'd had to drink, and how late it was when she'd gone to bed, she'd hardly slept. It was as if her mind went into overdrive and couldn't stop whirring. She'd been angry at Ross, yes, but he'd been really drunk, and she and Libby had been stupid to let them into the staff quarters. What were they thinking of? If Ziggy had caught them, he'd have gone mental. They should not have got involved. One of the other guys could easily have sneaked Ross into their room for the night, she was sure. The other two hotel managers weren't as strict as Manuel.

Well, what was done was done, as her mother always said. What she needed now was a shower and breakfast. She wished she had the whole day off instead of just the morning. Her head was throbbing and her back ached. She'd slept in her undies last night, so she turned to look at her back in the long wardrobe mirror and, as she'd suspected, it was already starting to bruise from where she'd landed on Eddie. She flushed as she recalled the feel of his hand on her breast again, then swiped the memory away. She wasn't going to think of that now. She was

going to shower, make a strong coffee, grab a bite to eat –
she'd missed breakfast but kept a packet of cornflakes in
the cupboard for emergencies – then go and lie by the
pool for an hour.

As she headed for the shower, her phone buzzed. She
hoped that wasn't Charlotte with even more wedding
instructions. She picked up her mobile and swiped the
screen.

R U UP? L x

Jess was surprised Libby was awake so early. Usually
she could sleep like a baby no matter what, *and* she had
the whole Sunday off. Lucky thing

Yep, just having a shower.

C U at the pool in an hour?

OK x

A couple of hours lazing by the pool with an iced cold
drink should make her feel better. And with any luck,
Ross and Eddie would spend the day recovering in their
room so she wouldn't have to see them.

***

Ross was sprawled on top of the bed, comatose. Eddie looked over at him, wondering whether to try and wake him, but decided to let him sleep it off. Best mate or not, he could do with a break from him. Looking after Ross was hard work. He wished he'd never come on this stag do. The restaurant was so busy this time of year, yet here he was, wasting his time drinking every day and trying to stop Ross from doing something stupid that would wreck his wedding.

Like kissing Jess.

Eddie winced as he recalled last night's events again. He couldn't believe that Ross had lunged at Jess like that. And was mortified that he'd made things so much worse by trying to help. He doubted if Jess would want to see any of them again, but he ought to find her and apologise for Ross's appalling behaviour last night, and for his own clumsiness. Then it was best if they gave the two reps a wide berth. The girls had been so friendly and helpful to them, at the risk of getting into big trouble themselves, and in return Jess had been manhandled. Twice.

He got up and padded across to the bathroom, turning on the shower and stepping in. Oww! Ice cold. He should have let it run a bit first. Jess could report them, he thought, as he smothered himself with shower lotion

87

under the now warming water, but he knew she wouldn't. Ross was lucky, it could have been a very serious situation.

If Carly got wind of it she would probably call off the wedding. Leave Ross standing at the altar. Like Yvette left him.

Unwanted memories of his almost-wedding-day filled his mind. He'd been so happy that morning. Yvette was the love of his life, at least he'd thought she was. He would have done anything to make her happy. As he'd got ready for the ceremony all he'd thought of was how beautiful Yvette would look walking down the aisle, how lucky he was, how perfect their life together would be. Ross had been his best man, had accompanied him to the church, waited with him as the minutes ticked by until it slowly dawned on Eddie that Yvette wasn't just being 'fashionably late,' but wasn't going to turn up at all.

It was Ross she'd eventually phoned. Eddie hadn't even been worth a phone call. Ross had broken the news to him that Yvette didn't love him. She was in love with someone else, the old school friend who had contacted her on Facebook and who she'd insisted was only a friend. Apparently, they'd been messaging each other, meeting up, falling in love – and Eddie had been oblivious to it all. It was Ross who had told everyone, cleared the gifts away, organised everything, and pulled Eddie through the dark weeks that followed. He owed Ross, and he wasn't going to let him down. He wasn't going to let Ross's wedding day be ruined over one drunken kiss. Carly wouldn't be hearing what had happened from him, and he was pretty certain Ross wouldn't blab, so, thankfully, his secret was safe.

Eddie turned off the shower, grabbed one of the white bath sheets hanging on the door and rubbed himself dry.

Ross was still snoring. Eddie hesitated. No, he wasn't going to wake him, even though he knew Ross would be mad at sleeping away half the day when it was his stag do. At least he couldn't cause any more trouble if he was asleep. He pulled on a pair of cut-off denims, a black vest and sandals, ripped a sheet of paper off the notepad supplied by the hotel and wrote AT THE POOL. TEXT ME WHEN YOU WAKE then looked around for the best place to leave it. He spotted Ross's phone on the floor by the side of his bed – that would do. Wrapping the note around the phone, Eddie set off to find Jess and Libby.

Breakfast would be finished now, but a coffee would keep him going until lunchtime. He ordered one – strong with only a touch of milk – from the bar and sat down to drink it, trying to think of what to say to Jess. He liked her and would like to get to know her more. Not that there was any chance of that after last night. She probably thought he was a total idiot.

Which he was.

And Ross would be a dumped idiot if Carly got wind of what he'd been up to.

His mind drifted to Carly. He'd been surprised when he met her, she wasn't the sort of woman he'd thought Ross would be attracted to. She was pretty enough with her chic black bob, dark eyes, high cheek bones and slender figure, but she was so... prissy. Everything had to be perfect and in the two weeks he'd known her when he came over last summer, he'd never heard her laugh. She was so controlling, so jealous. Still, they say you don't choose who you fall in love with, and Ross must love Carly if he was going to marry her. And he guessed she loved him, too, or why else would she want to marry him?

Love is strange. It sort of gets hold of you and blinds you to reason, and before you know it, you're giving up everything you want, everything you planned for, to please someone else.

And then they dump you.

Well, that was never going to happen to him again. He'd made sure he didn't allow anyone else close enough to wield that much power over him. Not that he lived like a monk. There were plenty of girls who were happy to have a casual relationship, to hook up for fun, so he hadn't gone without company the past three years. He'd always made the rules clear at the beginning, though, to make sure he was hurting no one. No commitment, no pain.

Coffee finished, Eddie strode out the back and over to the pool, keeping his eyes peeled for the familiar mass of bright red hair. There she was. Libby, too, both lying on their stomachs on sun loungers by the pool. They looked like they were sleeping. Well, it would be no wonder if they were. It had been a very late night. As he walked over he couldn't help noticing how cute Jess's bum looked from behind, tight but curvy.

He grabbed an ice-cold lemonade from the poolside bar and sat down, waiting for one of them to move. Then he could walk over and apologise on Ross's behalf, assure them that nothing like that would ever happen again. That he and Ross would keep well away from them and spend as much time as possible in one of the hotels where the other guys were staying. It was hard work keeping Ross out of trouble. He'd be glad when the wedding was over.

***

Jess turned over, opened her eyes and blinked in surprise when she spotted Eddie sitting at a nearby table, sipping a can of lemonade. He smiled and waved, rather awkwardly, when he saw her. She sat up and looked around. Good. There was no sign of Ross. She really didn't want to face him yet. Not that she wanted to face Eddie either, but it was too late as he was already walking towards them. Damn, it looked like he was intending to speak to her. This was going to be really awkward.

She nudged Libby with her foot. 'Eddie's coming over.'

Libby mumbled and rolled over onto her side.

'Well I didn't expect to see you here this morning,' Jess said as Eddie reached them. 'Where's Casanova? Sleeping it off?'

'He really is sorree,' Eddie told her. 'As am I, for my... clumsiness.'

Jess waved her hand dismissively, glad for the sunglasses concealing her eyes. 'Don't worry about it.' She lay back down and closed her eyes again.

She could feel Eddie's gaze on her but kept her eyes firmly closed until she was sure he had gone. He'd apologised, she'd accepted. There was nothing more to be said.

'That was a bit harsh.'

Jess opened her eyes and blinked at Libby who was now sitting up. 'I thought you'd dozed off.'

Libby took off her sunglasses and dangled them from her finger. 'No, I was pretending to be dozing to give you two a bit of privacy. Obviously, you'd both feel awkward about last night.'

92

Jess shrugged and tried not to think of lying on top of Eddie, his hand ... 'One of those things.'

'You can't fool me. I can tell you like him.'

'He seems nice, which is more than you can say for his mate.' Jess screwed up her nose. 'I guess it was kind of him to come and apologise for Ross, although Ross should have done it himself.' She hadn't meant to sound so unfriendly and dismissive to Eddie. She was just embarrassed.

'I bet he's too drunk. And ashamed.' Libby picked up the bottle of sun cream and smoothed some onto her arms. 'I wonder what his fiancée is like?'

Jess shrugged. 'I feel sorry for her. I wouldn't want to be marrying a guy who gets so legless he throws himself at a stranger. Although, to be fair, he did say his fiancée's name and seemed genuinely confused when he realised that it was me, not her.'

She looked around. There was no sign of Eddie. Probably gone to join his mates at one of the other hotels. She guessed he and Ross would keep a low profile until they left. What did it matter, she thought, as she reached for the sun cream Libby had just put down. They were just two guys over on a few days holiday. She'd never see them again.

Chapter Eleven

'So sorry to disturb you, Jess.'

Jess looked up at the sound of the familiar voice. She'd spent all afternoon running the kids' club and was now on a short break before organising the evening's entertainment. The break consisted of an iced tea by the pool and Eddie and Ross, both dressed up to go out, were the last people she expected to see.

'Ross wanted to come and apologise for his behaviour last night, didn't you, Ross?' Eddie nudged Ross sharply with his elbow. Jess had to admit that he did look very shame-faced.

Ross licked his lips. 'Eddie told me what happened. I'm sorry, Jess. I was totally out of it. I can't even remember kissing you.'

'I don't think kissing describes it. Slobbering over me is more like it,' Jess retorted.

Ross shook his head. 'I honestly can't remember anything from when we left the club until I woke this morning. I think once I hit the fresh air that was it. I really am sorry.'

'I hope you don't make a habit of kissing women when you're drunk, especially as you're getting married next week.' Jess was determined not to let him off lightly. 'I don't think your fiancée would approve.'

'God no, she'd go mental!' Ross looked horrified.

'So you're not going to tell her?'

'Definitely not. Carly's so jealous she'd call off the wedding.' He ran his hand through his hair. 'Look, I'm sorry. I'm a total prat. What more can I say?'

He seemed genuine. 'Okay, I'll forgive you.' Jess finally relented. 'Just don't drink so much for the rest of the weekend, eh? I know it's your stag do and everything, but you don't want to be doing something you'll really regret.'

'I won't. I'm only having a couple of drinks this evening. Definitely not going overboard,' Ross told her.

Eddie had stood back a little, leaving Ross to apologise. He stepped forward now. 'That's very good of you. Ross and I appreciate your understanding, don't we, Ross?'

Ross nodded and shuffled, obviously embarrassed. 'I guess we'll see you around, then.'

'Sure,' Jess nodded. 'Enjoy your evening.'

Libby and Charlie joined her as Eddie and Ross walked off.

'I'm guessing Ross came to apologise?' Libby asked. 'He looked dead embarrassed.'

'Yes. Must say I didn't expect him to. He's worried what his fiancée will say if she finds out.'

'Well she won't will she, unless he blabs? Eddie's not going to dob him in is he?' Libby said.

'Dob him in for what?' asked Charlie, pulling out a chair to join them.

Jess grimaced. 'He grabbed me and gave me a snog last night when he was drunk,' she said, not wanting to go into too much detail. Charlie wouldn't snitch on them, but even so, it didn't look good saying they were all in Libby's room. She suddenly realised how bad it would look to Ross's fiancée if it all got out.

'Gross,' Charlie sympathised. 'I hope you marked his card for him.'

'Too true I did. But now he's freaking out in case his fiancée finds out and calls off the wedding.' She shrugged. 'Anyway, they leave early Tuesday morning and I'm working all day Monday, so I doubt if we'll see them again. They'll be keeping a low profile now.'

'A lot of fellas get a bit carried away on their stag do,' Charlie said. 'Last bit of freedom as a single guy and all that.'

'If I ever decide to settle down and get married – which won't be any time soon – my hen do will be totally wild,' Libby announced.

Jess and Charlie exchanged amused glances. 'That doesn't surprise me at all,' Jess said. She stood up. 'I guess we'd better get this entertainment rolling.'

'Kurt's just setting up. Have fun,' Libby said with a grin.

'That's right, rub it in that you've got the whole day off, why don't you?'

The kids' evening entertainment was quite fun, especially if you didn't have to do it every night. One small hotel group Jess had worked with had a skeleton entertainment staff which meant that Jess and Gustaw, a Polish lad with a wicked sense of humour, had been in charge of the entertainment every evening. After a week of the same games and kids' songs sung in French, German, Russian and English it felt like every day was Groundhog Day. She enjoyed working at this hotel though, there were enough reps for them to swap about the shifts which meant plenty of variety. She set off to the entertainment area over at the far end of the pool where she could already hear the strains of The Macarena playing.

***

Eddie selected a clean shirt and pair of casual trousers out of the wardrobe. Two more evenings to go then the stag party was over, thank goodness. He'd had stern words with the other guys today and told them no more pranks, but he wasn't convinced by their assurances that they wouldn't play any. He knew that as far as they were concerned, that's what stag parties were all about, and they looked on him as a bit of a spoilsport. He didn't mean to be. He just didn't want anything to spoil this wedding for Ross. Like his own had been ruined.

As he buttoned up his shirt, he wondered what Jess would be doing. She was working tonight so maybe she was in another show. Tempting as it was, he wasn't going to pop into the lounge to check, the less time they spent in this hotel the better after last night's fiasco.

He got dressed and went to join Ross who was already propping up the bar with Greg. 'No sign of Libby and Jess,' Greg said. 'It's Libby's night off, so I thought she might be at the bar. Shall we have a quick look around for them and say hello before we go?'

Ross glanced awkwardly at Eddie.

'What's up?' Greg asked sharply.

'Nothing, but we're on a stag do, we don't want to be hanging around with two of the reps all the while. We want to have some fun,' Ross knocked back his drink. 'Come on, let's meet the others and head for a club.'

'I didn't know it was a woman-free holiday,' Greg grumbled. 'Well I'm going to look out for Libby tomorrow. I'm not going home without talking to her and getting her number.'

I wouldn't mind getting Jess's number, Eddie thought, as they walked out of the hotel. Fat chance of that after last night. She had been really cold with him on the beach, obviously not wanting to have anything else to do with them.

Shame. He liked her. It would have been good to keep in touch. Still, he could look out for her Tuesday morning and say goodbye. There was no harm in doing that.

Chapter Twelve

Eddie was going home tomorrow, Jess remembered, as she headed over to the pool – she and Libby were running the exercise session again. Would he look her up to say goodbye? Did she want him to?

'Did you meet up with Greg yesterday?' she asked Libby, who was jogging on the spot as part of their warm up exercises.

'No, I bumped into him in the bar and he said they were out on the razzle all afternoon, so I thought I'd better give them a bit of space after what happened.' She stopped jogging and reached for the bottle of water on the table. 'He asked me to meet him for a drink tonight, though, to say goodbye.' She uncapped the bottle and took a sip. 'Have you seen Eddie?'

'No. I imagine he and Ross will keep out of my way.'

'That's a shame. I know you liked him. You're going to say goodbye to him, aren't you?'

'It depends if I bump into him.'

All through the exercise session, she kept glancing at the faces of the people around the pool, searching for a mass of sooty dark hair and a cute goatee beard, half hoping Eddie would drop by.

There was no sign of Eddie all morning. Well, what did she expect? They were on a stag do, they'd be out making the most of their last day. And she had been frosty with him. Completely overreacted. He probably thought she was some prissy misery guts and decided to keep well clear.

'Fancy an hour on the beach? We've got a couple of hours before our next stint,' Libby asked when their sessions were over.

'Sounds good to me.' Jess reached for her beach bag and popped on her sun glasses. It was a beautiful day, the sun was warm, but not scorching hot yet, like it would be later this afternoon. 'Let's grab a drink first, though.'

They headed over to the pool bar, grabbed two bottles of iced water, and made their way to the sandy shore.

Jess took her flip-flops off, padding across the soft, warm sand, looking out for a spare sun bed. You could often find one on the beach at this time of the day, whereas the sunbeds around the pool were always snatched up early, with some of the guests sneaking out at the crack of dawn to put their towel over a sunbed so they could claim it before anyone else did.

'There,' she pointed to two empty loungers, with a parasol over the top. They were quite close to the sea too, an ideal spot.

'Perfect,' Libby agreed.

Jess lathered herself with sun cream and lay down on the sunbed, intending to relax for the next couple of hours, but to her annoyance her thoughts kept drifting to Eddie, wondering what he was doing, whether she would see him again before he left. She started to get restless. She needed to be up, doing something, to keep herself busy, not be bothering about a guy she had only just met and who'd be going home tomorrow. She sat up. 'I'm going for a paddle.'

Jess paddled for a while, letting the cool sea sweep over her feet as she gazed out at the stretch of sparkling blue water in front of her, teaming with holidaymakers swimming, paddling and playing with their children. In the distance a jet ski skimmed across the surface of the water, leaving a white foamy trail. She felt the tension leave her. It was a glorious day.

Forget, Eddie, he's only one of many holidaymakers you've met this summer. He isn't important. She closed her eyes for a moment, felt the rays of the warm sun on her face, filling her with peace. She opened her eyes, turned around – and blinked.

There was Eddie strolling towards her, his bronzed skin glistening in the sun, silver dog-tag lying on the mat of dark hairs covering his chest, black swimming shorts slung low on his hips. Looking stomach-churningly sensational.

***

It was her. Eddie stood still, watching for a few minutes as Jess paddled in the sea. He'd been hoping to see her so he could say goodbye. He'd looked for her at the pool but the exercise session had finished and, guessing she was off duty for a while, he thought she'd be inside somewhere. *Quelle chance* that he'd decided to have a walk along the beach to clear his head, pounding from yet another late night. He'd left Ross spark out, hopefully it would be at least another hour before he surfaced and headed for the beach.

He walked slowly over towards Jess. She turned as he reached her, as if she sensed him. He saw the look of surprise – and was that pleasure – on her face. 'Eddie.'

'*Bonjour*, Jess. I thought I would take a little stroll on the beach. It is such a lovely day.'

'Where's Ross?' she asked. 'Sleeping it off again?'

He nodded and waded in the sea beside her. 'After this holiday, I think I will never drink again.'

She smiled at him, a real smile that crinkled the corners of her eyes and made him think that perhaps she'd forgiven him for his clumsiness. 'Finding it hard to keep up, are you?' she teased.

103

'It is … *difficile*. I enjoy a drink, a cool beer on a sunny day, a glass of good wine or a malt, and champagne, of course – but I can never see the point of drinking yourself into oblivion. The English and their stag parties.' He shrugged. 'The guys, they put flowers in Ross's hair last night and made him wear a dress – one they picked up from the market. Then they took pictures and uploaded them onto Facebook. Crazy.'

She chuckled. 'Believe me, that's quite mild compared to some of the stag parties we've seen on the island. Especially over the other side, in Magaluf. Charlie worked there last season and he said it was totally wild. That's why this hotel, being a family hotel, has such a strict restriction on single sex party guests.'

Eddie nodded. 'Yes, I can understand it. It is lucky you were there to talk the manager around for us.' He couldn't stop looking at her. She was so pretty, so full of life. 'I think you like your job very much,' he said softly.

'I do, most of the time. It's not a 'forever' job, but I've had fun over the last few years.'

This surprised him. 'You are thinking of leaving? Of doing something else?'

'In a year or two, yes. I haven't decided what yet, though. But I don't want to be a travel rep forever. I want to get my own place eventually, so I'll need a regular job, not jetting off all over the world.' She stared down at the water rippling over her feet then raised her eyes to his. 'What do you do?'

'I have a restaurant in Marseille. We specialise in sea food but, obviously, cook other meals, too.'

She looked impressed. 'That's quite an achievement.'

'As is what you do,' he replied. 'You want to see the world, so you work hard to do that. In the couple of days I've been here I can see that it is a difficult and tiring job, but always you are polite and friendly to the customers. You are good at your job. Very good.'

'Thank you.' Their eyes met and he fought down the urge to reach out and touch her cheek, trace his thumb over her lips.

'Are you flying back to France tomorrow, or the UK?' Her question snapped him out of his thoughts.

'France – once I've seen Ross safely on his plane. I will fly over to the UK Friday morning for the wedding.' Eddie pulled a face. 'I will be glad when this wedding is over.'

'I've got a wedding to go to next weekend, too. I'm chief bridesmaid at my cousin's wedding. Can't say I'm looking forward to it. I haven't seen her for ages, and we never get on when we do meet.' She looked over her shoulder, squinting her eyes. 'Here comes Greg. I think he and Libby have a bit of a thing going.' She shot a sharp glance at Eddie. 'He isn't married or anything, is he?'

'Absolutely not. He likes to... how do you say? Play the field.'

'Well he's met his match with Libby. She'll outplay him and leave him standing. Shall we join them?' she paddled out of the sea, back over the beach to the sun-loungers. Eddie followed, wishing that Greg hadn't shown up just then. Jess seemed to have forgiven him for the stupid episode in Libby's room, and he'd enjoyed talking to her. He toyed with the idea of asking her if she wanted to keep in touch, but hesitated, not sure what her reaction would be.

***

The day passed quickly. Once Eddie and Greg had gone to meet the other lads, Jess and Libby had lunch and then were back on duty. It was past ten that evening before they finished. That's it, I won't see Eddie again, Jess thought as she and Libby sat in the bar for a last drink before turning in.

'I checked out Greg's Facebook this afternoon. You should see it,' Libby said, taking her phone out of her pocket and sliding open the screen.

'How much of it can you see? Isn't it 'friends only'?' asked Jess, leaning forward to peer at the screen.

'He sent me a friend request.' Libby looked up. 'Actually, I'm meeting him in a bit; he's slipping away from the others.' She got Facebook up on her phone and clicked onto Greg's page. As Jess had guessed, there were lots of fun photos of him larking around and several of him with different girls.

'He's a bit of a player,' Jess said.

'Yeah, he's fun.' Libby logged out of Facebook and opened a bag of salt and vinegar crisps. 'What about you and Eddie? It looked like you were having quite a conversation this afternoon. What were you talking about? Are you meeting him later?' She fired off the questions as she munched the crisps.

Jess shrugged. 'We didn't talk about anything much, and no, I'm not meeting him.'

'I'm going to get changed, then. I can't go out like this.' Libby was still wearing her uniform of a red tee shirt and black shorts. 'See you in the morning.' She jumped down off the bar stool.

'Libby…'

'What?

'Be careful. I mean, you don't really know Greg.'

'Stop being such a goose, I'll be fine.'

Of course she would. Libby knew how to take care of herself, and she guessed that Greg and the others weren't exactly strangers now.

Jess opened her bag of crisps, ready salted (she didn't like strong flavours) and bit into a large one. Well there'd be no chance of Eddie slipping away, even if he wanted to. As best man he had to look after Ross. She might as well face facts. She wouldn't be seeing him again. She was on duty from eight in the morning and they were leaving at ten.

Well what did it matter? Okay, he was incredibly sexy, but she'd soon forget about him. Every week sexy guys piled into the holiday resort. Eddie was just one of many.

Chapter Thirteen

Her drink and crisps finished, Jess stood up, yawning. She was shattered. As she picked up her bag she heard her phone ring. It was almost midnight, a bit late for anyone to call. She reached in her bag, took it out and checked the screen. Libby. Had she met up with the other guys too, and wanted Jess to join them? Well, she had no chance. Jess was working in the morning and didn't intend to have another late night.

'Jess, something terrible has happened,' Libby gabbled as soon as Jess answered the call. 'Ross has disappeared.'

'What do you *mean*? How can he have disappeared?' Thoughts raced through her mind, had Ross got so drunk he'd wandered out of the club and gone off by himself. If so, surely he was capable of getting a taxi to bring him back. Unless he'd conked out again, like he did the other night. He could be lying comatose on the pavement somewhere... Stop panicking, let Libby explain. 'Lib?'

'The guys, they decided to play a trick on him. They jumped him, blindfolded him, pretended they were kidnapping him and bundled him into a taxi.'

Jess groaned. A common stag party trick, but one she had never found particularly funny. 'And...?'

'They drove him to the middle of the town, got him out, and left him in a park tied to a tree. Then they went off to get a kebab. They were only gone about ten minutes they said, but when they returned to untie Ross he wasn't there.'

'So he managed to get free and is on his way back to the hotel,' Jess said. 'I'm sure he guessed who his 'kidnappers' were.'

'Matt reckons Ross had no idea it was them. Ross kept shouting out, asking who it was, but none of them spoke to him. Stupid bloody idiots. And…' she swallowed. Jess closed her eyes, groaning. How much worse was this going to get? Libby continued. 'They took off his shoes, and left him blindfolded, too. Matt said Ross didn't see where they'd taken him, so even if he managed to get free he wouldn't know his way back.'

'You mean Ross is wandering around drunk, with no shoes, in the dark, the night before he's due to fly home?' Jess asked, irritated. What an idiotic prank to play. 'Did you check out the area? He couldn't have gone far in ten minutes.'

'Matt said they looked everywhere. Me and Greg weren't with them, we'd left the guys at the club, we wanted to have a quiet drink by ourselves. Then Matt phoned us. We got a taxi and went straight over there.

There's no sign of Ross. We've checked the nearby streets too.'

'Where's Eddie?' she asked.

'Still at the club. He didn't know about the plan. Matt said the guys tricked Ross into going outside when Eddie went to the bar then jumped him – they'd already told the driver it was a stag party joke. But it's all gone terribly wrong.' She could hear the anxiety in Libby's voice. 'Can you come and help find him, Jess? The guys are really worried.'

Jess sighed. Honestly, men could be stupid sometimes. Especially when they'd had a few drinks. 'Where are you? I'll get a taxi over.'

Libby told her the name of the park, Jess keyed it into the notes folder on her phone, grabbed her bag and hurried out. There were usually a couple of taxis hanging about at the hotel entrance, but it was late now, so she hoped they hadn't given up for the night.

Luckily, she'd just reached the gate when a cab pulled up and two people got out.

'Wait!' Jess shouted, waving to the taxi driver. Then she realised the two people were Ross and Eddie.

'Ross! You're okay!' she said, relieved. 'I've just had a panic call from Libby. The others are looking for you.'

'They can keep looking. All night long,' Ross retorted. 'Serves them right for what they did to me. If it wasn't for Eddie I'd still be tied to that tree, shivering my arse off.'

'I thought they were planning something. I saw them shove Ross into the taxi so quickly followed them in another cab,' Eddie said. 'As soon as they walked off I untied Ross.' He stroked his beard. 'So, they're still looking for him?'

'Yes, and Libby's with them. They're in a right panic.'

'Good. Well don't tell them I'm here. They can search all night for all I care.' Ross looked furious and she didn't blame him, but she couldn't let Libby and the others keep searching for him. They were worried sick.

'I can't…' she started to say, but Eddie shook his head.

'We can't do that, Ross. It's not fair to involve Jess, and Libby is out searching, too. Besides, we've all got to fly home tomorrow, and we don't want to risk anyone missing the transfer coach.'

Eddie could have told them himself, but Jess guessed he'd set Ross free and sneaked him away to teach them all a lesson. She didn't blame him. She took her phone out of her pocket and selected Libby's number.

'Jess are you on your way?' Libby sounded agitated. 'We've looked everywhere for Ross. I think we might have to call the police…'

112

'No need,' Jess paused. 'He's just turned up in a cab with Eddie.'

'Eddie?'

'What's that? What's happened?' she heard Greg ask.

'Ross has turned up at the hotel with Eddie,' Libby told him.

'What?' Greg exclaimed. 'How?'

'Hang on and I'll find out.' Libby was speaking to Jess again now. 'How did Eddie find him?'

'Apparently, he got wind of their plan, followed them, and set Ross free,' Jess explained.

Libby's chuckle resounded down the phone. 'So, they've been running around in a panic for nothing? Serves them right.'

Jess could hear the other lads shouting and grumbling in the background. 'I'll be back in a bit, Jess. Thanks for letting me know. Glad Ross is safe,' Libby said, her voice laced with laughter. 'Good for Eddie.'

'Well I'd have left them to stew,' Ross said, scowling, as Jess ended the call. 'I'm going to clean up and go to bed.'

'He was pretty shook up when I got to him,' Eddie said as they watched Ross stomp off up the steps and into the hotel. 'He had no idea where he was or who had taken him. It's a good job I was keeping an eye on them all. I could tell they were planning something, all the looks they

113

were giving each other, and the whispering.' He shook his head. 'I knew they wouldn't be able to get through the weekend without playing a stupid prank.'

'It's a good job you guessed what they were up to. They hadn't gone far, had they?' Surely they wouldn't have left him out there for long.

'They were hanging about around the corner. I think they'd have been back in ten minutes or so, but I couldn't risk it, there's no telling what they'll do when they're drunk. Nor could I resist the urge to trick them back. It's been a nightmare trying to control them all weekend. I'm glad we're going home tomorrow.'

'Are you always this sensible, or is it because you take your best man duties seriously?' Jess asked.

'I like a laugh as much as anyone else, but stag night pranks can get out of hand, and I promised Ross I'd have his back. I don't want anything going wrong with his wedding.'

'Like it did yours?' The words were out of her mouth before she could stop them.

There was a pause and she was sure she heard him catch his breath. She should never have said anything. Now he knew that Tony had been gossiping about him. 'Sorry, one of the lads must have mentioned it.'

'It is no matter,' he nodded. 'Yes, like mine. And a good job, too, I realise now. I'm glad I didn't marry

Yvette, it would never have worked out. She did me a favour.'

He didn't sound bitter. Maybe she hadn't put her foot in it after all.

'Better to find out before you tie the knot,' she said.

'I think better not to tie the knot at all,' Eddie replied, sombrely.

Obviously, his experience with Yvette had turned him against marriage. Well, she couldn't say she blamed him. Few people were happily married, look at her parents, they seemed happy when she was little, but things soon started to go wrong. 'Well I hope it all goes well; the wedding I mean.'

'Me too. Then I can go back to my life in France and relax. I didn't realise how big a strain it was to be the best man.' He turned to her, and even though it was dark she could sense his eyes gazing into hers. 'I hope that your cousin's wedding goes well, too. I think you will make a beautiful chief bridesmaid.' He leant forward and kissed her on both cheeks, sending her pulse racing. 'Goodbye, Jess.'

'Goodbye,' she said a little too breathlessly. It was a kiss on the cheeks for goodness sake. Stop overreacting!

He was still gazing at her. Slowly he reached out his hand and tilted her chin with his finger. She held her breath as his head came closer then suddenly his lips were on hers, kissing her gently, his moustache lightly tickling her nose. It was a fleeting kiss that left her wanting more, but Eddie had released her and was already walking up the steps.

Jess wrapped her arms around her shoulders, watching him go in. He really was something. She wouldn't mind getting to know him better. A lot better. Shame she would never see him again.

***

Dammit, why did he kiss her on the lips? He hadn't planned to. He'd meant to kiss her on the cheeks then walk away, but she'd smelt so good, felt so good, he hadn't been able to stop himself. Hadn't wanted to stop. It had taken all his will power to cut short the kiss and walk away. She didn't seem to mind, but she hadn't kissed him back. He guessed that she wasn't as interested in him as he was in her. Which was a good thing. He had a feeling he could get really fond of Jess. Too fond. And the last thing he needed was to fall for a woman again. Especially someone like Jess who lived for the moment, travelled around the world with her job, and was a man magnet. No, it was better that she hadn't returned his kiss, because if she had, he doubted if he'd have been able to walk away.

116

***

'Jess!'

Jess spun around to see Libby and the lads staggering up the drive. 'Were you waiting for us?' Libby asked. She looked around. 'Where's Eddie and Ross?'

'They've gone inside. I think they're hoping to get a few hours' sleep before the flight tomorrow.' She looked at the others. 'You should all do the same.'

'Well this is it, babe. Goodbye.' Greg reached out and pulled Libby to him, swaying slightly. He wrapped his arms around her and gave her a long kiss, which Libby returned ardently.

I wish Eddie had kissed me like that. Jess imagined sinking into Eddie's embrace, feeling his lips on hers, kissing her slowly, deeper. She shook the thought from her mind. There was nothing between her and Eddie. Whereas Greg and Libby had obviously hit it off and intended to keep in touch. She left them to it.

***

Eddie lay awake most of the night thinking about Jess, how attracted he was to her, how her body had felt against his, how much he wanted to see her again. Finally, he

117

decided to get up early and try to find Jess before he left, ask her if she'd like to keep in touch. After all, what harm could it do to message each other now and again?

But he overslept, and by the time he'd woken Ross up, had breakfast – he'd ordered room service for them both – and packed, it had been time to go down to the lobby to catch the coach. He knew Jess was working and guessed she was probably on pool duty again, but there was no time to go and check. No time to say goodbye.

Maybe it was for the best. He didn't like the feelings she stirred up inside him, feelings he never wanted to experience again. Not after Yvette.

As he sat on the plane, leaving the Spanish island far behind, he wondered if he'd done the right thing. Beside him Ross snored softly. Eddie rested his head back in his seat and closed his eyes. He was tired. Too much drink and too many late nights. He closed his eyes and drifted off to sleep. His dreams were full of a girl with bright red hair and an infectious laugh.

***

Jess looked up as the plane soared overhead. Were Eddie and Ross on that, on their way back to England? She and Libby often got close to holidaymakers, it's hard not to when you see them every day, and some you missed more

118

than others. Some wanted to stay in touch, asked to exchange phone numbers or email addresses. She always refused politely, knowing that people acted differently when they were on holiday to when they were at home. She told them it was company policy so that she didn't seem rude. Out of sight, out of mind. There was always the next bunch of holidaymakers to entertain and befriend.

It was different with Eddie. She'd half-hoped he'd ask to exchange phone numbers or befriend her on Facebook, as Libby and Greg had done, and if he had she'd have been tempted to agree. He hadn't asked, though. Hadn't even sought her out this morning to say goodbye.

And a good job, too. He'd got under her skin far too much. That kiss last night...

She shrugged the memory away. She didn't need or want a relationship. No strings, no pain.

At least now they had all gone home, she didn't have to worry about Ross getting drunk and causing trouble at the hotel. Honestly, she didn't know how his fiancée put up with him. If she knew what he was really like she'd probably call off the wedding. And who could blame her.

Chapter Fourteen

The next few days flew by. There were constant, frantic messages from Charlotte about the wedding arrangements – it seemed like she was having a bit of a melt down and was convinced that something would go wrong on the day. She wanted to check that Jess was certain of the arrangements: what her duties were, what to do with the flowers, had her speech ready, etc, etc.

'She's driving me mental,' Jess said in exasperation. 'She's enough to put you off weddings for life! Honestly, does it matter if everything isn't perfect?'

'To be fair, I'd want to make sure everything was just right on my wedding day,' Libby replied, looking up from the task of painting her finger nails dark blue.

Jess stared at her in astonishment. Libby always seemed so laid back. Then she remembered how particular she was about what she wore, how she did her hair, even painting her nails to match her clothes, like now. Appearances were very important to Libby, so yes, she probably would plan her wedding in detail and want everything to look right.

'Maybe, but I can't believe you'd be as bad as Charlotte.'

'I hope not. I wouldn't want to turn into a bridezilla, but it's the bride's day, isn't it?' Libby expertly swept the nailbrush over her thumb. 'I mean you only get married once, well you hope you do, so you want it to be as perfect as you can get it.' She dipped the brush into the pot. 'I'd like a designer dress for sure, and to turn up in a sleek limo.'

Jess could hardly believe her ears. 'You've actually planned your wedding? You're not even dating anyone!'

'Not planned it. Well not in detail, but I have thought about it, yes. All women do. It's their big day.'

'I haven't.'

Now it was Libby's turn to look incredulous.

'Are you serious? Not even a little bit? You've never thought about what you'd like to wear? What sort of wedding you'd like... whether you want to get married in a church or on a beach, that sort of thing?'

'Of course not.' It was true. She had never thought about getting married. She had far too many things she wanted to do. And why would she think about getting married when she didn't have a serious boyfriend – had never even had one? She'd had plenty of dates, yes, some even lasting a couple of months, but that was as far as it got. The idea of planning her wedding was ridiculous.

'Well think about it now. What sort of wedding do you want?' Libby slipped the nail varnish brush back in the bottle and screwed it shut. 'You must have some idea.'

'I don't. Why should I? I might not ever get married.' The idea of committing herself to someone freaked her out. How could you promise to love someone forever when you had no idea how either of you would feel in a few years' time? If either of you would meet someone else? She couldn't bear the thought of tying herself down to one man, committing to a regular job and a mortgage when there was a whole world out there waiting to be explored.

'You will, eventually. Everyone does.' Libby leaned forward, eagerly. 'Go on, think about it. Imagine you were getting married tomorrow. To Eddie, maybe,' she added mischievously.

A picture of Eddie looking dashing in a dark grey suit, burgundy tie, his hair styled so that it was lifted slightly off his face, flashed across her mind. Whoa! She'd actually come up with a colour scheme. Scary.

'I knew it! You did fancy him,' Libby said, triumphantly. 'I can't believe you didn't at least FB friend him. Don't worry, I can get his details from Greg so you can contact him.'

'I don't want to contact Eddie. What's the point? Holidaymakers come and go. I don't feel the need to keep in contact with all the dishy men I meet, like you do.'

'Aha – you admit you think he's dishy then?'

'I'd have to be blind not to see that. Yes, he's dishy, but that doesn't mean I've got the hots for him.' She changed the subject before Libby could question her further. 'Anyway, talking about weddings, I still need to paint the soles of my shoes so that Charlotte thinks they're Louboutins. I don't want to leave it until the last minute in case it looks a mess and I have to take it all back off again.'

'It won't. I've done it before. You might need to put a couple of coats of nail varnish on, though. How many bottles of red do you have?'

'Half of one. I'll pop to the shop in my break and grab another bottle.'

***

'They've turned out well. They really look like Loubs,' Libby said when she dropped by later. She picked up the blue stilettos and turned them over to admire the red soles. 'I bet no one will know the difference.'

Jess grinned. 'I hope they fool Charlotte. I can't wait to see her face when I turn up wearing these. Mind you, I don't want her looking too closely because I reckon she'll soon spot they're not the real deal. I bet she's got a genuine pair.'

Libby grinned. 'She sounds a right snob, no wonder you're dreading it. Still, at least you'll have four days off. I can't believe Ziggy allowed you to do that when we're smack bang in the middle of the season. I'm so jealous.'

'He took a lot of persuading, and I've had to do sick cover,' Jess reminded her, thinking of last Sunday when she was supposed to have had the whole day off but had to do Tanya's afternoon shift. 'But, yes, I am looking forward to the time off. I wish I could have had a week, though. I'd like to spend some time with my mum and drop in on Becky and Mae. I haven't seen them for ages.' Becky and Mae had been her buddies since secondary school and they always tried to meet up when Jess flew back home. It was rare Becky could make it now she was settled down with Scott, her partner, and had a little baby, but Mae always turned up. Last time she'd brought her latest girlfriend, Anna. It had been a scream. They'd drunk and laughed so much that the evening had sped by and they'd been astonished to see that they were the only ones left in the bar when the staff politely asked them to leave as it was closing time. 'It'd be good to catch up with Gerri, too, if I have time.' She'd met Gerri at college and they'd kept in touch.

'What are you wearing with the shoes?' Libby asked.

'I was thinking of a casual top and distressed jeans. It's pretty informal. We're all meeting in the lounge of the hotel for a few drinks and a catch up. I expect Charlotte will be running through the schedule again, making sure we all know what to do. And Aunt Jean will be boasting about how much everything has cost, how clever Russell is, and how dazzling his prospects are.' She could imagine the scene. 'I'm dreading the whole wedding to be honest. Charlotte and Aunt Jean will have their noses in the air, bragging about how posh it all is, and I'll be biting my tongue trying not to bring them down a peg or two.' She sat down on her bed and sighed. 'I wish you were coming. I'll need someone to have a giggle with in the evening.'

'The rest of your family will be there, surely?' Libby asked.

'My brothers can't make it, so there will only be Mum, and she'll be so worried about doing something to upset Aunt Jean or Charlotte that I probably won't get a word out of her.' She shrugged. 'Never mind, I'm sure I can manage to smile and put up with them all for one day. I've had enough practise doing that with some of the guests.'

'Not to mention the drunken ones who try to snog you.'

'God yes.' Ross's drunken kiss had all but been forgotten. She'd been far too busy looking after and entertaining the guests to think about him. Although, images of Eddie's rugged good looks and soulful dark eyes had occasionally flashed across her mind when she lay in bed at night, but she always swiped them away.

'Remember to take lots of photos,' Libby told her. 'Especially of you in that dishy bridesmaid's dress.' She grinned. 'Just the outfit to snare the best man. It's tradition for the chief bridesmaid and the best man to hit it off, you know.'

'Well there'll be no chance of that. Honestly, Lib, he'll be dead boring, as will Russell. Charlotte's got as much personality as a door post and she's bound to pick someone just like her.'

She rummaged through the clothes hanging in her wardrobe and took out a bright orange silky shirt.

'What do you think? It's casual, but dressy enough for the evening.'

Libby looked at the shirt and grinned. 'Orange shirt, red hair and blue shoes. No one can accuse you of being obsessed with matching colours. If you ever do get married, you'll probably wear a rainbow coloured dress.'

'Now that sounds like an idea! And I'll get married in a wildflower meadow with a daisy necklace!' Jess rummaged through the wardrobe again and picked out a

126

couple more tops and a spare pair of jeans. 'Maybe I'll start packing my case now. I've only got a couple of days.'

She knelt down by the bed, pulled out her small purple-decorated-with-silver-stars-suitcase and lifted it up onto the bed.

'I bet you don't have a problem spotting that on the conveyor belt,' Libby remarked.

'That's the idea.' Jess opened the case and shoved her Loub-look-alikes, a pair of trainers, and a pair of sandals into the zip-up compartment on the one side, then folded her clothes neatly into the other side.

'Won't you need a dress for the evening do?' asked Libby.

Jess shook her head. 'No, Charlotte doesn't want us to change. She's keeping on her wedding dress and she wants us to wear our bridesmaids' dresses, so the photos are,' she made quote marks with her fingers '"consistent."'

Jess selected a few changes of underwear, put them in a carrier bag and then into the case. 'Right, now all I have to pack is my make-up and toiletries, and it's no good packing those until the morning I go.'

'Lucky you. I love weddings. I haven't been to one for ages.' A wistful look came over Libby's face. 'Everyone dresses up so lovely, the bride is like a princess. It's sort of magical.'

'Can't say it all appeals to me, but there you go. I'll try to enjoy it.'

'I bet Greg and the lads will all look hunky in their suits. I hope he puts some photos on Facebook so I can see them.'

An image of Eddie dressed in a charcoal grey suit and burgundy tie flashed across Jess's mind. The same image she had the other day. Strange. She didn't even know the dress code for Ross's wedding, so why should she get the same image twice? Libby was right though, they would look hunky. Especially Eddie.

Chapter Fifteen

'Shit, my suit jacket's a bit tight. It's all the booze and takeaways I had on the stag weekend. Carly will have a fit.'

Eddie looked over and saw that Ross was right, the buttons on his dark blue suit jacket looked like they were about to pop off. 'Leave it unbuttoned,' he advised.

'I can't do that. Carly will think it's slovenly.' Ross breathed in, but it didn't make much difference. He unbuttoned the jacket and sank down on the chair. 'What am I going to do? There isn't time to lose weight now. The wedding's in two days.' He ran his hand through his newly-trimmed hair. 'I wish I'd never gone on that stag do. It was a total disaster. I've put on weight and if ever Carly finds out about me kissing that holiday rep she'll kill me. Why didn't I just go out for a meal, like she did?'

Eddie watched him worriedly. Ross had finally forgiven the lads for kidnapping him and tying him blindfolded to the tree, but he'd been beating himself up all week about his drunken snog with Jess – or rather that he forced on Jess. He was convinced Carly would find out.

'Stop worrying. She's not going to find out. You and me are the only ones that know and I'm not going to say anything, are you?'

Ross looked up at him. 'That's the thing, we aren't the only ones who know. The other rep, Libby, told Greg and he told the other guys. They all know.'

Damn. Even so, they wouldn't dob Ross in, would they? Especially after the stunt they pulled! They'd lose his friendship for good if they did.

'They're your mates. They aren't going to say anything.'

'What if they tell their girlfriends? And the girls tell Carly?'

'They won't. Why should they? Blokes never talk about stuff like this. Everyone does stupid stuff on stag dos. Besides, Carly isn't friends with any of the guy's girlfriends.' Eddie walked over and put his hand on Ross's shoulder. 'Stop panicking. It's all going to be fine.'

'How can it be? My suit won't even do up and it's too late to get it altered.' Ross stood up. 'The only thing I can do is not eat for the next couple of days. I've got to lose a few pounds if I do that.'

Was he crazy? 'You can't not eat. You'll make yourself ill.'

Ross shot him a determined look as he unbuttoned his jacket. 'I'll do anything to make sure our wedding day is

130

perfect. I know everyone thinks Carly is stuck up and bossy, but that's just the way she comes across to strangers. I thought it at first too, but once I got to know her I realised what a wonderful woman she is. She's thoughtful and kind and far too good for me.' He took off the jacket and placed it carefully on the hanger. 'I love her, Eddie, and I don't want anything to spoil our day.'

He really does love her, Eddie realised in astonishment. He'd got the impression that Carly had been the one pushing the marriage, that Ross had been dragged along rather reluctantly, but he saw now that he was wrong. Ross wanted this wedding to go ahead as much as Carly did.

Well, it's a good job that he had his stag do abroad, because if Ross had snogged a girl over here there was no doubt it would get back to Carly. He should have guessed Libby would tell the other guys. It's the sort of thing she'd think was funny. Had Jess told anyone, he wondered. He remembered the tales she and Libby had shared with them; things other guests had done.

He was still embarrassed about the stupid way he'd groped her when he pulled her off Ross. Talk about making a situation worse. He shrugged the memory from his mind. Two more days and the wedding would be over. He could go home and forget all about it.

***

'Right, I've got to go. The pick-up coach is here,' Jess said as the coach to the airport pulled up outside the hotel. 'I'll message you when I land and send you pics of the wedding.'

'And a photo of the best man – especially if he's a hottie,' Libby replied.

'I told you, he's bound to be a nerd. I know the sort of guys Charlotte goes for, and the friends they have.' If they had any at all. Sleazy Simon certainly hadn't, and he had definitely been a creep. Jess gave Libby a quick wave and hurried out, pulling her case behind her. She'd be glad when this wedding was over. The only plus to it was seeing her family and friends again.

Once on the flight, Jess's thoughts drifted to the wedding. She'd been surprised when her mum had told her it would be *this* summer. Charlotte hadn't met Russell until the middle of last year, and they'd only got engaged at Christmas. Jess had expected the wedding to be next year so that Charlotte and Aunt Jean had time to plan it all and make sure everything was perfect, but, according to her mum, Charlotte had been planning her perfect wedding for years, right down to the font on the invitations. All she'd been waiting for was the right man to come along. It was a bit weird, Jess thought, recalling her conversation with Libby about planning weddings. She was almost thirty and had never met a guy she'd like to tie herself down to. It was always great at first, fresh and exciting, then she got bored. And how did you know if you could trust them? Look at how Ross and the others had behaved. It was as if they'd forgotten about their girlfriends as soon as they stepped onto the plane. Nope, marriage – or any kind of commitment – definitely wasn't for her.

Mum had told her in their weekly phone calls that Charlotte was a real bridezilla, having a hissy fit if anything went the slightest bit wrong. Surprise, surprise. Charlotte had been like that ever since Jess could remember. She was a right spoilt brat.

She wondered what Russell was like. Pompous, she guessed, and smarmy. She knew he was the manager of a software firm, Aunt Jean had proudly told her mum that, and how he was working his way up to the top. 'He'll be on the board soon, you wait and see!'

Well she'd soon find out. Charlotte had booked Jess and the other bridesmaids rooms at the hotel she was getting married in, to make sure that none of them were late for the wedding. She'd also arranged for a make-up artist and a hairdresser to tend to them all the next morning, so that they were all looking their best for the photographs. Typical Charlotte. She bet she'd persuaded –

or rather bullied – Russell into having his hair styled as well. She'll have chosen his outfit, of course, and told him how to spend his stag night. Cancel that. He probably wasn't allowed a stag night in case he had too much to drink or dared to look at another woman. Charlotte had always been controlling and possessive.

Jess would have liked to have gone home first, say hello to her mum and see how she was, but there was no time. The bridal party were all meeting for drinks in the bar at seven, which meant that by the time she arrived, Jess only had half an hour to freshen up and get changed.

She closed her eyes and rested her head back on the seat. This was going to be a difficult weekend. Only the thought of meeting up with Mae and Becky on Sunday night cheered her up.

***

The taxi pulled up outside the hotel. Impressive was her first thought. And madly expensive was her second. Obviously, she knew Charlotte would choose a posh hotel that would look good in the photos, but she hadn't expected it to be this grand. It looked like Charlotte, Uncle Gerard, and Aunt Jean had pulled out all the stops. She half expected there to be a red carpet on the floor!

She hadn't expected the taxi fare to be so much, either. Luckily, she'd had the foresight to change some euros for English money at the airport. She rummaged in her bag for her purse as the taxi driver got out, opened the boot, and took out her case.

'Thanks, keep the change.' She handed him a twenty pound note then hurried inside and over to the reception desk to check in. The receptionist gave her a key and instructions, adding 'Miss Dysall left a message to remind you that there's a meeting in the lounge bar at 7.00 prompt.'

Jess smiled. 'Thank you.' She glanced at her watch. The taxi had got caught up in traffic, so she now had even less time to freshen up and get ready. She hurried over to the lift.

The room was amazing, like something out of a magazine. Snow white bed linen and curtains to match, beech fitted wardrobes along one wall, with matching desk, coffee table and bedside units, a soft pale-blue pile carpet, and pale-blue and white tiles in the spacious en suite. She dreaded to think what the whole wedding would have cost. Apparently, Aunt Jean and Uncle Gerald had started a trust fund as soon as Charlotte was born, to pay for her university education and her wedding. What a waste of money. If Jess had been lucky enough to have a trust fund she'd use it to travel around the world. I mean, who needed a degree unless you wanted an actual profession – she was sure that Charlotte could have still got her job as a PA without it – and fancy wasting thousands on one day. She'd rather have a spectacular honeymoon – money spent on travelling and holidays was never wasted as far as Jess was concerned. Mind you, Charlotte would probably be having a spectacular honeymoon as well.

She opened her case and quickly unpacked it. Charlotte had the bridesmaids' dresses and Jess knew she'd be keeping them all safe until they all got ready in the morning. There was no way her fussy cousin would risk anyone spilling something on them. She hoped her dress fitted. Well, there was nothing she could do about it now. It was a wonder Charlotte hadn't demanded she go for a fitting as soon as she arrived in case the dress needed any last-minute alterations.

She barely had time to freshen up and change into her jeans and orange shirt when there was a knock on the door.

'Jessica! Are you there?'

Charlotte.

'Coming!' Jess hurried over and opened the door. Charlotte stood in front of her, immaculately made up and dressed to the nines in a fitted black dress revealing toned, sun-tanned legs. She looked Jess up and down, her eyes

136

lingering pointedly on the distressed jeans. 'Are you ready?'

'I just need to get my shoes. It's only a casual meeting in the bar, isn't it?' Jess grabbed her blue mock-Loubs and slipped them on. She saw Charlotte's eyes widen as she stared at the shoes and had to fight back a smile. It looks like she'd noticed the red soles and been completely taken in.

'You could call it that. I wanted us all to meet, get to know each other a little before tomorrow. I'll introduce you to Amanda and Danielle, the other two bridesmaids, and we can go through the schedule for the day, too, so you all know what's expected of you.'

Sounds fun. Not!

She hoped that the other two bridesmaids weren't as stuffy as Charlotte.

'Will your mum and dad be there, too?' she asked, hoping they weren't. She didn't think she could bear a whole evening listening to Aunt Jean and Uncle Gerald boast about how clever Charlotte was, how much the wedding cost, and the latest home improvements they'd had done to their mansion in Surrey.

'Mummy and Daddy will both be there. Daddy has taken a couple of days off work especially. He wants to make sure everything is perfect for my big day,' Charlotte told her. 'Mummy has been so helpful with the wedding

137

preparations. Especially as you – my chief bridesmaid – haven't been able to organise anything for me. Or even come over for a dress fitting,' she added petulantly.

Breathe in. And out. Now is not the time for an argument. Jess swallowed down the angry retort that sprang to her lips and said as pleasantly as she could, 'you knew I worked abroad when you asked me to be chief bridesmaid, Charlotte. And you knew I couldn't get any time off – not in the summer months. You're lucky I managed to swing it for the wedding.'

'I thought you could fly over for the weekend for a dress fitting, at the very least. And organise a few things for me – it's not that difficult with the internet.'

'It is when you work twelve hour shifts six days a week, which is what I do most of the time.' God, Charlotte had started already. She was dreading this evening, when Aunt Jean was bound to throw in a few gripes as well. Jess would try to keep the peace, but they had better not push too much. She was the one doing them a favour. They had practically begged her to be chief bridesmaid – well, Aunt Jean had via Jess's mum.

Charlotte pressed the button for the lift then turned and scanned Jess up and down. 'Oh dear, I think you might have put on a bit of weight. I hope your dress fits. Perhaps you should try it on now to make sure.'

What a bloody cheek. She might not be a stick insect, like Charlotte, but she wasn't fat.

'My measurements are the same as the ones I sent you, so there shouldn't be a problem,' she retorted, although she didn't know if her measurements were exactly the same, she never really bothered to weigh or measure herself, using whether her clothes fitted comfortably or not as a guide instead. Her job kept her on her feet all day so there was no chance of piling on the pounds, despite the chocolate and cream cakes she couldn't resist tucking into whenever she got the chance.

'I hope so. It's too late to get it altered now anyway, so you'll just have to breathe in.'

What a snob, Jess thought, as Charlotte floated into the lift. She couldn't wait for this wedding to be over with.

When they walked into the lounge bar it was quite crowded. Uncle Gerald stood up and waved them over. 'Ah, there they are,' Charlotte said. 'Get me a drink will you, Jess? A white wine with soda, please.' Then she strode off to join the others.

Yes Miss! Jess resisted the urge to give a mock-salute to Charlotte's retreating back and wove her way through the crowd to the bar. She pitied Russell, he had no idea what he was letting himself in for.

She ordered herself half a cider, a small wine and soda for Charlotte, and carried them over to the corner where

Charlotte's parents and a few others were gathered. She scanned the faces, wondering if any of them were Russell but then realised that, of course, he wouldn't be here. It was bad luck to see the bride the night before the wedding.

'Ah there you are, Jessica,' Aunt Jean said as Jess joined them at the table. She pointed to a silver-haired rather distinguished looking man on her right. 'You remember Uncle Albert, don't you? He's Charlotte's usher.' Then she turned to the two young women sitting beside Charlotte. 'And these are the other bridesmaids, Amanda and Danielle, Russell's sisters.'

'Danni,' Danielle whispered as she gave Jess a peck on the cheek.

'Mandy,' Amanda said, winking.

'And I'm Jess,' Jess added. Danni and Mandy seemed nice. Maybe this weekend wouldn't be too bad after all.

They chatted for a while, the usual stuff, where she worked, the wedding plans. When Jess went up the bar to get another drink, Danni followed her. 'I must admit I was surprised when Ross told us he was marrying Carly, I never thought he'd settle down and, well... Carly isn't his *usual* type.'

Carly? Ross? Jess paused. *It couldn't be.* It was just a coincidence.

'What's up?' Danni asked. 'You've gone a bit pale.'

'You called Charlotte, Carly and Russell, Ross...'

'Everyone does – except the parents, of course. Don't you?

Jess shook her head. Her mouth felt dry. She had a very bad feeling about this. She licked her lips. 'I've never met Russ...Ross. do you have a photo of him?'

'Sure.' Danni rummaged in her handbag. 'Didn't you get the wedding invitation? It had a photo of them both on it?'

'No, Charlotte emailed the details to me.'

Danni pulled out a cream slip of paper and handed it to Jess. 'There's Ross.'

Jess glanced down at the coloured headshot of Charlotte and a fair-haired man. His hair was shorter, and he was wearing a shirt and tie, but there was no mistaking him. It was Ross.

Ross who had got blind drunk on his stag weekend, lunged at Jess, and given her a fat, slobbery kiss.

Then another thought struck her.

If Ross was the groom, Eddie must be the best man.

Chapter Sixteen

'Are you okay, Jess? You're staring at that photo oddly.'

Danni's voice cut through Jess's thoughts. 'Er, yes.' Charlotte knew she was a travel rep for goodness sake, why on earth didn't she tell her that Russell was spending his stag do in Majorca? Surely, she knew that Jess was a rep there? Or maybe she didn't, Jess hadn't mentioned it to her and her mum might have simply said that she was working abroad. All their contact had been through email and had only ever been about the wedding preparations.

Now what did she do? Should she say that Ross had stayed at her hotel? It couldn't do any harm, surely, it would come out at some point and then it would seem strange that she covered it up. After all, she wasn't the one who'd done anything wrong. He'd said his name was Ross and his fiancée was called Carly. How was she supposed to guess it was Russell and Charlotte? Charlotte had never called herself Carly as far as Jess knew.

'He stayed at the hotel I work at, in Majorca, but he called himself Ross,' she added, 'And said he was marrying someone called Carly. She's always been Charlotte to me, so I didn't put two and two together.'

'Russell's family and friends have always called him Ross.' Danni gave her a searching glance. 'He behaved himself, didn't he? Eddie promised to keep an eye on him.'

Jess shrugged. 'I didn't actually see much of them, being a rep is a demanding job.'

Danni grinned. 'Six of them went, they wanted to go to Magaluf but Carly wouldn't hear of it. She's very insecure, always worries Ross is going to cheat on her. She booked them into a family hotel hoping that would keep them out of mischief.'

'There was a bit of a problem over that. Unfortunately, because it's a family hotel, no stag or hen parties are allowed, so two of the guys were sent to the sister hotel next door and two over the road,' she said. 'I was walking through Reception when they arrived so saw what had happened.'

'Really? Ross didn't say. Well, that might have been for the best. Gives them less chance of getting into trouble. I imagined them going back to one of their rooms and drinking through the night. They're a lively bunch. Except for Eddie. He's the sensible one.'

Jess shrugged. 'That's men on a stag do. I'm surprised Charlotte allowed him to go on one. I thought she'd keep his reins tight. What was her hen do like?'

'We went for a meal. You know, Carly – angel wings, L plates and 'kiss me' hats aren't really her style.'

Jess nodded but her head was whirling. What should she do? Charlotte was her cousin, and she was about to marry a man who had cheated on her.

Well not exactly cheated. It had been one drunken kiss. A kiss that Jess hadn't wanted. But would Charlotte believe that after Sleazy Simon?

'Fancy Ross staying at your hotel? What a coincidence.' Danni looked puzzled. 'I wonder why Carly didn't mention it to you seeing as you worked in the resort?'

'I don't think she knows where I work. I usually spend each season in different places. Besides, we aren't that close. We don't talk much.'

'I can see that. Yet she asked you to be her chief bridesmaid?'

Jess shrugged. 'Between me and you, I think I was the last resort. Charlotte hasn't got that many friends and the ones she has got probably didn't fancy the role, knowing how demanding she is. At least I'm not in the same country so not that readily available.'

'She is a bit …difficult…isn't she?' Danni agreed. 'I hope the wedding goes okay with no dramas.'

'Me too,' Jess replied. Somehow, she had to keep the drunken kiss – and the other stag party behaviour – a secret, or there would be hell to pay. She wouldn't put it past Charlotte to cancel the wedding if she found out. And guess who would get the blame? Jess, of course.

'Guess what, Ross and the guys were at the same resort that Jess works in, and Ross and Eddie actually stayed at her hotel,' Danni said as they joined the others at the table.

Charlotte's face froze. She stared at Jess as if she could hardly believe what she was hearing. 'You didn't mention this,' she said, icily.

'I didn't know until Danni showed me a photo of Russell. I've never met him, have I?'

'Surely the fact that he was on a stag do, his name was Russell, and he was marrying someone called Charlotte the very next week rang a bell with you,' Aunt Jean said frostily.

Awkward. She obviously had to explain why it didn't ring a bell, but would that get Ross in trouble? It might look like he was trying to conceal his true identity. But then he hadn't known who she was, had he? Best to stick to the truth as much as possible. 'The guys called him Ross, and he referred to his girlfriend as Carly,' she looked at Charlotte. 'I guess that's his pet name for you, but I didn't know that. If you'd told me he was going to Majorca I might have guessed who he was.'

'I didn't know you worked in Majorca.' Charlotte's tone suggested that if she had known she'd have made sure Ross went somewhere else for his stag do. She turned to her mother. 'Did you know?'

'For goodness sake, Jess is here, there and everywhere with her... *job*.' Aunt Jean said the word 'job' as if it was an insult. 'I can't keep track of her.' She glared at Jess. 'I still think you might have worked it out. It isn't that difficult.'

'Look, I didn't talk to them and get their personal details,' Jess defended herself. 'I was too busy working.'

Charlotte looked at her suspiciously. 'Surely Russell said he was getting married this weekend?'

'Yes, he did but so are lots of other people.' Jess tried to keep her patience. 'I told you he called himself Ross and called you Carly. How was I supposed to make the connection? They're two completely different names.' She could feel the anger rising. 'You've always called your fiancé Russell and I didn't know you went by the name of Carly.'

'I do now. Ross calls it me and it's sort of stuck. I like it, it sounds sort of bubbly. You can call me it, too. Everyone does,' Charlotte, or rather Carly as she now wanted to be called, looked almost friendly.

'I certainly won't be calling you any such thing,' Aunt Jean sniffed. 'Your name is Charlotte and I have no

146

intention of shortening it.' Then her eyes narrowed in suspicion. 'Danni said that Russell and Eddie stayed at your hotel. What about the other men, where did they stay?'

Jess explained about the hotel policy and how the new receptionist who had taken the booking hadn't realised that it was an all-male stag party. This led to a half hour interrogation from Charlotte and her parents about what the lads had got up to and how much she had seen of them, which she answered as vaguely as she could.

Aunt Jean and Charlotte seemed satisfied, but Jess felt very uncomfortable. She was sure that they would be interrogating Ross as soon as they got the chance.

Charlotte was now detailing the arrangements for the next day, when the hairdresser and make-up artist would come, what time they all had to meet, how to walk, how to talk... the list went on and on, but Jess was hardly listening. She forced a smile on her face and nodded in what she hoped were the right places. If only she could get away and Facetime Libby, ask her what she thought she should do. Libby would be busy with the evening entertainment right now, though. She'd try and catch her later when she went to bed, if it wasn't too late, Majorca was only an hour ahead.

'Where did you and Ros... Russell meet?' she asked when her cousin had finally stopped talking about the arrangements and everyone was now chatting idly to each other. She was sitting right next to Charlotte so felt obliged to make conversation and realised that she knew absolutely nothing about their relationship.

'In the supermarket, would you believe?' Charlotte chuckled and suddenly her face was transformed. She looked gentler, prettier, there was a soft dreamy look in her eyes. 'We both reached for some beans from a pile and brought the whole lot down. Tins were rolling all over the aisle. I was devastated, but Russell just laughed. We picked them all up and built the pile again, then he asked me out for coffee. And that was it.' Her eyes danced with happiness. 'I know we seem so different, Russell is carefree, a bit of a lad, I guess, but he's kind and funny and...' Her voice trailed off.

She really loves him, Jess realised in shock. She hadn't though Charlotte was capable of loving anyone. She always seemed so cold and aloof.

'Love at first sight, eh?' she teased.

Charlotte nodded. 'It was for me – and Russell said that it was for him, too.' She twisted a lock of hair around her finger. 'Sometimes I have to pinch myself to think I'm going to marry someone like Russell. He's so handsome,' she looked at Jess. 'Girls are always throwing themselves at him, but he assures me he'd never look at anyone else.'

Jess could hear the uncertainty in Charlotte's voice and could understand her feeling so insecure. Although Ross was good looking, he definitely wasn't Charlotte's usual type, but he seemed as besotted with her as she was with him. She'd be gutted if she found out about the kiss. And she'd blame Jess, of course. Everyone would blame Jess.

***

'Love the Loubs,' Danni said as she joined Jess at the bar a little later. 'I noticed Carly eyeing them up, too. Being a rep must pay well.'

Jess grinned. 'I'll tell you a secret if you promise not to tell Charlotte…'

'Cross my heart.' Danni air-drew a cross over her heart with her finger. 'Do you know a cheap resale website?'

Jess shook her head. 'They aren't Loubs.'

Danni stared down at the shoes. 'Really? But it's only Loubs that have red heels and soles.'

Jess slipped off a shoe, picked it up and handed it to Danni. 'Red nail varnish.'

Danni inspected the shoe, then her face broke into a wide grin. 'Hey, what a brilliant idea. I'm going to pinch it!'

149

'Libby, my friend, suggested it. You reckon it's fooled Charlotte, then?' Jess took the shoe back and slipped it on again.

'Definitely.' Danni paused as if wondering whether to say anything. Then continued. 'Look, can I speak to you for a minute? They're all busy talking over there,' she indicated at the rest of the wedding group. 'They won't notice if we slip outside.'

'Sure,' Jess agreed, puzzled. She guessed it was probably something to do with the wedding arrangements. Maybe Danni wanted to ask her to let her catch the bouquet. If so, she needn't worry, Jess had no intention of vying for it.

They took their drinks outside and sat at one of the tables.

'I couldn't help noticing that you looked really shocked when you saw the photo of Ross. As if...'she hesitated, 'well, as if something had happened. And you were quite cagey when Carly and her mum were questioning you about him.'

Was she? Heck, she hoped they hadn't picked that up. 'I was shocked,' she said. 'I didn't realise who Ross was when he was at the hotel.'

'Yes, but why shocked?' Danni pursued. 'Surprised I can understand. But you looked really stunned and uncomfortable. As if... well, as if he'd done something you didn't want to talk about.' She fixed her eyes on Jess's face. 'He hasn't, has he? I know what these stag dos can be like. And Ross, he's got a bit of a roving eye, but I thought he really loved Carly and wouldn't do anything stupid. Tell me he didn't do something awful like trash the hotel room or get off with someone.'

What should she say?

She hesitated a moment too long. 'He did, didn't he? I can see it in your face.' Danni leaned forward, her voice urgent. 'What did he do? You can tell me, I'm hardly likely to tell Carly, am I? I'm Ross's sister.'

Maybe she should tell her, because if all this did come out at a later date, and Aunt Jean and Charlotte tried to blame her, at least she could say that she'd told Danni.

'Okay, but look, I'm only keeping quiet about it because he was drunk and didn't realise what he was doing.' She quickly relayed what had happened. Best not to mention that he was lying on the sofa in Libby's room at the time.

'That was all, a kiss?'

'A *drunken* kiss. He was mortified afterwards. Apparently, he thought I was Carly.' She twiddled the stem of her glass. 'I know Charlotte, though, and she'll think it was more than that.' *Especially if she found out Ross was in Libby's room.* 'She can be really possessive and highly strung. She might even call off the wedding.'

151

Jess sighed. 'So you see why I looked so shocked. I had no idea he was my cousin's fiancé. I was trying to help out a guest, as a rep that's my job, and the manager would have thrown Ross out if he'd seen him in that state.'

Danni chewed her lip. 'He's a bloody idiot. But you're right, Carly will be furious if she finds out, so let's keep it under wraps. As you say, it was just a kiss. I was hoping he hadn't slept with someone. He hasn't actually got form for being faithful, but I think he really does love Carly, so I'm hoping he's a reformed character.'

'Eddie was watching him like a hawk, he wouldn't have had a chance to get up to anything much,' Jess said. She stood up. 'We'd better get back to the others now or they'll be wondering what's going on.'

***

It seemed as if the evening would never end, but finally she was back in her room and immediately messaged Libby.

R U up? Need to talk asap.

Wats up? Came the message back.

152

Jess hit the Facetime button and Libby's sleepy image immediately appeared on the screen.

'I was about to go to bed,' she said. 'What's the emergency?'

'Emergency? It's a total disaster! You'll never guess who Charlotte's fiancé is.'

'Is it someone famous?

'It's *Ross*.'

'*Ross*?' For a moment Libby seemed puzzled as the realisation swept over her face. 'OMG. You mean Stag Party Ross. The one who snogged you?'

'That's the one.'

'Bloody Hell! What did you do when you saw him? What did he do?'

'I haven't seen him yet. His sister – she's really nice – showed me a picture of Charlotte's fiancé and it was Ross. Apparently, he calls Charlotte Carly, and his proper name is Russell.'

'Blimey, who'd have thought it? Have you told your cousin that you met him?'

'Ross's sister told her. Danni saw my surprised look when she showed me his photo and asked if I knew him. Then she told Charlotte.' She paused. 'She really loves Ross, Libby, but she's dead jealous. Always has been. If she finds out about the kiss she might call the wedding off. And she'll definitely blame me.'

'Then don't tell her. It's up to him if he wants to confess and explain. I'd keep out of it.' She paused. 'I think you need to warn Ross though, otherwise he might be so shocked to see you he gives the game away.'

Libby had a point, but how could Jess arrange that? 'The thing is, I probably won't see Ross and Eddie until the actual marriage. I doubt if they will arrive until just before the ceremony.'

'Shame you didn't swap phone numbers with Eddie, then you could phone him and explain,' Libby said. Then she paused. 'Hang on, I could message Greg and tell him to tell Ross.'

'No, that will only make him panic. I need to see him face to face and assure him I won't say anything.'

They talked it over for a while, with Jess finally deciding to try and find Ross before the wedding tomorrow and warn him. 'I'll sneak away and go down to the ceremony room early and wait for him to arrive,' she said.

Chapter Seventeen

A phone call woke her at seven the next morning. It was Carly. Jess groaned as she swiped the screen to answer. What now?

'Morning, Jessica, just checking you're up.'

'The wedding isn't until two this afternoon...' Jess replied sleepily.

'I know but there's lots to do. We're all meeting for breakfast at eight and then the hairdresser and make-up artist will be here at nine. The morning will be gone before you know it.'

'Okay, give me time to shower and I'll be down.'

Jess made herself a cup of coffee first. Somehow, she had to slip away to meet Ross before the ceremony, tell him who she was and assure him that his secret was safe with her.

Danni, Mandy, and Charlotte had almost finished breakfast when Jess walked into the restaurant. She waved cheerily to them then helped herself to coffee and toast, ignoring the assortment of cereal and bacon and sausage and eggs on offer. She wasn't at all hungry. In fact, she felt a bit nauseous, wondering how the hell she was going to get a chance to talk to Ross, because if she didn't, her cousin's wedding could be ruined.

'You're late,' Charlotte said accusingly as Jess reached the table and pulled out a chair. 'I'm going up to have my hair and make-up done now and was expecting you to be ready, too.'

'Sorry, I won't be long.' Jess sat down. 'I'll come up to your room as soon as I've eaten this.'

Charlotte stood up, leaving her used cup and plate on the table. 'I'll carry on ahead. The hairdresser and make-up artist will be here soon.'

'She's a bit of a bridezilla, isn't she?' Danni remarked as Charlotte and Mandy walked off.

'A total nightmare, you mean.' Jess bit into her piece of toast. 'I dread to think what hairstyle she's got planned for us all.'

'Me too.' Danni finished her orange juice and looked squarely at Jess. 'Look, I keep thinking of what you told me about Ross. You need to warn him otherwise he might give the game away when he sees you.' She paused. 'Are you sure that it was just a kiss? I know what Ross is like when he's had a drink.'

'Yes, honestly. And I've already thought I should warn him. I'm going to slip down before the ceremony begins so I can speak to him.'

'Good. The last thing we need is for Carly to get wind of this. If anything goes wrong today, Mum will have a complete meltdown. Honestly, planning for this wedding has dominated our lives for months. Mum's lost over a stone with the stress of it all.' She picked up her bag hanging on the back of her chair. 'See you in a bit.'

'Sure. I'll be ten mins max.'

It was almost twenty minutes before Jess knocked on the door of Charlotte's suite and stepped inside to a chaotic scene. Her cousin was sitting in front of the mirror, hair scraped back, while the make-up artist was dabbing primer on her face. Aunt Jean was laying out the bouquets – white and silver roses mixed with yellow freesias – which had just arrived, on the bed, alongside the make-up artist's open case. Danni and Mandy were both sitting in chairs by the window, heads back, gel patches under their eyes. The bridesmaids' dresses were hanging from the curtain rail at the window, each covered with a plastic bag.

'At last,' Charlotte snapped. 'You need some eye patches for the bags under those eyes.' She pointed to a basket spilling with eye patches, face masks and other beauty aids. 'Shona will be doing your face next as you're the chief bridesmaid.'

Jess sighed and picked up a couple of eye patches. Anything to keep Charlotte happy on her big day.

The morning fled by in a flurry of makeovers, hairdressing, pampering, and primping. Charlotte was highly strung, snapping at minor details, and almost burst into tears when her mascara smudged.

'Come on, darling, it's not the end of the world,' her mother told her.

'I just want everything to be perfect. This is supposed to be the best day of life. I don't want anything to ruin it,' Charlotte said, picking up a tissue to wipe a tear from her eyes.

Jess bit her lip. She hoped she got a chance to catch Ross when he arrived.

***

'Hurry up, Ross, we'll be late!' Eddie shouted. The morning had been a strain. He'd stopped over at Ross's flat last night, they'd both sat up talking late, and yes, had a couple of drinks, too. Ross had been besieged by doubts. Was he doing the right thing? Was he good enough for Carly? And riddled with guilt, too, about the drunken kiss he'd forced on Jess.

'Look, forget it. It meant nothing, and Carly will never find out,' Eddie had told him.

Then Ross had told him that Carly was pregnant. They hadn't known about it for long and were keeping it quiet until after the wedding. 'If she finds out what I did she might cancel the wedding and then I'll probably never see my baby.' Eddie felt for him as he sat, head in hands. 'It's all such a mess.'

'Do you want to marry Carly?' he'd asked.

'Of course, I do. I love her.' Ross had got up and paced the floor. 'I want it to work out, Ed. I want my kid to have a happy family, like I've got.'

Eddie had wondered whether to suggest that Ross should confess to Carly rather than get married with it hanging over them. But he wasn't sure Carly would forgive him.

'I don't see how Carly would find out. We'll never see Jess again,' he reassured him. 'Try to stop worrying about it or Carly will sense something is wrong.'

Eddie didn't admit, even to himself, how much he missed Jess. He hadn't been able to get her out of his mind all week, the way her eyes sparkled, that infectious laugh of hers, the feel of her body against his when he'd so awkwardly pulled her off Ross.

'Where's my tie?' Ross asked, frantically tossing the cushions off the sofa.

Eddie sighed. They'd got up late, Ross had nothing in for breakfast so they'd had only a stale round of toast each, and his stomach was growling hungrily.

159

Ross was wearing his dark blue wedding suit and white fitted shirt, still open at the neck, and his silver-grey waistcoat was unbuttoned. The outfit was supposed to be complimented with a lemon tie – the same shade of lemon as the bridesmaids' dresses.

'Did you leave it in your room?

'I brought it out with me, so you could tie it for me,' Ross said, running his hand agitatedly through his hair. 'I put it down in here somewhere.'

Ten frantic minutes later, they found the tie stuffed down the side of the sofa.

'We've got to get a move on,' Eddie said as he smoothed out the creases in the tie and helped Ross knot it around his neck. 'The ceremony is in an hour.'

'I know.' Ross hesitated. 'Carly will turn up, won't she?'

'Of course she will. She adores you and she's looking forward to the wedding. She's spent months planning it.'

'So did Yvette,' Ross said. Then added. 'Sorry, mate…'

Memories shot across Eddie's mind: getting to the church with Ross, waiting eagerly for Yvette to arrive, Ross going to see where she was, then coming back, his face pale, Yvette had phoned him to say she couldn't go through with it because she loved someone else. Eddie could hardly believe it, didn't want to believe it. Yvette, like Carly, had planned the wedding right down to the last detail. She had even messaged him that morning saying how much she was looking forward to marrying him. And all the time she had been in love with someone else.

'Carly will be there,' he reassured Ross. 'Stop panicking. She is nothing like Yvette. It will all be fine. Now fasten your waistcoat, put your jacket on and let's get going.'

'What about my buttonhole?' Ross asked, looking around for it.

'They're being delivered to the hotel, we'll put it on when we get there,'

'Have you got the ring?' Ross asked as they made a frantic dash out of the house. Eddie opened the door on the driver's side and got in, Ross was far too nervous to drive. 'Yes, it's in my pocket.'

'Let me see.' Ross got in the car and slammed the door shut.

Eddie reached into his inside pocket, took out the ring box, and opened it to reveal the white gold ring with a smattering of sparkling diamonds that had taken Ross months of overtime to pay for.

'Satisfied?'

Ross nodded.

'Right, now let's get going and hope that we don't hit any traffic.'

***

'You look stunning,' Jess said admiringly as Charlotte stood before her. The meringue dress accentuated her slim waist and made her figure look curvier. Her straight dark hair was swept back into a smooth chignon, adorned by a delicate silver tiara glistening with what looked like diamonds, but were probably Zircon, and matching drop earrings. She'd never seen her cousin look so beautiful.

'Thank you. I hope Russell thinks so,' Charlotte said, turning to study her reflection in the mirror.

She really means that, Jess realised. She'd always considered Charlotte to have that blind confidence that only seems to come from being a spoilt child. But last night and this morning she'd seen how insecure her cousin really was. And how much she idolised Ross. She knew she was making the right decision not to tell her about that stupid, awful kiss. How could she destroy Charlotte's happiness over a single drunken mistake?

But would Ross – or Eddie – give it away when they saw Jess? She had to find them and warn them first, let them know that she hadn't spilt the beans. She couldn't leave it until they walked down the aisle.

Chapter Eighteen

The problem was sneaking away without anyone noticing. Charlotte seemed determined not to let Jess out of her sight.

'Right, now let's take one of you with your chief bridesmaid. Closer.' The photographer motioned for Jess to move closer to Charlotte. She obliged, smiling when he told her to, but all the time her mind was whirling as she tried to think of an excuse to leave once the photographs were over.

Finally, with only twenty minutes to go, she took action. Checking her phone and pretending she'd received a text, she said, 'Mum's just arrived. I'm going to pop down and say hello.'

'What... *now*? It's nearly time for the ceremony.' Jess could hear the panic in Charlotte's voice.

'I'll be real quick. I'm all ready, I can meet you down there.' The ceremony was taking place in the private wedding suite, at the back of the hotel. 'I haven't seen Mum for months. I just want to talk to her before it all starts.'

'OK. Make sure you're waiting for me outside the ceremony room when I arrive,' Charlotte told her. 'I can't walk in without you.'

'I'll be there. I promise.' Jess picked up her posy and left the room before Charlotte could call her back. Surely Eddie and Ross would be here now.

She took the lift down and made her way through the corridor, past the lounge, and towards the wedding suite. Pushing open the double doors, she stepped inside.

She paused as she took in how splendid it all looked. The long room had been partitioned off for the ceremony, so she was now standing in the reception area. The round tables and chairs were covered in pure white tablecloths, with a lemon runner along the middle of each one, the same colour as the bridesmaids' dresses, and lemon sashes were tied with a big bow at the back of each chair. Large lemon candles placed in shimmering glass bell jars stood in the middle of each table, while lemon runners and tapered lemon candles in silver candelabras adorned the top table – where the bride, groom, their parents, chief bridesmaid, and best man would sit. It looked spectacular. Charlotte had spent so long planning this. Jess couldn't let her cousin's wedding day be ruined. She had to speak to Ross.

Hearing footsteps behind her, she spun around then caught her breath as Ross and Eddie walked in.

***

'Jess!' Eddie couldn't take his eyes off her. She looked sensational in that dress. Lemon shouldn't really go with that bright red hair, but it did. Her hair was swept up off her face in a messy bun with tendrils hanging down each side, highlighting the incredible bone structure of her face, her long neck, while her strapless dress with its nipped in waist emphasised her curves. She'd looked gorgeous the night she'd starred in the 'Songs of Broadway' show, but it wasn't a patch on how she looked in this bridesmaid's dress.

Bridesmaid's dress? As the impact of this suddenly dawned on him, Jess blurted out, 'thank goodness I've caught you both before the ceremony.' She paused. 'Ross, the Carly you're marrying is my cousin, Charlotte.'

Ross gaped at her, his mouth opened and closed like a fish gasping for air, but no sound came out.

'Your cousin?' Eddie repeated, his mind racing. 'Carly is your cousin?' It couldn't be. Why hadn't Jess known? She'd said she was going to be chief bridesmaid at her cousin's wedding, so how could she not have known that Ross was the man her cousin was going to marry? Surely as chief bridesmaid she'd know all the details.

165

'Bloody hell! You're Jessica. The cousin who works abroad?' Ross ran his hand through his neatly coiffured hair. 'Why didn't Carly tell me? She must have known where you worked.' Suspicion brightened his eyes. 'Is that why she booked me into your hotel? So you could keep an eye on me?'

'Don't be daft. I had no idea who you were. I didn't know many details about the wedding. Charlotte – Carly – and I haven't spoken for years. I've never called her Carly. She only asked me to be chief bridesmaid because she doesn't have anyone else to do it. She made all the arrangements, all I had to do was show up, hold the train, and smile for the photos.' Jess sounded genuine. 'I had no idea what her fiancé looked like until your sister showed me a photo of you both together last night. It was a right shock, I can tell you.'

Merde, this was getting worse and worse. Carly was her cousin so Jess was bound to tell her what had happened. Then Carly would call off the wedding. Eddie was immediately taken back to three years ago, standing at the altar, waiting for Yvette.

He couldn't let Ross go through that. Not just because of one stupid drunken kiss.

'Does Carly know?' Ross's voice came out as a squeak.

166

'She knows you stayed at the hotel I work at, and the trouble with the bookings, but not about anything else.' Eddie could see the sparks flashing in Jess's eyes. 'And I want it to stay that way, right?'

'Thank you.' Ross swallowed. 'But why?'

'Because Charlotte's mad about you and I don't want to break her heart. It was a one off drunken mistake on your part and you won't repeat it again. Will you?'

'No, of course not.' Ross swallowed. 'Thank you.'

'Don't thank me. I'm not doing it for you. I'm doing it for Charlotte.' She jabbed Ross in the chest with her finger. 'And you'd better make sure you never ever do anything like that again, do you hear me?'

'I won't. I'm sorry, Jess. I'm so ashamed.'

'So you should be!'

'Jessica, what are you doing here?'

Jess spun around to face Aunt Jean, her lips pursed. 'I thought you were going to find your mother?'

'I am. I wanted to take a quick look at the wedding decorations first to make sure everything was in order. As chief bridesmaid, it's my responsibility to make sure today goes perfectly.' Jess waved her right hand to encompass the room. 'Doesn't it all look lovely? And the smell from the flowers is so... fresh.' She was gabbling, Eddie thought, in panic. Her aunt would guess something was wrong.

'I see, and then you bumped into Russell and Eddie so decided to renew your acquaintance?'

Was it his imagination, or was Aunt Jean's voice laced in suspicion?

'They came in as I was about to leave.' Jess turned back to them and smiled so wide she looked almost manic. 'You both couldn't believe it when you saw me, could you?'

'No, it was a… surprise,' Eddie replied as casually as he could. '*Un petite monde*, as you say.'

Ross's face had visibly paled. Carly's mother was scrutinising him, her eyes narrowed. 'Are you feeling ill, Russell? You look very pale. You didn't have too much to drink last night, did you?'

Ross shook his head. He seemed unable to speak. Eddie put his hand on his shoulder. 'It's just nerves. Don't worry, he'll be fine in a few minutes.'

'Good because my daughter has worked hard to make this day perfect, and I don't want anything spoiling it. Do you understand?' Her eyes swept over them all as if she knew their guilty secret.

'Nothing will go wrong. Everything is under control,' Eddie assured her.

'Excellent. Now you two had better go to the ceremony room right away. The Registrars are waiting for you, they have already spoken to Charlotte. Come along,

Jessica. Charlotte needs you to hold her train, there will be plenty of time to speak to your mother later.'

Mrs Dysall spun on her heels and walked back out of the room. Jess mouthed, 'Chill. It'll be okay,' then followed her out.

'Fuck. That was a close shave.' Ross pulled out one of the chairs and sunk down on it, propping his elbows on the table and resting his head in his hands. 'If Carly gets wind of this, she'll dump me.'

Eddie glanced at his watch. The ceremony was due to start in just over ten minutes. This was not the time for Ross to go to pieces.

'She won't, you heard what Jess said. She's not going to tell her. Now pull yourself together. You've got to go and talk to the Registrars before the ceremony, remember? We'd best go through.'

At that moment, one of the Registrars stepped into room. 'Mr Greaves?'

Ross looked up. 'Yes?'

'Are you ready to answer some questions before the ceremony?'

'Sure.' Ross got to his feet and followed her into the other room, with Eddie close behind him.

A few guests were already sitting in there, waiting. Eddie hurried past them to the front row, where he sat waiting for Ross who was now sitting at a table at the front talking to the Registrars. All he could think of was that Jess was here. Jess who he thought he would never see again. Gorgeous, vivacious Jess who made his heart beat a little faster whenever he looked at her.

Like Yvette used to do.

He was never going there again. All he had to do was get Ross through this day and he was free. Tomorrow he would fly home and Jess would be a distant memory.

Chapter Nineteen

She'd done the right thing, she knew she had. As Ross turned to watch Charlotte walk through the arch of flowers in the middle of the aisle, she could see from his expression that he adored her. He didn't take his eyes off her as she walked gracefully along the red carpet, head held high, her bouquet clasped in both hands. Jess and Danni walked slowly behind her, holding the long train of the wedding dress in one hand, and their posies in the other. Mandy followed them.

Eddie had turned to watch, too. Jess felt her cheeks glow as his eyes rested on her, she hoped that she wasn't blushing, or didn't stumble. It was just her luck to fall flat on her face with everyone watching her. She spotted her mum and smiled at her as she walked past. She looked really smart, in a lilac shift dress with a matching three quarter linen jacket trimmed with white, and a white hat to match. She looked a bit slimmer, too, less tired, and there was a glow about her. Then Jess noticed the man sitting by her side, his hand resting on Mum's. He was handsome, in a mature kind of way, with thick grey hair and smiling eyes peering through half-rimmed glasses. Who was *he*? Mum hadn't mentioned that she'd been seeing anyone. It had been years since her parents had split up, and her dad had already remarried, so it was about time Mum found a bit of happiness. She'd ask her about him later.

When Charlotte reached Ross's side, she handed her bouquet to Jess. She took it and sat down on one of the chairs at the front, resting the bouquet and her own posy on her lap. Eddie moved to a chair on the other side. Jess might not be one for weddings, but she had to admit that it was a lovely ceremony, and both bride and groom looked extremely happy. There was a dicey moment when the Registrar asked if anyone knew of any reason why the bride and groom shouldn't be married. The room fell totally silent. Jess felt her heart pound and had to stop herself from looking over at Eddie, sure he was feeling nervous, too – and Ross – well, Ross looked totally calm. His eyes were soft, lost in the beauty of his lovely bride. Jess doubted he even heard the question being asked. Luckily the moment passed, and the Registrar continued with the service. A wave of relief swept over Jess as she listened to Carly and Ross say their vows and exchange rings. When Aunt Jean had walked in on them she was sure they'd been rumbled. And they would have been if she'd arrived a few minutes earlier, she would have overheard everything. Her aunt definitely suspected something though, because as soon as they had walked

172

out of the wedding suite she'd glared at Jess. 'I don't know what was going on in there, Jessica, but nothing had better spoil this wedding for Charlotte. Do you hear me?'

Jess had nodded and assured her nothing was going on, Ross and Eddie were merely surprised to find out they were all attending the same wedding, but she was inwardly seething. Damn Ross for putting her in this situation. If she'd known who he was when he turned up in Majorca, she'd have given him a wide berth.

Never mind. It's over now. I can relax and enjoy myself, she thought as she followed Charlotte and Ross into the reception area. She felt acutely aware of Eddie walking by her side, he looked so gorgeously hunky in that suit, she had to force herself to keep her eyes focused ahead.

The bride and groom took their seats in the middle of the table and Jess sat to one side whilst Eddie sat on the other. As she took her seat, Jess couldn't resist a quick glance at Eddie and he met her gaze with a smile. Maybe this wedding wouldn't be so boring after all.

Jess searched the crowd of guests, finally spotting her mum sitting at a table to the left and gave her a smile and a wave. As soon as the formalities were over she'd nip over and have a quick chat with her and meet the mystery man she was with.

First came the speeches. Eddie's was hilarious. He related several incidents of mishaps he and Ross had got up to when they were younger, jested about how Ross was secretly a superhero, and even produced some mock up photos of Ross dressed as superman in ridiculous situations, such as rescuing a woman from a burning building and lifting a derailed train off the track. The room was in uproar, Jess laughed so much she had to dab the tears from her eyes with the serviette, and even Charlotte cracked a smile. Eddie had cleverly managed to get the correct balance of being funny without revealing anything that would cause a problem for Ross and Charlotte. And Jess bet that there was plenty he could divulge! Eddie probably had his secrets, too. Someone as fit as him would have a past. Then she remembered about his fiancée jilting him on his wedding day and realised that today must be very hard for him. She wondered if it brought back painful memories, although whenever she sneaked a glance at him he seemed happy enough.

Uncle Gerald's speech was the usual 'proud father of the bride' affair, full of tales of Charlotte's brilliant childhood and his pleasure at welcoming Ross into the family. Jess tuned out about halfway through. Then she realised that it had all gone eerily quiet and everyone was staring at her.

'Sorry?' she asked blankly.

'It's time for your speech, Jessica,' Aunt Jean said, her plum-lipsticked lips forced into a tight smile.

Shit! She hadn't written a speech. Had forgotten that she was meant to. Now what could she do? The only memories she had of Charlotte weren't exactly glowing.

'Jessica?' Aunt Jean repeated.

Okay. There was no way she could get out of this. She had to give a bloody speech. Jess took a gulp of wine and rose slowly to her feet. Deep breath, Jess, and smile. Think of it like the times you have to talk to the guests. You can do this.

She smiled at everyone and plunged in. 'First I'd like to thank you all for coming here today and sharing this wonderful occasion with us. And to congratulate Charlotte and Ross... Russell on their marriage. I'm sure you'll all agree that they make a lovely couple, and Charlotte looks totally stunning in her wedding dress.' She half turned towards the bride and groom. Everyone clapped. So far, so not yet disastrous. 'I'd also like to thank Eddie for being best man, and the other bridesmaids, Danielle and Amanda – who I'm sure you'll all agree look beautiful in their dresses – not Eddie of course, he's not wearing a dress...' peals of laughter erupted, 'although he does look rather nice...' more roars of laughter and she felt her cheeks flush. Damn, first she's gibbering and now she's blushing. She remembered that Eddie had finished his

175

speech with a toast to the bride and groom so she said, 'now let's all have a toast to the bride and groom.' She reached for her wine glass, knocking Charlotte's glass over in the process, and stared in horror as a red river spread over the white tablecloth. 'Oh, I'm so sorry,' she stammered in dismay, reaching for a serviette, but Eddie had already grabbed one and deftly mopped up the spilt wine then refilled Charlotte's glass.

'For goodness sake, Jessica, be careful, that could have gone over Charlotte's dress,' Aunt Jean snapped, her lips pursed in disapproval.

'Sorry,' Jess said again. She raised her glass. 'Here's to the bride and groom. May they have many happy years together.'

Everyone raised their glasses and repeated the toast, then Jess sat down, relieved that it was over.

The formalities now finished, the food was served and everyone tucked in. Jess was surprised at how much she was enjoying herself. The banter between Ross and Eddie was hilarious, and Danni and Mandy were very friendly, sharing even more anecdotes of when Ross and Eddie were both younger. Jess roared with laughter as Danni regaled her with a tale about the night Eddie and Ross had decided to camp out in the back garden when they were young, had been woken up in the night by the family cat creeping into their tent, its shadow making it look like a monster, and had run out screaming.

'Can I say in my defence that I was only eleven years old,' Eddie said, his eyes sparkling with amusement. 'And that Ross ran out of the tent first.'

'See how brave I was – facing the monster to give you chance to get away,' Ross jested.

'Yes, that's why you legged it straight into the house and locked the back door, leaving me in the garden alone with it,' Eddie added to another roar of laughter.

Eddie and Ross obviously had a deep bond. No wonder Ross had wanted him to be best man, and Eddie had been determined to look after his friend, no matter what.

Jess watched Eddie talking to Ross's father. They looked comfortable with each other, affectionate, almost like father and son. Eddie glanced up as if sensing her, and his lips curved into a smile. He's a lovely man, she thought. The sort you could trust. She couldn't imagine why anyone would want to jilt him at the altar to run off with an old school friend they'd reconnected with on Facebook.

After the meal, everyone started to mingle and Jess went over to speak to her mother.

'Hello, Mum.' She kissed her on the cheek. 'How are you?'

'Jess, darling, you look beautiful.' Pam Kaine stood up and hugged her. Jess inwardly groaned as she said, 'you really should wear dresses more often.'

Jess bit back the retort that she felt more comfortable in jeans, shorts or leggings, knowing her mum meant well. 'Thanks. You look pretty good yourself.' Radiant was more like it. She'd never seen her mum look so happy. She turned pointedly to the mystery man, who'd now stood up, too, his arm placed casually around her mother's waist.

'Jess, this is Phil.' Mum paused. 'We've been going out together a few months now.'

'Hello, Jess.' Phil held out his hand, his face wreathed in a smile that spread to his eyes. 'Pam's told me a lot about you. Nice to meet you, at last.'

She shook Phil's hand, momentarily stunned. Mum and Phil were obviously quite serious about each other so why hadn't Mum mentioned him?

'I was going to tell you, but we've hardly had chance to talk,' Pam said, looking very awkward. 'And it's not the sort of thing I wanted to say by text.'

Jess felt guilty. Mum was right, it had been ages since they'd spoken on the phone. Jess sent her a 'how are you? I'm still alive,' text every week but that was about it.

'I'm really pleased for you, Mum.' she said, giving her a hug. She meant it, too. It was time her mother had something good happening in her life, someone to care for her.

Phil looked pleased. 'Do sit down and chat to us a while, Jess. It'll be good to get to know you a little. I'm looking forward to hearing all your 'repping' tales.'

He looked a nice man, Jess thought. Kind, caring. 'Oh, it's not as exciting as it sounds,' she replied. 'I do enjoy it, though. No two days are the same.' She pulled out the chair next to her mum and they all sat down for a chat.

***

There was a break for an hour or so for the staff to clear the room ready for the disco that evening so some of the guests mingled in the bar, others went to their rooms.

'Are you going to join us in the bar, Jessica?' Aunt Jean asked as they stood up to leave the table.

'I'll go and freshen up first and then I'll join you,' Jess told them.

'I hope you're not intending to change, Charlotte wants you all to remain in your bridesmaids' dresses,' Aunt Jean reminded her.

'I know.' Actually, Jess longed to change out of the dress into her jeans, but she knew it was important to Charlotte. I've got through the worst of the day, she told herself, as she made her way over to the lift, now I can have some fun. Maybe she'd even have a dance with Eddie. Isn't that what the chief bridesmaid and best man were supposed to do? She wouldn't mind getting to know him a little more now they could both relax and enjoy the wedding.

First though, she wanted to phone Libby, let her know that everything had gone okay. They'd pulled it off. Ross and Charlotte were married, and it had gone like a dream. Panic over.

Chapter Twenty

Eddie watched Jess dancing around with a couple of little girls, the lemon bridesmaid's dress sashaying around her legs. She was the whole package: pretty, sexy, and fun. Although he'd been dismayed when he first realised she was the chief bridesmaid, convinced she'd spill the beans to her cousin – the sisterhood and all that – he had to admit he'd been delighted to see her again. He'd thought about her a lot since the stag party last weekend, wishing he'd left her his number so they could keep in touch, and now here she was. He couldn't believe his luck.

The song finished, and Jess smiled as she said something to both children, then walked over to join Eddie. He pushed back his chair and stood up.

'Let me get you a drink. Dancing like that must be thirsty work.'

She grinned. 'Thanks, I'd appreciate that.' She sank into one of the chairs and kicked off her strappy gold sandals. 'A white wine spritzer, please.'

He'd longed to chat more with her during the wedding breakfast, but as they were sitting at opposite ends of the head table it had been difficult. She'd laughed – really laughed – at the jokes in his speech, chatted away to everyone, been so friendly and fun, like a ray of lemon sunshine in the room. Her own speech – obviously completely off the cuff, had been funny – and she hadn't freaked out when she'd knocked over the glass of wine. She seemed nice, funny, kind, uncomplicated – and incredibly sexy. He'd decided he'd like to get to know her more, and now was his chance to talk to her, if he could get her to sit still long enough that was. The children were drawn to her, and she seemed happy to entertain them – he guessed that's why she was so good at her job. She was still talking to some children when he returned with her drink. He presumed they were asking her to dance with them, but she smiled and shook her head, pointing down to her still sandal-less feet, obviously telling them that her feet hurt. The children waved and walked away.

'I think you have a fan club,' he said, putting the spritzer down on the table in front of her. 'I guess you spend so much time with children in your work that entertaining them comes naturally to you.'

'Yes, but to be honest I've always been surrounded by kids. My mum was a child minder for years.' She reached for the glass. 'Thanks.'

'Do you have brothers and sisters, too?' he asked, genuinely interested, and listened intently as she told him about her two older brothers – explaining that neither of them had attended the wedding as one was backpacking around the world and wasn't due home until tomorrow, and the other 'didn't do weddings' – and how her mum had struggled to keep the roof over their heads since her dad walked out when Jess was a toddler. Her eyes sparkled when she spoke, her expression was animated. She clearly loved her family.

Then she asked him about his family and his life in France. They talked for ages, one of them going to the bar every now and again to refill their glasses. Eddie was so wrapped up in her company that he didn't notice the evening slipping by, the occasional amused glances they got from the other guests, the music changing. It wasn't until he heard the DJ's voice announcing the last dance, ('Grab your partners, folks, this is a smoochy one,') that he realised the evening was almost over. He had to have one dance with Jess before they said goodbye, feel her arms around him, her body close to his. He leaned over the table and placed his hand on hers.

'Dance with me?'

Her emerald eyes met his and for a moment it was as if the world had stopped spinning. Then she nodded. Wordlessly they both got up, walked hand in hand onto the dance floor, then melted into each other's arms and swayed to the music. It was more like a prelude to lovemaking than a dance. The smell of her intoxicated him, her touch as she wrapped her arms around his waist sent his blood pressure racing, the feel of her body against his ignited fire in his loins. He fancied her like crazy. He couldn't let her walk out of his life.

'I could do with some fresh air. How about you?' he whispered in her ear when the dance had finished.

'Sure.'

They walked outside, side by side, down the path towards the fountain, in silence, then sat down on the bench in front of it, still holding hands.

Jess sighed and looked up at the inky black sky. 'It's been a lovely day. I didn't expect to enjoy the wedding so much. I was sort of dreading it.'

'Me too, I'm not one for weddings,' he agreed. Especially as the last wedding he attended was his own and he'd been dumped at the altar. 'But I'm glad I came, and that we got the chance to see each other again. Look…' he hesitated. What was he doing? He said he'd never fall for a woman again. He shrugged the thought away, he wasn't falling for Jess, he only fancied her. There was nothing wrong with that. 'How about we keep in touch? We could exchange phone numbers, have a chat now and again, maybe even meet up.'

Jess cocked her head to one side, a small smile playing on her lips. 'That would be great, but you live in France, and I live wherever my job takes me, so meeting up might be difficult.'

'Difficult but not impossible. I'm sure you have time off and I can manage the occasional weekend off, too. Do you think you might fancy a weekend in France?'

Jess nodded slowly. 'A weekend in France sounds very nice.'

'Then let's arrange it. Soon.' He slipped his arm around her shoulder, gazing into her eyes. They shimmered invitingly back at him. Still holding her gaze, he leant forward until his lips grazed hers, softly, fleetingly, then deeper, hungrier as she returned kiss for kiss. Then kissing wasn't enough, he was holding her to him, running his fingers down her neck, her back, and her hands were in his hair, down his back, tugging at his shirt.

***

What was she doing? Anyone could walk out on them. Jess reluctantly eased herself out of Eddie's embrace. 'Whoa! Let's take a step back here,' she said breathlessly. Maybe they could meet up now and again – France wasn't that far away. She didn't want to say goodbye to him. She hadn't felt so attracted to anyone for a long time, if ever. And those hot kisses – it was all she could do to pull away.

'Let's go up to my room,' Eddie said. 'We can have a couple more drinks. I don't want the night to end yet.' His eyes were dark with desire, his voice soft, husky.

Did she want to go back to his room?

You bet she did.

He held out his hand to her and she took it. Arms wrapped around each other's waist they walked inside and over to the lift.

Keeping one arm around her waist, Eddie unlocked the door to his room. Jess stepped inside, glancing around quickly. It was similar to hers with its beech wardrobes and white bed linen on the double bed, two armchairs, a desk and a tray with tea making facilities, a bottle of wine and a couple of glasses on the side. Eddie's suitcase was open on the floor in one corner. Like her, he obviously hadn't thought it was worth unpacking for one night.

'Take a seat and I'll pour us the wine,' Eddie walked over to the desk and opened the wine whilst Jess kicked off her sandals and sat on the edge of the bed.

'You know, I think Charlotte and Ross might actually make a go of it,' she said as Eddie poured the wine into the two glasses. 'She really seems to love him. Which is totally amazing. I didn't think she was capable of loving anyone. And they seem so unsuitable but...'

'I agree, I thought the same.' Eddie sat down beside her and passed her a glass. 'When I first met Carly I thought Ross was making a terrible mistake, but she is good for him. She has made him more... responsible.'

'And Ross has made Charlotte softer. You might think she's still prissy and demanding, but you should have seen her before she met Ross.'

'That is what love is supposed to do, bring out the best in people,' Eddie said.

'I wouldn't know,' Jess said lightly. She took a swig of her wine. 'I've never been in love.'

Eddie turned to her and she could see the surprise on his face. 'Really? Never? Not even a teenage crush?'

'Never.'

'I don't know whether to envy you or pity you.' he said softly.

That surprised her. 'Why? From what I can see falling in love is a load of hassle. Most people give up their life and dreams for someone then end up getting their heart broken.' She took another swig of wine. 'I can't see the point.'

His face was an unreadable mask as he stared down into his glass, his fingers clasping the stem so tightly she feared it might break. *Me and my big mouth. Why did I have to say that when I know he got jilted? He must have been heartbroken. Maybe he still is.*

He raised his head and turned to her, his expression unreadable. 'Yes, that is true. I vowed I would never fall in love again. Never give anyone else that power to hurt me.' He paused. 'Then I see people who are happy, whose faces light up when they are together, who lift each other up, and I think that for some people it works. For some people love is a wonderful thing.'

'But not for us?' she said it lightly but in truth she was testing. She wanted to make sure that he understood the rules. This was fun only. She didn't want to be responsible for breaking his heart again.

He took a swig of his wine and shook his head. 'No, not for us.' Then he put his glass down on the table and reached out for her. 'This is definitely pleasure only.'

'Pleasure'. The way he said the word sent shivers down her spine. 'Definitely,' she murmured, wrapping her arms around his neck.

Chapter Twenty One

The shrill sound of an alarm dragged Jess out of her sleep the next morning. She opened her eyes and stared at the white and silver striped wall. Where the hell was she? Just as she tried to recollect, a hand snaked around her waist and Eddie kissed her on the back of her neck, then her shoulders. '*Bonjour, ma douce.*'

Memory flooded back. She turned around and kissed him. 'Morning, sexy.'

She'd gone and done the cliché, slept with the best man. A smile hovered on her lips. And what a night it had been. Okay, yes, she'd had a bit too much wine, but she wasn't that drunk that she hadn't known what she was doing. She fancied Eddie, he fancied her, and they'd taken precautions. What harm had they done? Even so, she'd rather not announce it to everyone. She glanced at her watch. Seven thirty. 'What time is breakfast served? I need to get showered and changed before anyone spots me.'

'Carly wants us all seated by nine o'clock. That is why I set my alarm.' Eddie nuzzled her neck. 'Don't go yet.'

'I have to. I can't turn up for breakfast dressed like this.'

'Then come back to me after breakfast. When are you going home?' he asked, in between feather kisses down her neck.

'Tuesday. You?'

'Tonight.' He raised himself up on one elbow, liquid chocolate eyes holding hers. 'Let us spend the day together, Jess. Please. I don't want to say goodbye to you so soon.'

She didn't want to say goodbye to him, either. Not yet. 'I'd love to,' she said, wrapping her arms around his neck and pulling his lips down on hers.

***

As she showered back in her room – which she'd managed to sneak into without being noticed, thank goodness – her mind drifted to Eddie. She'd never met anyone like him. He was fun and sexy, but also kind and loyal at the same time. In her experience those four qualities didn't normally go together. Last night had been fantastic, but it wasn't just the sex, it was the way he treated her. As if she was precious. As if he really cared. Of course she wanted to spend the day with him, but she'd arranged to spend the afternoon with her mum, and her brother, Ned, was coming over too. She hadn't seen him for ages. She'd have to tell them she'd come along later,

190

Eddie was flying home at six. She'd go over then and spend a couple of hours with her family before she met Becky and Mae.

She would miss Eddie. She was glad she'd agreed to keep in touch. They'd swapped phone numbers and connected on WhatsApp last night, talked about visiting each other when they could. She doubted if they'd manage it often, but she was glad they'd still be friends. Friends with benefits, she thought, remembering last night with a smile.

The rings of her phone brought her out of her daydream. That'll be Charlotte making sure that she was ready. She turned off the shower and grabbed a towel. The wedding had gone spectacularly well, thank goodness. Charlotte and Ross had looked so loved up. Amazing as it seemed, her cousin had found someone she loved more than herself.

Jess thought back to her conversation with Eddie last night about how she had never been in love, recalling the dark cloud that had swept over his face. Charlotte and Ross might be happy now, but it wouldn't last. It never did. Her parents had seemed happy enough for a while, but it turned out Dad hadn't been happy at all.

Love was overrated, but friendship and fun were worth holding onto. Especially if it was with someone like Eddie.

***

After the wedding breakfast, Eddie and Ross were waiting for Jess in the reception. 'I wanted to say goodbye and to thank you, Jess, for not telling Carly.' Ross held out his hand to her. 'You could have ruined yesterday – and the rest of my life – but you didn't. I'm really grateful. It must have been difficult for you with Carly being your cousin.'

'It's fine. Don't worry about it. Just make sure that you don't do it again,' Jess told him.

'I won't. I love Carly. It was a mistake. I was drunk. I'll never cheat on her again.'

'And just when did you cheat on my daughter?' asked an icy voice behind them.

Aunt Jean.

Shit.

Jess registered the look of horror on both Ross and Eddie's faces and took a deep breath before she turned around, her brain going into overdrive. How could she salvage this?

'He didn't 'cheat' on Charlotte,' she said. 'I think you must have misheard.'

'I most certainly did not. I know perfectly well what I heard.' Her aunt's eyes flicked from one to the other of them, her expression stern. 'And it's obvious you're

192

covering something, you all look guilty as sin. Explain yourselves.' She folded her arms and waited.

'Cheat is too strong a word,' Jess said slowly, playing for time and hoping she'd get inspiration on how to get them all out of this mess.

'Really?' Aunt Jean's eyebrows shot up her forehead. 'Then what word should we use?'

'It was just a kiss. A drunken kiss. That's all,' Ross stammered.

'A *kiss*?' The outrage on Aunt Jean's face and the way she repeated the word 'kiss' made it sound like Ross had admitted to an orgy.

'Not even a kiss, actually, more…' Jess desperately tried to defuse the situation, embarrassingly aware that other guests were looking over at them curiously.

'Who. Did. You. Kiss?' Jess winced as Aunt Jean emphasised every word.

'It was me,' she said quickly. 'Ross – Russell – was drunk.' *Better not say he was asleep on the sofa in Libby's room as, that would call for even more awkward explanations.* 'He kissed me.' A hiss of horror escaped from her aunt's pursed lips, so Jess gabbled quickly. 'Honestly, it was a mistake. Ross was so drunk he forgot where he was and thought he was kissing Charlotte.'

'It's true, it was a terrible *erreur*,' Eddie agreed. 'He was so mortified when he realised…'

193

'I think you'd better tell me this from the beginning,' Aunt Jean said very slowly. 'Because I'm struggling to understand how Russell could mistake you for Charlotte even if he was extremely drunk.' She obviously thought there was no comparison between Jess and the utterly divine Charlotte. 'And why Russell was with you in the first place.'

Damn. This was getting worse and worse.

'Well, you see …' Jess started to say, but Aunt Jean held up her hand to silence her. 'I want to hear it from Russell.'

Before Ross could explain, Charlotte walked in, dressed in a fitted pale blue suit and white stilettos, Danni and Mandy were behind here. 'So here you all are,' she trilled. 'I wondered where you'd got to, Ross. We need to be going soon.' She swept up to them and slipped her arm through Ross's. He looked so guilty he might as well have had 'I got caught out' stamped all over his face. 'What's the matter?' she asked, looking from one to the other.

The silence hung in the air for a few awkward moments and then Aunt Jean said, 'Russell is just explaining to us how he got so drunk that he kissed Jess on his stag do, apparently thinking it was *you*.'

Shit! Jess saw Charlotte look confused, then furious. 'You did what?' She swung her hand back and smacked

Ross across the cheek. 'How dare you!' Then she took a step towards Jess, 'And as for you...'

'Whoa! Don't you even think of doing that to me because I'll slap you right back,' Jess warned her.

'It was not Jess's fault,' Eddie butted in.

'I can explain...' said Ross, holding his now-glowing cheek.

'You'd better make it good or I'll be having this marriage annulled,' Charlotte told him, hands on hips. 'And you'll never see this baby,' she patted her stomach. 'I can promise you that.'

'Baby!' Aunt Jean echoed, her face incredulous, steely blue eyes flitting from Charlotte to Ross.

'Yes, I'm almost three months gone. We were going to tell you when we came back from the Honeymoon, when we'd had the three-month scan.'

Wow! Pregnant. This made the situation even worse. Jess glared at Ross. How dare he put her in this situation. 'I think you'd better explain to Charlotte because I'm not taking the blame for your drunken behaviour,' she told him. 'It was bad enough being on the receiving end of your slobbery kiss when all I was trying to do was prevent you being thrown out on the street.'

'Thrown out on the street!' Charlotte almost screamed the words. 'What the hell were you doing, Ross?'

'Carly, you must listen...' Eddie protested. 'Nothing happened. It was a kiss. Ross was drunk. He thought Jess was you.'

Charlotte's eyes almost popped out of her head. 'You thought I was her!' she pointed a quivering finger at Jess. 'How could anyone possibly mistake me for *her?*' She shuddered as if the very idea was repulsive.

Count to ten, Jess, she's pregnant and hysterical. If you upset her and she loses the baby you'll be ostracised by the family for eternity.

'Charlotte, calm down, dear. You shouldn't be getting upset in your condition.' Aunt Jean put a reassuring hand on her arm, but Charlotte immediately swatted it away.

'How can I possibly not be upset when my... *husband*... has been snogging my cousin?' she screeched, swinging around to glare at Jess. 'I might have guessed you'd try and get your claws into him. You bitch. You just can't leave any man alone, can you? Just because you can't keep one of your own.'

Jess was furious. How dare Charlotte try and paint her as a jealous man-stealing freak. 'If you think I fancy him,' she pointed a finger at Ross, 'you're mental! Now you had better explain right now, Ross, because I'm getting sick of being the scapegoat here. I am trying very hard not to retaliate because of Charlotte's condition but I'm not taking the blame for this.'

Ross stammered out the whole story, skimming over the bit about pulling Jess down on top of him so tightly that she couldn't move, and how Eddie had to rescue her and ended up with his hands on her breasts. He made it sound like he'd given her a peck on the cheek rather than a full on slobbery snog.

'So, you just kissed Jess on the cheek?' Charlotte demanded.

'Er, not on the cheek exactly.'

'How exactly?' Her voice was dripping with ice now.

'Well it was on the lips, but only for a second then I realised she wasn't you. I'm sorry, Charlotte. I would have told you but I didn't want to upset you.'

'You didn't want me to call off the wedding, more like.' Charlotte spat out. 'And where were you exactly when this happened?'

Jess saw the panic in Ross's eyes. So did Charlotte.

'Where. Were. You?' she repeated.

'I can explain,' Eddie butted in quickly. 'Ross was very drunk, and it was late. The manager wouldn't have let him in if we'd gone through the reception so Jess and Libby, they took us through the staff entrance.'

'Libby?' Charlotte asked sharply.

'Another rep. My friend.'

'And how exactly did you both come to be with Ross and Eddie?' snapped Aunt Jean.

As Jess quickly explained she could tell from the hiss that escaped Aunt Jean's lips and the stony look on her face that this wasn't going down well at all. And she couldn't really blame her. Okay, Charlotte had made some nasty accusations about her, but Jess had to admit that this was sounding pretty bad. She took a deep breath.

'Look, Charlotte, it sounds worse than it was. I would have told you, but I knew it was a genuine mistake, so why ruin everything?'

'If it was a genuine mistake why didn't you mention it when you saw the photo of Ross? You said he was staying at the hotel. Why didn't you say that he got drunk and kissed you?' She jabbed her finger at Jess. 'Because you felt guilty, that's why.'

'Guilty! I've got nothing to feel guilty about.' Jess retorted. 'I kept quiet because I knew how it looked and I didn't want to ruin your wedding day. Besides', she added, 'I did tell Danni.' She turned to Danni, hoping she'd back her up.

'That's right, she did,' Danni stepped forward. 'She didn't know whether to tell you or not, but we decided it was best not to.'

To Jess's amazement Charlotte's eyes suddenly filled with tears. 'I can't believe you've done this to me, Ross. I thought you loved me.' Her bottom lip was trembling.

198

An upset Charlotte was harder to be annoyed with than a furious one. Jess instinctively stepped forward to comfort her cousin, but she recoiled. 'Keep away,' she spat. 'You've done enough damage. You've ruined my wedding.'

'I'm so sorry, Carly. Please forgive me.' Ross looked terribly upset. 'If you'd just let me explain.'

'I don't see how you can explain this, Ross. I really don't.' Charlotte pulled a tissue out of her pocket and wiped her eyes. 'I think our marriage is over before it's even begun.' She turned on her heels and stormed off.

Chapter Twenty Two

'Carly!' Ross chased after her. He looked so devastated that Jess felt really sorry for him. She hoped Charlotte didn't go through with her threat to end the marriage. It was obvious she and Ross loved each other. And there was a baby on the way, too.

For a moment they all stood in awkward silence. Aunt Jean spoke first. 'So this is why you came down earlier, to warn Russell. I never thought he was good enough for my Charlotte. There was something about him I didn't trust, and now I know why.' She pointed a finger accusingly at Jess. 'If you'd have told us the truth last night I might have been able to stop the wedding. Now, everything's a mess. My poor daughter is pregnant and married to a philanderer.'

'That's exactly why I didn't tell you.' Jess fought down the anger welling inside her. She might have guessed Aunt Jean would blame her.

'You've always been jealous of Charlotte. Isn't stealing her boyfriend once enough for you? Oh no, you have to try and do it again, and right before her wedding too. I bet you couldn't believe your luck when Russell

200

turned up at your hotel. I bet you guessed who he was and made a play for him. Just like you did with Simon.'

'How bloody dare you!' Jess was fuming but Aunt Jean was already marching away, after Carly and Ross.

'What did she mean about you and Carly's other boyfriend?' Eddie asked quietly.

Damn, trust her aunt to bring up that horrible business with Simon in front of Eddie. 'You know that what happened with Ross wasn't my fault,' she reminded him.

He nodded slowly. 'And Simon, the other boyfriend?'

'That wasn't my fault either, and it was years ago. Simon – who was a total freak and I didn't fancy in the slightest – made a pass at me, I turned him down. End of.' An image of Simon crossed her mind. Sleazy Simon. He was beyond disgusting and had a habit of looking at you as if he was undressing you with his eyes. She'd been totally creeped out when he came on to her.

'Then why did your aunt say that you made a play for him?'

He didn't believe her. She could see the doubt written all over him. Well who the hell did he think he was? She barely knew him, she didn't have to explain herself to him. Just because they'd spent the night together didn't mean he owned her and she had to explain all her past to him.

She shrugged her shoulders. 'Please yourself what you believe. I don't have to justify myself to you.' Then she walked back into the hall.

***

Eddie watched her go, his mind racing. He liked Jess. A lot. But he didn't like people who cheated. Like Yvette had done to him.

Okay, the incident with Ross hadn't been Jess's fault. He'd been there, he knew that. Even so, her aunt seemed adamant that she'd cheated with one of Carly's previous boyfriends. Could that be true? Surely Jess wouldn't do that to her cousin? Jess was friendly, she had to be, it was her job. She was the sort of woman that attracted men. Beautiful, fun, outgoing. Whereas Carly was – well, she came across as very difficult to him. He could well imagine why a boyfriend of hers would prefer Jess.

Perhaps Jess hadn't encouraged him, like she hadn't encouraged Ross. But if so, why didn't she explain what had happened instead of walking off?

Maybe he should go after Jess and apologise. He hadn't meant to sound so damning. He didn't want them to part like this. Last night had been fantastic. And it wasn't just the sex – brilliant as it was – it was the easiness and warmth of her personality. He felt like he could talk to her for hours, *had* talked to her for hours. She was fun, honest, uncomplicated, and exactly what he needed right now.

He'd woken up in the early hours of the morning, raised himself up on his elbow and lay there for a while watching her sleeping. She'd looked so beautiful, so peaceful as she lay there. He'd even fleetingly imagined what it would be like to wake up to her every day. A wave of loss had swept over him when he thought of never seeing her again, and he'd decided he'd fly over to Majorca to see her as soon as he could take a few days off.

Now he wasn't so sure.

He couldn't think about it now, he had to try and sort out this mess with Ross and Carly or this would be the shortest marriage on record.

***

She'd booked out of her room so the only place to go for any privacy was outside. Jess wandered out and sat down on the wall around the fountain. The wall where she and Eddie had kissed last night.

She was fuming. Why should she get the blame for this? She was the victim here and had only kept quiet so as not to cause trouble between Charlotte and Ross. Well she wished she'd told her now. Mind you, even if she had, Charlotte and Aunt Jean would have still said it was her fault.

What angered her – and hurt – the most was Eddie's reaction. As soon as the episode with Sleazy Simon had been mentioned his face had frozen over like a glacier. It was clear that he actually believed that she had tried to steal Charlotte's boyfriend. Judged her without waiting for an explanation. He had no right to cross-examine her like that and then to refuse to take her word.

She thought back to Charlotte's engagement to Simon, five years ago. Jess had still been living at home, working in a local office, helping her mum look after the kids she minded. They'd been invited to the engagement party and Mum had insisted they went. Jess hadn't wanted to go. She and Charlotte had never hit it off, they had always been like chalk and cheese. She'd never liked Charlotte's choice in men either – they were all stuck up mummy's boys and Simon was no exception. She'd agreed to dance with him out of sheer politeness when he'd asked, after all, he was going to be family. She'd been shocked when he turned up at her work declaring his love for her. She'd made it quite clear that she wanted nothing to do with him. But he wouldn't take no for an answer, and had followed her home asking her to let him in. In the end,

Ned had threatened him to clear off or else he'd *be* cleared off.

The scene that followed when Charlotte found out was awful. The engagement was broken off, Aunt Jean and Mum fell out big time, and Jess was so sick of it all that when she saw an advert for travel reps in the local paper, she applied immediately. Two weeks later she was on her way to Crete and the start of a new career.

She might have known she'd get the blame again. Well thank goodness she was going back to Majorca on Tuesday. The sooner she was out of here, away from them all, the better.

Her phone buzzed. It was a text from Libby.

How did it go?

Jess went to text back then changed her mind and called instead. Libby answered the call immediately. 'That was a quick reply. Either you're bored, or you've got some goss to tell me.'

Jess sighed. 'Charlotte found out about Ross kissing me.'

'OMG! You're kidding me!' Libby squealed down the phone. 'How? What happened? Is the wedding off?'

Jess explained as best she could with Libby butting in every now and again with comments like 'what a cheek' and 'for goodness sake it's not like you went to bed together.'

'What's the situation now?' Libby asked.

'I've no idea. Charlotte's threatening to have the wedding annulled – not sure they can actually do that if they did the deed last night, but it's looking like it could be the shortest marriage in history.'

'Shit! Really? That's a bit OTT.'

'I know, but to be fair, she did seem genuinely upset and the fact that they were in the staff quarters didn't go down well – Eddie told them that. And to make it worse she's pregnant – almost three months.'

'Double shit.'

'Yep. Anyway, they've disappeared to talk things over and no one's seen them since. I guess I'll have to wait. They're supposed to be leaving for their honeymoon in,' she glanced at her watch, 'half an hour. I'm sitting at the fountain trying to avoid everyone's accusing stares as obv I'm the femme fatale in all this.'

'Keep your chin up, hun. Ross was at fault… not you.'

'Try telling Charlotte and Aunt Jean that.'

'I will if you give me their phone numbers,' Libby offered.

Not a good idea. She could just imagine the message Libby would send them. 'No need. I'm a big girl. I can take it. See you Tuesday.' As she ended the call she saw her mum walking towards her. She guessed Aunt Jean had told her what had happened and now Mum wanted to hear Jess's version.

'Look, don't worry, Jess, I'm sure Charlotte and Russell will make up.' Her mum sat down beside her and put her hand comfortingly over Jess's. 'I know what your brothers are like when they've had too much to drink, don't know one hand from the other.'

'It's not fair though, Mum. I only kept quiet to avoid all this. I didn't want to ruin the wedding.' She turned to face her. 'It's not like I wanted Ross to kiss me. He was holding me so tight I couldn't get away, Eddie had to pull me off him.'

Pam tutted. 'Trust Jean to blame you, again. Just like she did with that horrid business over Simon. I knew there would be some rational explanation.' She patted Jess's hand. 'They'll make up, you'll see. Come on, let's go back inside. I don't see why you should sit out here. You've done nothing wrong.'

As they walked back inside, Eddie came over to them, looking relieved. 'Carly and Ross have made up. They're coming down in a minute to leave for their honeymoon.'

Chapter Twenty Three

'There, what did I tell you?' Pam patted Jess's hand. 'I'll see you inside.'

She hurried on in, leaving Jess and Eddie looking awkwardly at each other. As if they were strangers, had never torn each other's clothes off last night, writhed on the bed, caressed each other, kissed until they had to come up for air, made wild love that had left her body shuddering. As if Eddie hadn't held her gently in his arms this morning, told her that she was 'gorgeous, amazing, sexy' and didn't want this to be goodbye. As if they hadn't swapped phone numbers, promised they would keep in touch.

Finally, Eddie broke the silence. 'I'd better go, too. I must say goodbye to Ross, I'm flying home tomorrow and won't see him for some time.'

They had planned to spend the day together before Aunt Jean had painted her as a bunny boiler who couldn't keep her hands off someone else's fella. Now Eddie couldn't wait to get away from her. Just because his fiancée cheated on him didn't give him the right to class her as the same. She had never, ever gone out with anyone else's guy, and never would. Well stuff him. He could think what he wanted.

She shook her head. 'I'll be off, too. Mum's asked me to have dinner with them – my brother's coming over. I haven't seen him for ages.' She stretched up and kissed him on the cheek. 'Bye, Eddie. Have a safe flight.'

***

She was flying back in two days' time, and there was no way she was going to let what had happened ruin the rest of her short break with her friends. She and Charlotte had never been bessie buddies, so she was hardly likely to see her again for years. And as for Eddie, well, she could do without complications like that in her life. One night together and he thought he had the right to question her, to demand an explanation over something that happened years ago and was totally not her fault. Forget it. He could go back to France and stay there.

Sunday afternoon at her mum's was a riotous affair. Ned turned up with his latest girlfriend, Starburst, who he'd met when backpacking in Thailand. A delicate, elfin-faced girl with glossy liquorice hair and big brown eyes, she was apparently tougher than she looked as Ned informed them she was a black belt in Karate and had fought off a would-be mugger somewhere outside

Bangkok. Jess hadn't enjoyed herself this much in ages. She was pleasantly surprised by how Phil slotted in with the family, Jake had obviously met him several times and had an easy relationship with him, and Ned seemed at ease, too. As for her mum, she was positively glowing. Jess couldn't remember the last time she'd seen her look so happy. Probably way back in Jess's childhood before Dad had decided he wanted a new life without them.

'So, Jess, is it good to be home – even if only for a short while?' Phil had turned to her and was waiting for her reply.

She nodded. 'I miss this crazy lot when I'm away. And so much seems to happen, I feel out of the loop whenever I come back.' She grinned. 'I guess it's my fault, I should keep in more contact with everyone, but the days fly by. You wouldn't believe the hours I work.'

'I would! My daughter, Jenna, is an air hostess, so is often away from home, working all hours. She tells me that flying to other countries isn't as glamorous as it sounds and that sometimes all she sees is the airport.'

'Oh, I'm luckier than that. I'm based in the hotel a lot, but we do get the occasional days off so I get to look around a bit.' She popped a crisp into her mouth and chewed it before asking, 'Do you see your daughter often? Has Mum met her?'

'Not a lot, she lives in London and yes, Pam has met her once. They got on very well.' He leaned forward a little. 'I realise it was probably a shock for you to see me with your mum. She didn't want to tell you over the phone, she thought it was best face to face. I want you to know that I think she's a wonderful lady and I intend to look after her.'

What a gent, he looked so sincere. Jess smiled. 'Good, it's time someone did. She's worked so hard all her life.' She looked over at her mother laughing merrily at something Ned was telling her. 'It's good to see her so happy.'

Phil seemed pleased at this and they chatted pleasantly for a while, with him asking about her job and seeming genuinely interested in her replies. He's a nice man, Jess thought when he finally went over to join her mother. She watched as he slipped his arm around her mum's waist and Mum looked up at him, smiling. They seemed so happy together. Beside them, Starbust sat on Ned's lap, her arm wound loosely around his neck, his arm around her waist. They looked so... together. As if they belonged to each other.

Like Ross and Charlotte had been – until the drunken kiss was mentioned. She shrugged. It had probably all blown over by now and they were enjoying their honeymoon. In a few months they'd have a baby, too.

Their own family unit. For the first time in her life that made her feel a bit wistful. Her mind slipped back to the night before, when her body had been entwined with Eddie's. Waking up to him sleeping beside her, his arm around her waist. It had felt good. She'd thought that maybe they actually had something going on. Until he'd shown just how little he thought of her.

She shrugged. She was well out of that. She glanced at the clock. Time to meet Becky and Mae.

She picked up her coat and bag and said her goodbyes, exchanging kisses and hugs with her brothers, promising to be back over soon.

'I'm staying over at Mae's tonight,' she told her mum. 'I'll be back tomorrow, but not sure what time.'

'That's fine, darling. Whatever's best for you. Make sure you say goodbye to me before you go on Tuesday, though.'

'I will,' she promised.

***

Eddie stared out of the plane window, his mind running back over this morning's events. Last night with Jess had been really special. He'd felt a bond with her. It hadn't been the same empty sex he'd had with the women he'd slept with since Yvette. He liked Jess and he felt that she liked him. They'd talked and laughed. It had seemed like they'd made love rather than had sex. It was the closest he'd felt to a woman since Yvette. Actually, ever. He'd loved Yvette, but he'd never felt he could talk to her, confide in her, like he had with Jess. Her touch hadn't ignited a fire in his body like Jess's had. They hadn't laughed, caressed each other, rolled over into each other's arms as soon as they woke like he and Jess had done this morning. He hadn't kept waking in the night, reaching out to make sure Yvette was there, like he'd done with Jess.

When he'd held Jess in his arms this morning it had felt so good. He hadn't wanted her to go. He wanted to stay like that, with her in his arms, forever. He sensed that she hadn't wanted to get out of bed either, for the moment to end, so had suggested they spend the day together. Her face had lit up and she'd agreed. It was all fine until Carly's mother overheard Ross talking to them.

No. That wasn't where it went wrong. It went wrong when Carly's mother accused Jess of trying to steal another boyfriend of Carly's. She'd made it sound like Jess was flighty, would go off with anyone. That she wasn't to be trusted, like Yvette. And for a moment he'd believed it. Jess had sensed that, too. He'd seen the look she gave him, how her face had clammed up. That's why she'd said goodbye so briskly. She was annoyed that he'd doubted her. Yet she hadn't thought enough of him to explain. He would have believed her, he just wanted to hear the explanation. The fact that she wouldn't give him one had made him think that she was guilty.

That's why he hadn't gone after her, he realised. Because Carly's mum had made him stop and think. He liked Jess. *Really liked her.* Wanted their relationship to be more than a casual fling. And there was no way he was going to get in deep with someone who would cheat on him like Yvette did. He lay back in the seat and closed his eyes. He was best out of it.

***

It was a fantastic evening. Becky looked a little tired – sleepless nights with the baby – but there was a contentedness about her. Mae had brought Anna along again and they were both so obviously in love. Everyone was happily coupled up.

Her thoughts once again turned to Eddie. She pushed them away. She didn't want to be part of a couple. And she definitely wasn't going to go ga-ga over a guy she barely knew and had only spent one night with. No way. He'd be back in France by now, slipping back into his life and not giving her a second thought. Well, she wasn't going to give him a second thought either.

But she couldn't help checking her phone to see if he'd texted before she settled down to sleep on Mae's rather lumpy sofa.

He hadn't.

Chapter Twenty Four

Seven months later.

The months had flown by. When the summer season had finished in October, the reps had all been offered the chance of going home until April when they would be called back again or being transferred to winter holiday work – *Time of Your Life* ran holidays all over the globe. Jess and Libby had both opted to be transferred and had managed to get a placement together in Switzerland until the end of February. Now Jess had a month off before working in Majorca again, so she was flying home for her mother's wedding.

She'd been surprised but pleased when Mum, her voice bubbling over with excitement, had phoned her to tell her that she was getting married. 'I chose March because I knew you'd be home then for a few weeks,' she'd said. 'And... I want you to be my bridesmaid. Will you?'

Jess had been really touched. 'Of course I will. I'm so pleased for you, Mum.'

So here she was again, packing her case ready to fly home for a wedding.

'Is it weird being bridesmaid at your mum's wedding?' Libby asked.

'A bit,' Jess admitted. 'I'm pleased for her though, and I'm glad she asked me.'

'At least there'll be no dramas with the groom this time, and I guess the best man will be too old to flirt with,' Libby teased.

Jess had tried not to think of the disastrous events at Ross and Charlotte's wedding. Over the last few months she had firmly thrust the memory of Eddie out of her mind, but Libby's jesting words brought it all flooding back. Mum and Phil were having a small family wedding, but Mum had told her that Charlotte and Ross were too busy with their new baby girl, Rosabelle, to attend the wedding. She'd arrived in January, a couple of weeks early. Aunt Jean and Uncle Gerald were coming, though. Jess didn't relish seeing them again, but she would put a smile on her face and be polite, for Mum's sake.

'At least you'll be able to have a fitting for your dress this time,' Libby told her.

Mum and Phil had chosen spring colours for their wedding. Mum had sent a photo of her outfit – an elegant African violet shift dress with a matching three quarter coat – they agreed that they would buy Jess's dress and shoes early next week. The wedding was less than two weeks away and Mum had already done 'research

217

shopping trips' and found a few dresses for Jess to choose from.

'Yes, and there'll be no drama, I hope. Thank goodness Charlotte isn't coming.'

'Have you heard any more from her? I guess she and Ross are okay now?' Libby asked.

Jess shrugged. 'As far as I know.'

'They haven't invited you to the christening, then?' Charlotte and Ross were having a christening this coming Sunday.

'No. Danni and Mandy – Ross's sisters – are the godmothers.'

'What about the godfather?'

'I've no idea.' Jess carried on packing.

'I wondered if it might be Eddie. He is Ross's best friend, after all.'

That stopped Jess in her tracks. It was a possibility. Which meant that Eddie would be coming over to England. Would only be a few miles from her...

But what did it matter? Months had passed since she last saw him, and she'd heard nothing from him. Not even a Merry Christmas or Happy New Year text. Whatever they'd had between them hadn't weathered the first storm. She shrugged carelessly. 'Who knows? I'm not bothered if he is.'

Libby scrutinised her sharply. 'Are you sure? I never did understand why you two didn't keep in touch.'

'Because it was obvious that Eddie has trust issues and that's not something I want to deal with.' Jess snapped her case shut, zipped it up and padlocked it. 'Anyway, it was ages ago now. Do you still keep in touch with Greg?'

'Not really. I mean we're FB friends but nothing else. But then I didn't sleep with him.'

If only she hadn't slept with Eddie. Even now, memories of the night they spent together sometimes crept across her mind as she was drifting off to sleep at night. She felt like they'd really connected, but obviously he hadn't felt the same way. Not that it mattered. It was history now.

***

Mum met her from the airport, all smiles. Jess had never seen her so happy. Talk about a glowing bride.

'I'm so glad you're stopping for a few weeks this time instead of dashing off after a couple of days,' Mum said as she opened the boot for Jess to put her suitcase inside. 'It'll be lovely to spend some time together before I go on honeymoon.' They were going to Cyprus for a week. 'I've still got some last-minute shopping to get – shoes and my going away outfit. And your dress and shoes, of course. I

219

thought dusky blue for you, it would go nicely with my outfit.'

'Sounds good,' Jess nodded. 'I could do with going shopping for some new clothes and shoes.' She'd slung on her false 'Loubs' today but they were getting shabby now. A new pair of jeans and a couple of tops would be good, too. She'd saved up enough money while she was working to treat herself and the summer clothes would be hitting the shops now.

Mum was in non-stop-chatter mode as she slid the car into gear, checked the mirrors and headed off, weaving her way in and out of the traffic, braking so suddenly as a car pulled out on them that Jess gasped in alarm. She'd forgotten how erratic Mum's driving could be. Her mother continued, totally oblivious to Jess's wincing whenever she took a corner sharply, slammed her brakes a little too hard, or raced onto the roundabout before an oncoming car could reach them, and carried on chattering about the wedding.

She's really loved up, Jess thought in surprise. It was a bit... she mentally searched for a word to describe how she felt listening to her mum chattering on about Phil, their wedding, their honeymoon, their plans for the future. Embarrassing was too strong, awkward didn't fit it, either. Odd. That was the only word she could think of to describe it. Her efficient, no nonsense, sensible mother had suddenly turned into a gushing bride. Odd. But nice.

'Oh, I'm sorry, love, here I am rabbiting away, I'm all me, me, me when I haven't seen you for months and haven't even asked about your news.' They were now, thankfully, turning onto their street, and Jess suppressed the sigh of relief that almost escaped her lips as her mother pulled up outside the family home. Well, *that* was an experience!

'I haven't got much to tell,' she said with a smile as she unbuckled her seatbelt and opened the door. 'I'm busy working most of the time, and when I'm off I go skiing or hit the clubs, depending what time of day it is.'

'No man, then?' Pam was out the car now, peering over the roof at Jess, a searching look on her face.

'No man.' Jess shrugged her shoulders. Why did the newly coupled/engaged/married always try to make it sound like being single was a crime? As if not finding someone to entwine your life and heart around made you a total freak. She was perfectly happy being single and carefree, thank you very much.

'You and Eddie, Ross's best man, seemed to get on well. I thought you might have kept in touch.' Mum opened the boot and Jess reached over and grabbed her case quickly, it was heavy so she didn't want her mum lifting it out.

Yeah, they had got on well before Aunt Jean had decided to destroy her character and Eddie had decided she was too much like his two-timing 'jilt him at the altar' fiancée to take a chance on. She pushed away the still stupidly raw memory of how hurt she'd been. 'I hardly knew him, Mum.' She put the case down onto the pavement. 'Besides, I like being single. I can do what I want when I want.' She grinned. 'I'm happy for you, though. You've been on your own too long.' She gave her mum a hug. 'Come on, you can show me your outfit and tell me all your plans.'

Phil was in the kitchen, very much at home as he put the kettle on, spooned coffee into cups, took a packet of biscuits – chocolate hobnobs, Jess's favourites – out of the cupboard, opened them, and slid some onto a plate. It had never occurred to her that he'd have already moved in. Stupid of her. Of course he would have. In just over a week's time he would be her stepfather. Which was seriously weird. But seeing the way he slid his arm around Mum's shoulder, hugged her to him, tenderly kissed her on the forehead, and the way Mum beamed back at him, Jess was pleased. Her mum deserved some happiness at long last.

Unsettling how the tenderness reminded her of Eddie, though. How he'd weaved an arm around her shoulder and pulled her into him, kissing her gently on the forehead. His kiss hadn't stopped there, though. It had moved downward until it found her lips, got deeper, more urgent...

Stop it, Jess! She blinked away the memory to see both her mother and Phil looking rather worriedly at her.

'Are you alright with Phil being here, Jess?' Her mother sounded anxious.

'The lads are fine with it. Pam and I never stopped to think how you'd feel.' Phil's cheeks were slightly flushed and he'd dropped his arm from Mum's shoulder. She'd embarrassed them.

'Of course not. Why should I? It's Mum's home and I don't actually live here, I just drop in now and again.' She gabbled. Then she realised that they might want to change that. Might want her to move out of her hardly-used childhood bedroom so they could have the house to themselves.

'Actually, I've been thinking. I ought to get a flat of my own instead of hogging that bedroom. It isn't fair on you that I drop in and out like this.'

'Don't be silly. It's not worth you paying for a flat you're hardly going to use. There will always be a room for you with us, won't there Phil?' Pam turned towards Phil and he nodded in agreement.

'Of course. Now let's all sit down and have a cuppa. You must be tired after the flight, Jess.' Pouring boiling water into the mugs, he passed one to her and one to Pam.

Jess joined her mum sitting at the table while Phil remained standing, leaning against the kitchen cupboard. After a while he took his mug outside, leaving them to talk. Which they did, re-boiling the kettle and making more coffee, then going upstairs to see Mum's outfit and pictures of the flowers and the cake.

'I'm so glad you've come home for the wedding, Jess,' Mum said, giving her a peck on the cheek. 'It wouldn't be the same without you here.'

'I wouldn't miss it for the world, Mum.' Jess gave her a hug. 'I'm going to take a shower now and freshen up. Leave you to go and chat to Phil. You both must have lots to discuss.'

Pam headed downstairs and Jess crossed the landing to her bedroom. She opened the door and looked around at the red poppies dotted across the white wallpaper, the curtains of the same design, the bedspread. Vibrant red cushions, red carpet. Her teenage bedroom. But she wasn't a teenager anymore, she was almost thirty years old and now that Mum was getting married it was time she moved out and got her own place.

Mum was right though, she thought, lifting the case that Phil had thoughtfully brought up for her onto her bed and opening it. It wasn't worth renting a flat that she would hardly use.

Maybe it was time she rethought her life. Got herself a more stable job. Grew up, put down roots and got herself a permanent home.

Chapter Twenty Five

Jess. Eddie paused as he walked away from the till and stared at the woman to his right He'd only been back in England two days and already he was imagining he'd seen Jess. How crazy was that? Okay, the long hair dangling in wavy tendrils down her back was definitely the same traffic light red, and she stood leaning slightly on her right leg – just like Jess. But it couldn't be. He skimmed his eyes over the bright yellow top, down to the skinny jeans, resting for a second or two on the pert butt then down to the blue suede shoes. Could it be? As she moved her foot he caught a glimpse of red sole, slightly chipped off in one corner, and a smile tugged at the corners of his mouth. Yes, it was Jess. But what was she doing back in the UK?

He knew she hadn't been invited to the christening. He'd checked before he'd accepted Ross's plea to be godfather to their daughter, Rosabelle, not wanting to risk bumping into Jess again. It had taken a while to drive her out of his thoughts, his dreams, but he'd finally done it. The last thing he'd expected when he dashed into this shoe shop to buy a smart pair of black shoes to go with his suit was to find Jess here.

She hadn't seen him yet. She had her back to him, looking at a selection of skyscraper-heeled shoes. He watched as she selected a black one from the shelf and pondered over it. Would she paint the soles of those red, too?

If he turned away now and walked out of the shop, she wouldn't know he'd been there. He could forget he'd seen her. He hesitated, part of him longing to speak to her again, to see those gorgeous green eyes gazing into hers. As he fought an inner battle with himself, Jess swung around. 'What do you think of these, Mum?' she asked the woman next to her. Then her eyes widened as she noticed Eddie, and they both stood rooted to the spot, staring at each other.

It was her mother, Pam, who broke the silence.

'It's Eddie, isn't it? Are you over for the christening?'

He nodded, stepped towards her, murmured, 'Delighted to meet you again, Mrs Kaine' and she replied 'Pam, please,' as he kissed her on both cheeks then wished he hadn't because now it would be rude not to kiss Jess on the cheeks too, but if he touched her soft skin with his lips how would he be able to tear himself away?

Jess was looking at him like she wished she was anywhere but here, then quickly took a step back signalling that she didn't want him to greet her in the same way. 'Hello again.' Her voice was cool. Distant.

He nodded. 'You are home for a visit?'

'Mum's wedding. It's a week Saturday.'

He glanced towards her mother again and smiled. 'Congratulations.'

'Thank you.' Pam paused. 'Look, we were just about to take a break. Why don't you join us for a coffee? There's a lovely little café on the High Street and we can have a catch up.'

He was about to reply that he would be delighted to but was too busy when Pam tapped his arm. 'Come on, you can spare half an hour.'

He registered the panic in Jess's eyes, gave her an apologetic smile, and followed her out of the shop.

***

Damn. Why did Mum have to invite Eddie for a bloody coffee? Surely she could see how awkward they both were with each other. Mum barely knew Eddie so there was only one reason she could have done it, she was perishing matchmaking again. She'd attempted to match Jess up with a few guys in the past, but Jess had managed to shake off the awkwardness with a grin and shrug, muttering 'mothers', and swiftly extract herself from it without too much embarrassment. This time though, Mum had definitely over-stepped the mark. Jess had made it quite clear to her yesterday that she had no desire to renew her acquaintance with Eddie. Yet here Mum was, making her have a cup of coffee and chat with him, not caring that Eddie looked as reluctant about it as she was.

'Grab a table, I'll get the coffees.' Her mother indicated a table in the window.

'No, allow me,' Eddie protested.

'I most certainly will not. I invited you to join us,' Pam insisted. 'Piece of cake anyone?'

Jess shook her head, not trusting herself to speak as she walked over to a different table to the one her mother had indicated – a small act of defiance – leaving Eddie to follow. She sat down with her back to the wall and forced a smile on her face as he pulled out a chair and sat down opposite her. No point being rude and petulant. She was grown up enough to have a cup of coffee with him, even though after a night of fantastic sex he'd made her feel like a tramp who made a habit of stealing her cousin's boyfriends. 'Sorry about my mother. She does kind of take over.'

'Not a problem.' He leaned back casually in his chair and flicked his gaze over to her. 'It's good to see you again, Jess. How are you?'

'Fine. Busy. I've been working in Switzerland over the winter and have come home for a few weeks for Mum's wedding. I'm bridesmaid – again,' she added. 'How about you?' She steadily met his gaze, determined not to give any sign of how awkward she felt.

'I'm here for a week. I go back the day after Rosabelle's christening. I gather you aren't going?'

She'd like to have bet he'd made sure she wasn't going before he came over. 'No, but Mum and Phil are. I'm not exactly Charlotte's favourite person, am I?'

Eddie leaned forward, placed his elbows on the table and linked his fingers underneath his chin. Chocolate whirlpool eyes gazing unsettlingly into hers. 'I'm sorry. That isn't fair of her. Ross was the one at fault.'

'Yeah, well, they've made up so it's easier to make me the scapegoat.' She shrugged, lowered her gaze a bit then wished she hadn't because now she was looking at his long fingers and remembering how sensually they had caressed her body. She lowered her gaze to the silver dog-tag visible through the v neck of his T-shirt, resting on a cluster of dark hairs, hairs she'd ran her fingers through. Feeling the heat rise to her cheeks she glanced away, over at the bar, and saw with relief that her mother was heading their way, carefully balancing three cups of coffee and a plate of miniature fancy cakes on a wooden tray. 'Ah, here's Mum with the refreshments. And she's bought cakes, too.'

'Ah good, you two have made up, then.' Pam placed the tray down on the table, then put a cup of coffee in front of Eddie, another in front of Jess, and the third one in front of a vacant seat. Taking the plate of cakes off the tray she placed them in the middle of the table, put the tray down at the side of it, and sat down. 'I knew you would as soon as you started talking,' she said, a satisfied look on her face.

God, she was infuriating. Deep breaths, Jess.

Sensing that Jess needed time to control herself, Eddie took charge of the conversation, turned to Pam, and charmingly started asking about her wedding plans. That was it, she was on a roll. Within a few minutes Jess had fought back the anger and irritation enough to join in the conversation, and for the next half hour they talked lightly and pleasantly.

Finally, his coffee now finished and having been persuaded to eat one of the tiny but extremely delicious cakes, Eddie glanced at his watch and announced that he had to go.

'I'm meeting Ross at three,' he said and his tone of regret actually sounded genuine. 'It's been a pleasure to talk to you both.' He kissed Pam on both cheeks. 'I wish you every happiness in your forthcoming wedding.' His soft lips found Jess's cheeks and brushed them lightly. 'Bye, Jess.' Then he was gone.

Leaving her cheeks tingling and his new shoes in the bag by the table.

Jess didn't notice them until she stood up a few minutes later, ready to continue her shopping.

'He's left his shoes behind,' she said, picking up the bag and handing it to her mother. 'Perhaps you can give them to him when you see him at the christening on Sunday.'

'He said he'd bought them for the christening so he's going to need them in the morning,' Mum replied. 'Haven't you got his phone number? You could text him and tell him we have them. He might not have realised that he's left them here and could be looking everywhere for them.'

She had a point. And yes, Jess did still have Eddie's phone number. She'd gone to delete it a few times over the past few months but then had decided against it. Somehow, knowing that she had a way to contact him – not that she ever intended to – made her feel better.

'I do but...' If she contacted him he'd know she still had his number. That she hadn't deleted it. Then he'd think she'd been hoping he'd contact her. Which she hadn't. Well not after the first month or so. Not much, anyway.

'Then send him a message,' Mum urged. 'Before he goes and buys another pair of shoes.'

She guessed Mum was right. She reluctantly took her phone out of her handbag, scrolled down to Eddie's number in her contacts list, and wrote him a quick text.

Hi Eddie, you left your new shoes behind. Do you want Mum to give them to you at the christening or do you need them before?

She pondered for a minute on how to sign off. A kiss seemed too friendly and 'best wishes' was too formal. In the end she selected the smiley face emoji and placed her name underneath it. Then she pressed send.

'Done. Now let's get on with our wedding shopping. I'm popping around to Becky's later.'

They spent the rest of the afternoon shopping for wedding shoes and Jess's dress. Mum had already spotted a few she liked, and they both finally agreed on a gorgeous dusky blue one with a sweetheart neckline and floaty skirt – a perfect pairing to her new white shoes. Mum wanted them both to have white shoes and handbag.

***

Eddie was on his second pint, trying to act interested as Ross went on and on about baby Rosa, Carly, and the woes of married life which seemed to be a relentless cycle

233

of sleepless nights, fraught tempers, and microwave meals.

'I tell you, mate, I didn't realise how hard it would be,' Ross told him. 'Rosa, well she's cute, but she's full on. Me and Carly hardly have time to even hold a conversation these days. The house is a tip, all the meals taste of plastic, and as for sex, well I've forgotten what it's like.' He tipped his glass up, gulped a long mouthful then put it down again. 'I expected me and Carly to have a few years together as a couple before we had kids.'

'Then you should have been more careful,' Eddie pointed out.

'I was. Always. Except for that one night when we'd had a drink. One bloody night of unprotected sex. We'd have been okay if Carly had stayed on the pill.'

'You said it made her ill,' he pointed out. 'It doesn't suit some women. You can't expect her to take all the responsibility.' *Mon Dieu*, Ross was getting on his nerves. He had only been married seven months or so and already he was complaining. Carly didn't seem happy, either. She looked tired and was snappy and grumpy. He wished now that he'd insisted on staying in a travel lodge rather than their spare room where he had to constantly listen to them both bickering. It was difficult to remember how happy they'd looked on their wedding day.

Maybe he could still get a room somewhere, give them some space. He didn't think him staying there was helping the situation, especially as Ross wanted to go out drinking with him in the evening, which made Carly even more snappy.

'Look, Ross, it's really kind of you and Carly to put me up,' he said. 'But I've booked a hotel room for the rest of the week. It'll give you both a bit of space'

Ross sulked. 'There's no need for that. I like having you to stay.'

'It's not fair on Carly, she's got her hands full looking after the baby.' Eddie leaned his elbow on the table and stroked his beard thoughtfully. 'I know things are a bit difficult for you both right now, Ross, but it'll pass. Carly will get used to the baby and cope better.' He paused. 'You could help her a bit, you know. Rosa is your baby, too.'

'I try to, but Carly won't let me near Rosa. She doesn't trust me to do anything right,' Ross grumbled. He gulped down the rest of his drink and stood up. 'I don't blame you for booking into a hotel, mate. I wish I could.'

'You don't mean that. You love Carly and Rosa, you know you do.'

Ross picked up his jacket and shrugged himself into it. 'Yeah, I do. But I don't like being at home right now, I can tell you that for nothing.'

Eddie watched him, worried. He hoped things weren't as bad as they sounded. Ross and Carly had almost split up straight after the wedding and now it seemed as if they were on the point of it again.

He reached into his jacket pocket and took out his phone to check the time. His heart did a fluttery leap as he saw a text from Jess. She'd kept his number. How many times he'd hoped over the past few months that he'd get a text from her! But why was she contacting him now? Then he noticed that it had been sent hours ago – he'd turned it onto silence when Rosa was having a nap that morning. Puzzled, he opened the text and read it. It was straight to the point, telling him he'd left his shoes behind at the cafe. He'd forgotten all about them, he'd been so distracted at seeing her again.

'Who's that?' Ross asked.

He didn't want to tell him, to let him and Carly know that he'd seen Jess again, that she'd texted him. They'd ruined it for him last time, he didn't want that to happen again.

'Charles. Something to do with work. Anyway, I'd better get back to yours, pick up my things and sign into my hotel.'

Book a hotel more like. He hadn't even got a room yet, not that it would be a problem, there were enough hotels in the city, one would have space.

No, the problem was what to say to Jess. He wanted to see her again.

He selected reply and started to type.

So sorry, Jess, I've only just noticed your text. I put the sound down on my phone earlier so as not to wake Rosa. Any chance of picking the shoes up tomorrow evening? I could meet you somewhere.

Then, before he had chance to change his mind, he pressed send.

'Can't you stay and have another drink?' Ross asked petulantly.

Eddie shook his head. 'And neither should you. You should be at home helping Carly. And don't give me that excuse that she won't let you do anything. You need to try harder. You can see she's exhausted. Make her a cup of coffee or run her a bath. Anything to let her know you care.'

'It's okay for you to preach, you don't know what it's like,' Ross retorted. 'Wait until you're settled down and got a kid, mate. Then you'll wish you appreciated your freedom more.'

Yes, he was definitely doing the right thing clearing out and leaving them to it, Eddie thought as he followed

Ross to the taxi rank. And the way Ross was going, Carly
would be sending him packing soon.

Chapter Twenty Six

Jess felt ridiculously excited to be seeing Eddie again. First date, schoolgirl crush sort of excited. She took ages deciding what to wear, trying out different styles with her hair. What the hell was the matter with her? Anyone would think she'd never been for a drink with a guy before.

Her mum noticed, of course. 'So you're meeting Eddie to give him his shoes?' She asked in a false 'not at all interested' voice. 'Are you meeting your friends afterwards?'

'Yes.' She was meeting Mae and Anna at nine, which gave her just over an hour with Eddie. Long enough to catch up and an excuse to get away before things got awkward.

'You don't usually make so much fuss about what to wear when you're meeting Mae,' Pam commented.

Jess glanced at her, but Mum's face was non-committal – deliberately, she suspected. 'Well we might go on to a club afterwards. Don't wait up,' she added. 'I'll probably be back late.'

'No problem. Enjoy yourself.' Jess cringed at the look that passed between her mum and Phil. They were so obviously hoping she and Eddie would hook up together. Well there was no chance of that. That ship had sailed. Still, it would be good to see him again.

***

Eddie glanced at his watch. They'd arranged to meet ten minutes ago and there was still no sign of Jess. He guessed she was being deliberately late – as women often did. He ordered himself a shandy (he was driving so would only have the one) selected a table in the corner, took out his phone, swiped the screen, and busied himself catching up on emails – Charles was dealing with most of the restaurant stuff but there were still a couple of things needing his attention. It would help pass the time and make him look busy when Jess arrived. He didn't want her to think he'd been waiting for her, watching the door every few minutes to see if she came in.

Even though that's exactly what he was doing.

The door opened and his heart skipped to attention before she even stepped into the room, as if it sensed her presence. Not that she stepped in, that was too slow, too normal for Jess. She burst in like a ray of sunlight illuminating the room, her long hair shimmering in the light as it flowed around her shoulders like flickering flames. Her figure-hugging purple maxi dress clinging to

240

every curve, the long slit up the side revealing toned still-suntanned legs, the short cream faux-fur jacket topping off the simple outfit to give a hint of glamour. He doubted if she had dressed like that for him. She was obviously going out.

She paused at the door, glancing swiftly around the room, her face breaking into a smile when she spotted him, returned his wave, and made her way over.

'Hi, sorry I'm a bit late.' She handed him the bag with his shoes inside. 'Here you are, I'd better not put it on the table in case you're superstitious.'

'Thank you.' He put the bag down on the floor as she pulled out a chair and sat down opposite him. 'And are you superstitious?'

'No, I think it's a load of rubbish, but my mum is. I put some new shoes on a table once and she went ballistic. She lost her purse the next day and swore I'd brought her bad luck.' She grinned. 'How about you?'

He shook his head. 'No – but I admit that I always try to avoid walking under a ladder – although that's more for safety reasons than bad luck.' He rose. 'Let me get you a drink. I would have got you one in, but I didn't want to presume that you'd be drinking vodka and coke.' He let his gaze drift over her dress. 'You look like you're going out?'

'Yep, meeting a couple of mates and going onto a club.' She went to get up. 'I'll get myself a drink. No worries.'

He motioned her to sit down. 'Please, allow me. Especially after you've gone out of your way to bring me my shoes.' He rose. 'What would you like?'

'Pinot grigio and lemonade, please. I'll leave the hard stuff till a bit later this evening.'

***

She watched as he made his way to the bar, trying not to remember the toned body under the tight-fitting jeans, his hands caressing her body, gently at first then... She shook the memories from her mind. That was one night, never to be repeated. And that's the way she wanted it to stay.

'So, you've been working in Switzerland?' He put the drink on the table, his arm lightly brushing against her back sending moth wings shuddering down her spine, then sat down opposite her. 'Do you ski?'

'Yes, not too brilliantly, mind, but I'm not a complete novice.'

'And how long are you home for?'

She took a sip of her drink. 'Until the end of the month – I've got some temping office work to tide me over.' She'd managed to organise a few odd days with an agency she'd worked for last year. 'Then I'm back to Majorca.' She wrinkled her nose mischievously. 'Can't wait.'

'You miss working away?'

'It's nice to have a couple of weeks off and catch up with friends and family, but yes, I love my job. The people, the weather, living in different countries. It's great.' Her eyes danced with enthusiasm.

'I'm sure it is. Do you ever tire of it though? And of not having a proper home?' He leaned back in his chair. 'You mentioned before that this isn't something you want to do for the rest of your life.'

She forgot she'd told him that. She ran her finger around the rim of the glass while she gathered her thoughts. 'I'm not sure,' she admitted. 'I've been thinking about it quite a lot just lately. I'm twenty-nine. Maybe it's time I got myself a more stable career, my own flat, a car, and all the other boring grown up stuff.' She grinned at him. 'I do enjoy being a rep though.'

'I guess there isn't an age limit to being a rep. Some people do it all their lives,' he pointed out. 'Even when they are married.'

'Well I don't intend to get married, but if I did I wouldn't want to be working away from home all the time.' She frowned. 'The trouble is I don't know what else I want to do. I'd hate doing a regular nine to five job in an office, and I love socialising with people.'

'Maybe receptionist or customer service work would suit you,' Eddie suggested.

'I'm still indoors, though, tied to a desk. I hate that. That's the sort of temping work I usually do when I come home for a month and I can just about stand it because I know it's only for a short time.' A strand of hair fell over her shoulder and she flicked it back. 'What about you? How long have you owned the restaurant? Do you have many staff working under you?'

He took a swig of his shandy. 'A couple of chefs and waiting staff. And I co-own it with my business partner, Charles. He deals with the admin and I deal with the cooking.'

'Really? Do you do all the cooking?'

'*Non*, I am the *Chef de Cuisine* – Head Chef you call it. I cook at my restaurant a few days a week, other days my chefs take over. Which is why I manage to take the occasional week off, like now.'

She leaned forward. 'Tell me more. What sort of stuff do you cook?'

She listened attentively as Eddie told her about his little restaurant in an upmarket coastal region in Marseille, his speciality fish dishes, pausing to take a drink as he relayed how he'd always loved to cook as a child, used to help his grandmother in the kitchen, but his father, an admiral in the navy, frowned upon it, looked on it as something a boy shouldn't be wasting his time doing, and even though his restaurant got three star Michelin reviews and even attracted some celebrity clientele, his father still disapproved and tried to talk him into getting a 'proper job'.

'You must miss your mother. And your grandmother,' Jess said softly.

For a moment she saw pain flicker across Eddie's eyes and instinctively reached out to put her hand reassuringly on his. Their eyes met, and her heart beat a little faster. Her throat tightened as he placed his other hand on top of hers, the pain in his eyes now replaced by a softness that held her transfixed.

'I've had enough!' Suddenly the chair beside her was pulled back with a screech and Ross plonked a pint of beer down on the table, spilling some of it, then sat down. 'If I don't get out of that house I'll go mental, I swear I will.'

The special moment gone, both Jess and Eddie stared at Ross in surprise.

'You've walked out and left Carly to cope alone again?' Eddie demanded. It was obvious that he was disgusted by Ross's behaviour. 'You can't keep doing this, Ross.'

'I can't stand it, Eddie. All she does is moan, and all the kid does is scream.' He picked up his pint and took a long swig. Then he looked from Eddie to Jess, his expression a big question. 'What are you two doing together? Are you still seeing each other?'

'I bumped into Eddie when I was shopping with Mum yesterday and he left his shoes behind so I'm returning them – I'm meeting some friends soon at a nearby club,' she added quickly in case Ross thought she'd dressed up especially for Eddie. Which she had, but she wasn't about to admit it.

'Never mind us. I've told you, you should be more patient. It's not easy for Carly, either. She's cooped up all day with Rosa and it's all new to her. She needs your help.'

'How can I help her when she yells at everything I do?' Another long gulp of beer. 'I tell you, I can't take much more of this.'

'You could probably do with a night out together. Can't Aunt Jean babysit so you can have some couple time?' Jess suggested. She'd seen this happen with couples before when a new baby arrived. They got so wrapped up in the baby they had no time for each other. Becky and Scott had been the same at first.

Ross glared at her. 'She would, but Carly won't leave Rosa. She thinks no one else knows how to look after her. It's a bloody nightmare.'

Jess could imagine. She knew what Charlotte could be like. 'It's early days yet,' she said. 'You need to be patient. Charlotte will relax a bit as Rosa gets older.'

'I doubt our marriage will last that long!'

Eddie drew in a breath. 'I know it's difficult, Ross, but you need to go home. Walking out and spending the evening in the pub isn't going to help. It'll just make Carly more upset.'

'Eddie's right. It's not easy for Charlotte, being stuck at home all day with a young baby when she's used to being out at work, mixing with adults.'

'Carly's always upset. Nothing I do is ever right so I might as well enjoy myself for once. At least then I'll be getting moaned at for something I've *actually* done.' He downed his drink and stood up. 'Anyone want another?'

'I don't think you should, Ross…' Eddie's protest was interrupted by the sound of Ross's phone buzzing. 'I bet that's Carly now, wondering where you are.'

'Well she can wonder. I'm not answering it,' Ross said sulkily. He took the phone out of his pocket, placed it down on the table, and went to get another pint.

The phone buzzed again, Charlotte's image flashing on the screen, the vibrations pulsating into the table seeming to convey the anger she was feeling.

'How did Ross know you were here?' Jess asked, trying to ignore the incessant noise.

'Ross and I had a drink here yesterday. I was staying with them but they're not getting on at all, so I've booked into a hotel. I can see them splitting up if they carry on.'

'Oh no, that'd be awful. We must do something,' Jess said. 'We've got to make Ross go home.'

The buzzing was getting more and more persistent, the phone almost bouncing along the table with each new call. Charlotte was obviously determined to get hold of Ross. He shouldn't be ignoring her like this. Jess picked up the phone, marched over to the bar with it, tapped Ross on the shoulder, answered the call, and thrust it into his hand as soon as he turned around.

'Ross!' Charlotte shrieked. 'Where are you? Rosa's ill…'

Jess saw Ross pale as he listened. 'I'm coming home right now,' he stammered.

'Want a lift?' Eddie had joined them at the bar.

Ross nodded. 'Carly said Rosa's really ill. We might have to take her to the hospital.'

'Maybe you'd better come, too, calm Carly down,' Eddie told Jess.

'I think that'd be the last thing she wants,' Jess replied, but Eddie had grabbed her arm and was pulling her along with him. Before she knew it, she was out of the pub and in the backseat of Eddie's hire car.

Chapter Twenty Seven

Eddie drove fast but carefully. Fifteen minutes, and several panicky phone calls from Charlotte later, they pulled into the drive of Ross's semi-detached house. Ross was out of the car, leaving the door wide open, and unlocking the front door before Jess or Eddie had undone their seat belts.

Jess hesitated. 'I don't think Charlotte will be pleased to see me. Perhaps I should stay in the car.'

'Please come inside. We might need you.' Eddie's voice was soft, persuasive.

He was right. If Rosa did have to be taken to hospital Charlotte was going to need all the support she could get. She could message Mae and Anna, they'd understand. She might be able to catch up with them later.

If anyone had asked Jess what she thought Charlotte's house would be like she'd have said immaculate, everything tastefully furnished and nothing out of place. She definitely wouldn't have imagined the lounge covered in baby clothes, packets of nappies, un-ironed washing, and empty bottles. Nor to find her 'never be seen without make up' cousin without so much as a sweep of blusher on her face, wearing a milk-stained sweatshirt and jogging bottoms, and hair scraped back in a ponytail. Charlotte was pacing the room, the screaming baby wrapped in a blanket, lying over her shoulder.

'What's the matter with her?' Ross asked. 'Why is she screaming?'

Charlotte turned to him, her face etched with anxiety. 'I don't know. She's been like this for an hour. She won't stop. She's got a temperature and look, she's covered in a rash.' She walked over to the sofa and sat down, Ross beside her, undoing the baby's sleep suit to reveal a red rash all over her stomach. 'What if it's...' she paused as if she couldn't bring herself to say the word. 'Meningitis.'

'Oh God! We need to call an ambulance. Fast!' Ross jumped up and took his phone out of his pocket.

'Hang on. Have you tried the glass test?' Jess asked. She turned to Eddie. 'Please can you fetch a clean glass from the kitchen? A tumbler's best.'

Charlotte stared as if she'd only just noticed Jess. 'What's *she* doing here?' she demanded. Then in a softer voice, as if what Jess said had just registered. 'What glass test?

Jess took the glass that Eddie handed her and walked over to the sofa. 'It's the recommended way to check for meningitis,' she said. 'You press the glass over the rash and look through it. If the rash fades, it isn't meningitis. Can you undress Rosa so we can try it on her tummy?'

250

Charlotte nodded, took the blanket off Rosa, and gently eased the baby's arms out of the sleepsuit. Rosa screamed and kicked her little legs, as if protesting about being disturbed. Jess bit her lip as she saw the angry, red rash all over the baby's body. She remembered one of the children her mum minded having meningitis. The rash had looked a bit like this at first, then quickly spread all over the body in red and blue blotches. They'd just got the child – Ben – to hospital in time. Ben had been lethargic too though, but Rosa definitely wasn't.

'This is going to be a bit cold, darling,' Jess said soothingly as she pressed the tumbler on the baby's tummy, her eyes fixed on the rash. She could sense that everyone else was holding their breath. To her relief, when she looked through the glass, the rash had faded.

'It's gone!' Charlotte sounded like she was about to cry with relief. 'Does that mean she's okay?'

Jess pressed the glass against Rosa's tummy again, just to make sure. The rash definitely faded. She looked up and saw the hope in Charlotte's eyes. 'It isn't meningitis,' she confirmed.

'Thank God!' Charlotte burst into tears and Ross placed his arms around her shoulder, pulling her towards him in a loving embrace.

'You are sure, aren't you?' Ross asked.

'It's a pretty accurate test,' Jess said. She felt Rosa's forehead. It was hot. And no wonder, in the thick sleepsuit and blanket. She was dribbling, too. Jess grabbed a baby wipe off the table, cleaned her finger with it then felt Rosa's gums. They were burning.

'Then what's wrong with her? Why did you put your finger in her mouth?' she could hear the anxiety in Charlotte's voice.

'I think she's teething, and over-heated.' She took off the sleepsuit, leaving the baby in just a vest and nappy. 'Do you have any teething stuff for her?'

'What sort of stuff?' Charlotte looked bewildered. 'What am I supposed to give her? I didn't think she was old enough to be teething.'

'It can start really young. Teething granules are best for a baby this age. You just open the packet and pop them into her mouth.'

Charlotte shook her head. 'I didn't know…'

'We'll go and get some,' Eddie offered. 'Come on, Ross.'

'Could you get me a cold flannel please Charlotte, so I can cool Rosa down?' Jess asked as the men went out of the door.

Charlotte jumped up and went into the kitchen, returning a minute later with a damp, white flannel. She watched anxiously as Jess placed the flannel on Rosa's forehead, then lay the baby girl over her knee and placed the flannel over the back of her neck.

'Look, the rash is going.'

'As I thought, she was too hot,' Jess said. 'You've got heating on in here, so a sleepsuit is enough. She doesn't need to be swaddled, too.'

'Mum said babies like to be swaddled, it settles them and helps them sleep.'

'Yes, but maybe use a thin shawl rather than a thick blanket. Have you got a shawl?'

Her cousin disappeared into the bedroom and returned with a thin lace shawl. 'What are you doing with Eddie anyway?' she asked as she handed it to Jess.

Jess quickly explained about going shopping with her mum yesterday, bumping into Eddie, him leaving his shoes behind and her returning them to him.

'He asked me to have a drink with him, then Ross came in. When we heard Rosa was ill Eddie insisted on driving Ross over and asked me to come with them in case I could help,' she finished.

'And why would he think you could?' Charlotte pouted.

'Because Mum used to be a child minder, remember? I grew up with kids and I work with them now.'

Charlotte looked at Rosa lying contentedly over Jess's knees, one fist thrust in her mouth. 'Well, you *have* helped,' she admitted reluctantly. Then she took a deep breath and added. 'Thanks.'

It must have taken her a lot to say that. Jess smiled at her. 'No worries. It's not easy looking after a little baby, is it? I remember things because of all the children Mum looked after, but I bet I won't be so calm if I have a child of my own. They're so defenceless, aren't they? And you feel so responsible.'

'I know. I'm terrified something's going to happen to her. She cries such a lot and she won't sleep. I can't keep on top of things. Just look at this mess.' Charlotte swept the room with her hand. Then her eyes filled with tears. 'I'm so tired.'

'Look, you cuddle Rosa and I'll do us a cup of coffee. I don't know about you, but I could do with one.' Rosa grizzled as Jess passed her over then snuggled up to her mother and chewed her fist again.

Suddenly Charlotte's eyes rested on Jess's clothes. 'Oh gosh, you're all dressed up to go out. I've ruined your evening.'

'I'm only meeting a couple of friends, it's fine. I've texted them to say I'll be late. They'll carry on to the club and I can meet them there.'

'But Rosa has dribbled on your dress.' Horrified, she pointed to a wet patch on the front of Jess's purple dress.

'Don't worry, I can clear that up,' Jess told her. 'But first, let me do us both a coffee.'

Jess had cleared up the dribble with a baby wipe – which still left a wet stain but one that should dry out – and was finishing her coffee when Eddie and Ross returned with teething granules and a teething ring. 'We'll freeze the teething ring in a bit,' Jess said, popping it into the steriliser first. 'Rosa should settle down once she's had the granules, so she probably won't need it until tomorrow, and it'll help her better if it's cold.'

Half an hour later, Rosa was fast asleep in her cot.

'I hope she sleeps through the night.' Charlotte rested her head against the back of the sofa and wearily closed her eyes.

'Why don't you go to bed, too,' Ross said gently. 'You look exhausted. I'll look after Rosa if she wakes.'

Jess stood up. 'Yes, rest while you can. We're going now.'

Charlotte's eyes sprang open. 'You'll both come around again, won't you? Friday night? I'll do something to eat and we can have some wine.'

'That's a great idea. Say you'll come,' Ross agreed.

Jess hesitated. She was so stunned that her usually snooty cousin was actually inviting her around for the evening that it didn't register at first that she was asking

Eddie, too. Not until she heard him say, 'I'd love to. What about you, Jess? Can you make Friday?'

'Er…'

'Oh, please say you will, Jess. Me and Ross haven't had people around for ages and you've been so good with Rosa. I want to thank you.' Charlotte urged.

Jess found herself nodding in agreement, saying that eight o'clock would be fine for her, and telling Charlotte not to go to the trouble of cooking as they'd all have a take away.

As it was raining outside, Eddie insisted on giving Jess a lift to the club where she was meeting Mae and Anna. She hurried over to his car, wondering how the hell returning his shoes had turned into an invite to spend an evening with Charlotte and Ross. With Eddie. As if they were a couple.

Chapter Twenty Eight

'I'm not sure how we got roped into that,' Eddie said as he started up the car then switched on the windscreen wipers and lights. He glanced at Jess. 'Are you okay with it?'

'I am if you are,' she said. 'It feels a bit strange, though. I mean, me and Charlotte have never got on, and now she's invited me to dinner.'

'Did you fall out because of the Simon thing?' Eddie had his eyes on the road, but she sensed her answer was important to him.

'Well it didn't help. Not that it was my fault. Simon was a creep and I had no idea he had a thing for me until he started turning up at my work then practically threw himself at me.'

Eddie indicated left, slowed down and pulled up at the side of the road. Then he turned to her. 'I owe you an apology, Jess. I had no right to judge you like that. Especially after...'

'We'd spent the night together,' she finished for him. 'No, you didn't. I'm not in the habit of going after a guy who's already taken. No matter what you and Charlotte might think. Okay, Ross was drunk and didn't know what

257

he was doing. But Simon stalked me. He wouldn't leave me alone.'

'That must have been worrying for you.'

It had freaked her out at the time to be honest, but luckily growing up with brothers had taught her how to deal with men. 'It wasn't pleasant, but what made it worse was the way Charlotte blamed me. We've never got on. She's a spoiled, adored only child, whereas I'm one of three, and definitely *not* spoilt. I thought she was a stuck-up snob, and she and her parents have always looked down on us.'

'Yet you came to her rescue tonight and have agreed to have a meal with them on Friday – even putting up with my company.'

She stared past him, out of the window at the raindrops slithering down. Why had she agreed?

'I felt sorry for her. She's always been on top of things, super-efficient. But tonight she seemed lost, out of her depth. She's got no experience with babies...'

'Not like you. You were marvellous with Rosa.'

She licked her lips, kept her eyes on the rainy window. 'I guess it's probably really hard for Charlotte, coping with Rosa. She's always been able to control everything in her life and suddenly she has this little baby that screams all night and she has no idea what to do.' She paused, remembering how distraught her cousin had looked when they arrived. 'She was terrified Rosa had meningitis.'

'That explains why you helped her tonight, but not why you agreed to go to dinner on Friday – and with me, too.'

'I didn't feel like I could refuse. They both obviously wanted company.' She met his gaze now. 'I can back out if you prefer to go by yourself? Pretend that I'm ill.'

He reached out and caressed her cheek with his fingers. 'I don't prefer. I wanted a chance to talk to you again. To apologise and ask if we can start over.' His fingers traced her lips now, sending pinprick shudders down her spine. 'Can we? Will you give me another chance, Jess?'

***

A car went past, lighting up her face and he saw the conflict in her eyes. He didn't blame her. He should have given her a chance to explain about Carly's ex. He'd been so untrusting ever since Yvette, so ready to doubt any woman he was with, so quick to look for signs of fickleness. He liked Jess. *A lot.* She'd been kind to them in Majorca, helping them sort out their hotel rooms, she'd looked after them when Ross was drunk, and look how he'd repaid her. Yet still she'd kept Ross's mistake a

259

secret and got herself into trouble with her family in the process. And tonight, despite everything, she'd gone to her spoilt cousin's rescue.

He cupped her face in his hands, held it gently and gazed into her eyes. 'Please give me another chance, Jess. We were good together, weren't we?'

Suddenly her face broke into a smile. 'Okay,' she said softly.

'Thank you.' He leaned forward and kissed her gently, his heart lifting as she returned the kiss. For a few minutes, they were lost in a deep, sensual kissing session until the horn of a passing car broke the spell.

'I guess we'd better save this for somewhere more private, before we get arrested,' he said, reluctantly releasing her. He wanted to ask her to come back to his hotel room where he had a bottle of wine cooling in the fridge, and a double bed with a comfy mattress, but resisted, knowing it would sound as if he'd only apologised to her so he could get her into bed again. He'd been an idiot, and she'd given him a second chance. He didn't want to mess it up. Then he remembered that she was meeting friends anyway, he was supposed to be dropping her off at the club. 'How about meeting me for dinner tomorrow night?'

She shook her head. 'I've arranged to meet another friend tomorrow, sorry. I could make lunch, though, or maybe Thursday?'

'I've promised to lunch with Ross's parents tomorrow, but yes, Thursday would be good. Shall I pick you up? About eight?'

'Eight is fine.'

***

It's amazing what could happen in one day, Jess thought, when she returned home from clubbing in the early hours of the morning. Yesterday she had no idea that not only would she bump into Eddie again, but she'd end up agreeing to another date, and would also be asked to dinner by her stuck-up cousin who had actually been quite pleasant.

She'd been so aware of Eddie in the car last night, of his presence besides her, his hand grazing her knee as he changed gear, the smell of his aftershave, his magnetism. That hot kiss had reignited her feelings for him again and she'd half-hoped he'd ask her back to his hotel room for a drink – Mae and Anna wouldn't have minded if she'd cancelled – although it had been a fantastic night, so she was pleased she hadn't. It was best to take their time and not jump into bed with each other again. Even if she did really want to.

She'd missed Eddie. She hadn't realised how much until she'd seen him again yesterday, until he'd held her in his arms. He brought out feelings in her that she had never experienced before.

'See you tomorrow, *ma chérie*. You'll be in my dreams until then,' he'd whispered as he kissed her goodnight before she got out of the car.

She took off her make-up, pulled on her pjs and snuggled up in bed. As her head touched the pillow she wondered if he would dream of her.

She dreamed of him.

***

Her mum was incredulous when she found out about Charlotte's dinner invitation.

'Since when did you two get so pally?'

'Since I went to her rescue.' Jess explained about the previous evening's events. 'She was in a real state. Thank goodness Rosa was just teething and hot. Charlotte's so scared of her catching cold she tends to overwrap her.'

'Yes, Jean's been worried about her but whenever she tries to help Charlotte accuses her of interfering and undermining her as a mother.'

'She's probably right, you know what Aunt Jean's like.' Jess helped herself to a chocolate digestive out of the biscuit tin. 'Anyway, I'm off to meet Gerri now. I might stay over so don't wait up.'

'I never do,' Pam pointed out. 'You work abroad most of the year so I presume you know how to take care of yourself.'

'And that is what I love about you, Mum.' Jess gave her a kiss on the forehead and with a wave and 'see you,' was out of the door.

Mum had offered to lend her the car saying she didn't need it that evening, so Jess drove over to Gerri's then they both walked to the local pub. It was good to get out and indulge in a bit of gossip. An evening with Gerri was just what she needed to take her mind off Eddie.

Gerri had met a new man, Aiden, and was full of it. 'He's a hunk,' she said as they paid for the drinks and carried them over to a table by the window. 'As soon as our eyes met over the coffee machine I just knew. He said he felt it, too.'

For the next half hour she talked non-stop about Aiden. Jess learnt how he'd recently joined the Promotions department of the web design company that Gerri worked at, how he was single, fit – he played football for the county – and had a flat in a much-coveted area of the town. He was driven, producing some fantastic ideas for promoting the company, and he was sweet, telling Gerri that she was the most amazing woman he had ever met. Jess had never seen her friend look so happy. Her eyes were sparkling and her cheeks glowed. She hoped the romance lasted this time. Gerri always took break ups hard.

'Well enough about me, what's going on in your life?' Gerri asked after she'd returned from the bar with another vodka and coke each. One with a straw in it. Gerri always worried that the coke would stain her teeth. 'Are you over that Frenchman yet?'

Over him? Jess stared at her in surprise. What a strange thing to say. Had she given her the impression she was upset about Eddie? She vaguely remembered mentioning him to Gerri when they'd met for a quick coffee the day before she went home after Ross and Charlotte's wedding, but she hadn't gone on that much, had she?

'Don't look at me like that. You know you were pretty cut up about the way he ditched you.' Gerri took a long sip with her straw. 'Not that I blame you. Fancy believing your aunt and cousin and not giving you chance to explain.'

'Actually...'

'You're back with him!' Gerri butt in, her face oozing delight. 'You are, aren't you?'

'I was never actually 'with him' as you put it. We weren't dating.' No, they skipped that bit and went straight to sleeping together. 'But yes, I am seeing him.' She briefly explained what happened yesterday. 'I'm meeting him tomorrow for a drink and then we're having dinner with Charlotte and Ross on Friday.'

'That's fantastic. You really liked him. I know you did.' She sucked up another strawful of her drink. 'Hang on, I thought you and your cousin didn't get on.'

'We don't. Well, didn't. We do a bit now. Maybe.' Jess grinned, picking up her glass and taking a swig of the dark liquid. 'I'll let you know after tomorrow night. If we last the evening without falling out with each other.'

'Are you and Eddie dating now?'

Jess wrinkled her nose. 'Not dating exactly. Just enjoying each other's company while we can. Eddie's flying home Monday and I return to Majorca soon.'

Gerri looked disappointed. 'You can keep in touch with each other, though. France isn't far, and you get days off, surely?'

'Not many.' Jess thought about it. Would she want to keep in touch with Eddie? Maybe. She wasn't sure. 'Let's see how it goes,' she said noncommittally.

'Good idea. Have you heard from Becky and Mae?' Gerri asked, changing the subject.

'I met Becky earlier this week and was out with Mae and Anna last night. They're still loved up. We'll have to see if we can all have a night out together before I go back.'

They passed the rest of the evening chatting pleasantly about mutual friends and reminiscing about their college days. As they always did. Jess felt happy and very light-headed when she finally slipped into the bed in Gerri's spare room. She took her phone out of her bag to put on the table beside her bed and saw that she'd had a message from Eddie. Two hours ago.

I did dream of you it said. *Looking forward to tomorrow.* xx

Eddie always wrote out his words in full instead of using text speak as most people do. She read it again. Two kisses. One kiss was friendly. Two kisses were … she wasn't sure what they were, but definitely more than friends. Had he been waiting for her to reply? She glanced at the time. One thirty. Very late, but he'd turn his phone down if he was in bed, wouldn't he?

Me 2. xx,

She keyed in then pressed send. At least he'd see it in the morning.

A few seconds later, just as she lay her head on the pillow, her phone pinged. She picked it up.

☺ xx

She smiled, snuggled down under the duvet and fell fast asleep.

Chapter Twenty Nine

Eddie texted Jess the next day offering to pick her up. 'It'll save you getting a taxi,' he said.

She got herself in a ridiculous flap wondering what to wear. She didn't want to look like she'd made too much of an effort, but definitely wanted to make an impression. She finally decided on black jeggings, a cornflower blue top and the pair of black skyscrapers she'd been looking at when she bumped into Eddie at the shoe shop the other day. She pulled on her favourite multi-coloured jacket over the top and grabbed her bag.

Eddie spotted the shoes as soon as she got into the car – he'd text her to say he was outside. 'You bought them, then?'

'Yep. My blue ones are about to fall apart.' She pulled the door to and fastened her seat belt. 'Where are we going?'

'A little country pub with a log fire,' he said, leaning over to kiss her lightly on the lips before starting the car. 'Do you fancy it?'

She did. Spring was here but the evenings were still cold. It'd be nice to sit beside a crackling fire with a glass of cider. The thought made her feel nostalgic. Working abroad was great, but there were some things she missed. Autumn, her family. She peeked at Eddie as he pulled up at some lights. Maybe she'd miss him, too.

He glanced at her. 'Okay?'

She nodded. 'What have you been doing today? Have you seen Ross again? How's Rosa?'

'Much better. The granules help a lot, as does the teething ring. Ross and Carly seem a bit more relaxed.'

'That's good. I'm surprised she asked us over tomorrow night when she's got the christening on Sunday. I thought she'd have too much to do.' Charlotte liked everything to be perfect, so Jess had imagined she'd be spending all her spare time sorting out what to wear, what to dress Rosa in, what food to get.

The lights changed, and Eddie pulled away. 'Her mum's taking care of the christening.'

They chatted away easily as Eddie zoomed along the dual carriageway, then turned off down some winding country lanes before pulling up outside a picture postcard black and white pub. 'Hey, this is really quaint! Is this one of your favourite places?' she asked as they got out of the car.

Eddie walked around to join her and linked his arm through hers. It felt good. Comforting. 'I've never been here before. I found it online, it looked good so I thought we'd check it out.'

'You were Googling places to go tonight?' she asked.

'I wanted something special for our first date.' He leaned towards her and kissed her tenderly on the nose. 'It *is* a date, isn't it?'

She thought about it for about a nanosecond. 'I guess it is.'

It was a fun evening, full of chatter and laughter, sharing titbits from their past, laughing over some of the incidents in Majorca. Sitting together on the leather sofa beside the crackling fire, Jess sipping cider, one shandy for Eddie then he switched to orange juice. Jess felt that she didn't want to move. She wanted to sit here forever, sitting by this man, talking, laughing, his arm loosely around her shoulder. She didn't want to say goodnight and go back to her childhood bedroom. If I had my own flat I'd ask him to come back with me, she thought. She wondered if he might ask her back to his hotel room for a night cap. She'd slipped her emergency kit into her bag just in case: a clean pair of knickers, deodorant, toothbrush, lipstick and a fold up hair brush.

Eddie squeezed her tight. 'I guess it's time we went. It looks like this place is about to close.'

'I feel awful that I've been sitting here sipping cider while you've had to stick to orange juice because you're driving,' Jess told him as she stood up and gathered together her coat and bag. 'I'll ask Mum if I can borrow her car tomorrow then I can drive us both to see Charlotte and Ross and you can have a drink.'

'That's very nice of you but I don't mind.' Eddie placed his arm around her waist as they walked out. 'I've got a bottle of wine in my hotel room. I can have a drink there.' He pushed open the doors and they both stepped outside into the cold evening air. He turned to kiss her. 'Fancy joining me?' he asked when they both came up for air. 'I can get you a taxi home later.' He kissed her again. 'If you want to go, that is.'

'Well I can't leave you to drink alone, can I?' She smiled at him. 'It wouldn't be fair.'

'Absolutely not.' They walked over to the car, hand in hand.

***

She hadn't gone home. They'd flung themselves into each other's arms as soon as Eddie closed the door, kissing, caressing hungrily as if they had been waiting for this moment all evening. Neither of them suggested it, it was as if by mutual consent that they undressed each other, not urgently tearing at their clothes, but slowly, sensuously, tantalisingly taking off each item one by one. Then Eddie scooped her up and carried her over to the bed.

'Are you sure you want this?' he asked as he lay down beside her, his breath warm on her neck.

271

'You bet I do,' she answered, pulling him closer.

***

Light streaming in through the window woke him. Aware of a body wrapped around his, he turned and looked at Jess sleeping on her back next to him, her long lashes spread out like fans on her cheeks. A small smile was playing on her lips, as if she was dreaming.

Was she dreaming of him, he wondered? As he had dreamed of her.

Ever since he'd met her he had dreamed of her. She was, literally, the woman of his dreams. Maybe it was time he admitted his feelings for her. Gave them a chance.

Jess stirred and turned over onto her side. Eddie edged closer to her back and wrapped his arms around her. He wanted to wake up like this every day, next to Jess.

***

Jess stirred sleepily. Eddie's arm was around her waist, his body spooned against hers. She felt relaxed. Cosy. Loved.

Loved?

Where had that come from? Okay, so she liked Eddie and there was undeniably chemistry between them. Make that a sizzling attraction. But love? Yet, as she lay there, cocooned in the warmth of his embrace, his naked body against her, listening to his soft snores, that's how she felt.

She didn't want to move and spoil the moment. Then she felt him stir. The hand around her waist started to move upwards, to softly caress her breasts as he kissed her softly at the back of her neck. 'Morning, *ma chérie.*'

She turned to face him, pressed her breasts against his chest. 'Morning, *mon beau.*' The French words sounded clunky in her English accent. She blushed a little, but his eyes twinkled with amusement.

'Did you sleep well?' he asked, between planting feather light kisses on her forehead, then her nose, her lips, her neck.

'Very well.' She kissed his strong, smooth shoulder, his mouth now on her breast, out of her reach. 'Did you?'

'Exceptionally. In fact, I feel quite energised.' His kisses were working their way back up her neck now until they found her mouth. 'Fancy a replay?' he whispered.

She wound her arms around his neck and pulled him tighter.

***

'Let's spend the day together,' Eddie said when they'd made love yet again, and were sitting up in bed, naked,

273

sharing the breakfast he'd ordered via room service, slipping on the fluffy white complementary hotel robe only to answer the door and take the tray, then shrugging it off again.

Jess nibbled on her piece of toast and thought about it. She'd intended to do some last-minute shopping before going to Charlotte's tonight. She still had a wedding present to get for her mum and she wanted to get a present for Rosa. She hadn't bought her anything when she was born, and now felt a bit mean. But a day with Eddie sounded too enticing to refuse. She wanted to spend as much time with him as she could.

'I'd love to, but I've got some shopping to get. And I'll have to go home and change first. I can't wear these clothes again today.'

'We can go shopping together,' Eddie told her. 'I need a new shirt for the christening and a present for Rosa. I've no idea what to get so you can help me choose.' He kissed her tenderly on the forehead. 'I'll take you home first and wait while you change. Deal?'

'Sounds good to me,' Jess agreed. She finished her orange juice, put the glass back on the tray and pushed aside the duvet. 'Okay if I have a shower first?'

'Be my guest. There's a hairdryer on the side if you need it. And a clean towel on the rack.'

'Thanks. As she slid out of bed he clasped a hand around her waist and pulled her back towards him, nuzzling into her neck. 'Want me to join you?' he whispered in her ear. 'I reckon the shower's big enough for two.'

'If you do we'll never get to the shops.' She tilted her head back further, meeting his lips as they came down on hers. 'I think you've had quite enough for one day.'

He was on his knees now, pressing her against him. 'I don't think I could ever get enough of you.'

She smiled and pulled away, playfully tapping his shoulder. 'You know what they say, always leave them wanting more.' She crossed the room to the en suite, then turned to blow him a kiss. 'I'll be five minutes.'

***

'That was ten minutes,' he said when she stepped out, wrapped in the soft white hotel towel, her wet hair cascading over her shoulders. He was sitting on the bed, still naked, watching the news on the TV.

'It's all yours now,' she said with a smile. 'Let's see how long you take.'

'You sure you won't join me?' he asked as he sauntered past her.

She grinned. 'Another time.'

'Rejected already,' he said in mock-dismay.

Jess waited until he'd disappeared into the en suite before rifling through her bag for her clean knickers. She didn't want him to realise she'd brought another pair with her, it made it look like she'd planned last night. Expected it. Or even worse, as if she was always prepared just in case she hooked up with a man she fancied, and they ended up in bed together. Not that there was anything wrong with that. She was single. And careful. But no matter how open-minded a guy was, they liked to think that they were the only one who had ever swept you off your feet and made you get so carried away with passion that you couldn't resist them.

Mind you, Eddie was the only one who had made her feel so... she didn't know how to describe the feeling of warmth that started in the pit of her stomach when she saw Eddie, then gradually spread through her body like a warm glow, the ease she felt in his company, the intense attraction for him. The desire that they had more time together. The growing reluctance to say goodbye.

She ran the hairdryer quickly over her hair, sprayed on her deodorant, then pulled on her underwear and jeggings. She was reaching for her jumper when the bathroom door opened and Eddie walked out, drying his hair with the towel, his body taut and glistening, the silver dog-tag pendant shining against his dark chest hair.

'It's no good trying to tempt me,' she said as she slipped on her shoes. 'I'm dressed and I'm not getting undressed again.' She forced her gaze away from his oh-so-fit body, picked up her bag and searched for her lipstick, determined not to give in to the desire to undress again and get back into bed with him. Half the morning had gone already, and they had things to do today.

He grinned. 'I reckon it wouldn't take much to persuade you, but you're right, we don't have time.' He picked up the hairdryer she'd left plugged in on the bedside table.

Turning back to the mirror she watched in amusement as he altered the setting then used it to dry the hair on his chest, before moving it lower down to dry his... Well that's the first time she'd seen someone use a hairdryer there!

She concentrated on applying her lipstick, determined not to let her eyes stray – well not much – whilst Eddie stood behind her, still naked, part-drying his hair then brushing it, smiling teasingly at her in the reflection.

Finally, he moved away, pulled on light grey boxers, a pair of dark brown casual trousers and a cream V-necked top before striding back over to her and kissing the back of her neck. 'Stay with me again tonight?'

She turned her head to his. There was no point in playing games, there was too little time. She wanted him

277

as much as he wanted her. 'Okay. I'll put a change of clothes in an overnight bag when I go home.'

He sat down beside her and pulled her into an embrace. 'I want to spend as much time as I can with you before I go home on Monday.'

'Me too,' she said between ardent kisses.

Then she remembered something. 'I promised Mum I'd go wedding shopping with her again tomorrow. We both still need a hat and I'm at work next week.' She was starting a temping job in customer services at a local hotel. 'Afternoon shifts,' she added. 'I can see you Monday morning before you go?'

'And tomorrow, when you've finished shopping? *Oui?*'

'You bet,' she said, unable to resist one last kiss. 'Now let's go.'

Chapter Thirty

Jess was relieved to find her mum and Phil out when she arrived home. She might be nearly thirty and living away from home most of the year, but she still felt awkward at stopping out overnight and returning home with a guy. Especially without letting them know first. She left Eddie in the lounge drinking a cup of coffee and answering emails on his phone, while she quickly changed and packed an overnight bag.

She was halfway down the stairs when the house phone rang. 'Can you get that, please?' She called to Eddie. She knew that many of her mum's friends still used the landline for a chat rather than the mobile.

'It's an estate agent for your mum,' Eddie said as she walked in.

'An estate agent?' Jess was puzzled. Surely Mum wasn't thinking of selling up? She took the phone off Eddie. 'Hello, this is Jess, Mrs Kaine's daughter. Can I help you?'

She listened in astonishment as the estate agent asked her to let her mother know that they would send a photographer around at ten tomorrow and have all the details for the house sale ready to sign before she went on honeymoon. Jess murmured a polite response, finished the call and sank down on the sofa, stunned. Mum hadn't said a word about selling the house.

'Jess?'

She looked up at Eddie. 'Mum's selling up. The estate agent is preparing the details now and sending a photographer around tomorrow. Why hasn't she told me?'

'Perhaps she's waiting for the right moment.' Eddie sat down beside her and squeezed her hand. 'I guess now that they are getting married, she and Phil want to buy a house together.' He looked at her concerned. 'Are you upset about it?'

'Not upset, exactly,' she said, trying to assess her feelings. 'This is my family home, the only home I've ever known. We all grew up here. And I've always had my room to come back to.' She couldn't believe how much this was affecting her. Don't be so bloody selfish, Jess. It's time Mum had a bit of happiness in her life, of course she and Phil would want a new home together.

'I'm sure there will be a spare room for you to stay in. Although you did say you were thinking of getting a flat,' Eddie reminded her.

Yes, she'd mentioned that to Mum and Phil, and they had replied, 'There will always be a room for you with us'. So why hadn't Mum told her she was selling up, then?

'Take no notice of me,' she said, giving Eddie a quick kiss then standing up and grabbing her bag. 'It just came as a shock. I guess I expected Mum to live here forever. I'm glad she's marrying Phil and that they're getting a place together.' She put the phone back in its holder and scribbled a note to her mum on the pad next to the phone, telling her that she was going out again and would be home tomorrow morning, ready for their shopping trip, then added a PS: *The estate agent phoned. He's coming around to take photos tomorrow.*

'Now let's go shopping,' she said brightly.

As she closed the door behind her she felt a wave of sadness, but she pushed it away. She was totally not going to spoil this for Mum. She deserved a new life.

***

'What sort of christening present do you get a little girl?' Eddie studied the display of gifts in the jewellery shop. 'Would this be suitable, do you think?' He held up a delicate silver bangle. 'I could have her name engraved on it.'

'It's lovely, but I think it might be something Aunt Jean will get, or maybe even Charlotte and Ross.' Jess scanned the shelf, flitting from one item to another. 'How about this? It's pretty and unusual, perfect as a present from her godfather.' She carefully picked up a silver angel decoration with a bell that tinkled softly. 'You could have *Rosabelle* and the date she was christened engraved on it.' She pointed to the sign on the side of the shelf. 'See, they do engraving here.'

'It's beautiful,' Eddie agreed. He was glad Jess had come shopping with him. The bell was ideal, and not the sort of gift he'd have thought of getting himself.

'I think I should get her something, even though I'm not going to the christening.' Jess frowned as she studied the gifts on the shelf. Finally, she selected a silver hairbrush. 'I'll take this, it's a little keepsake for her.'

'Will you get it engraved?' Eddie asked as they both walked over to the till with their items.

'I think I will. Just her name, though, not the christening date.'

When both their presents had been engraved and gift-wrapped, they went for lunch. They'd just sat down with their coffees and ham salad paninis when Jess's phone rang. She took it out of her bag and glanced at the screen. 'It's Mum,' she said swiping the screen to answer the call.

'Hi Mum… no don't worry… it's fine… honestly I didn't think anything of it.'

Eddie watched her, a frown creasing her forehead as she tried to get a word in. It sounded like Pam was upset over something. 'Please don't worry, Mum. You do what's best for you and Phil. I mean, I don't actually live with you, do I? I just bunk down in my old bedroom now and again.' Another pause. 'I'll see you tomorrow, Mum, and we'll talk about it then. I'll be back about eleven, after the photographer's been, so we can go shopping.' She ended the call and looked up at Eddie. 'Sorry about that,' she said. 'I guess you got the gist?'

He nodded. 'Your mum's upset because you spoke to the estate agent and she wanted to tell you herself…'

'Got it in one,' she cut her panini in half. 'She's assured me that I'm always welcome to stay in their new spare room whenever I come back to the UK.'

'Everything is okay then?' Eddie asked.

'Yes, it's fine. Mind you, I'll have to clear out the stuff from my room before I go back to Majorca. The house will probably be sold before I'm back in the UK again. And believe me there's a lot to clear out, I've still got stuff there from my childhood.' She bit into the panini. 'Hmm, this is delicious.'

***

Jess helped Eddie choose a shirt for the christening– white with fine black stripes and a neat button-down collar – looked for a wedding present for Mum and Phil – she decided on a beautiful engraved silver clock and photo

283

frame – then bought a bottle of wine and box of luxury dark chocolate mints to take to Charlotte and Ross's that evening.

The afternoon seemed to whizz by in a flash, and before she knew it, Eddie was looking at his watch and saying that they needed to make tracks as Carly and Ross were expecting them at seven and he needed to drop the christening present off at his hotel first. Which was great as it would give Jess chance to freshen up, too.

**

Jess felt a little apprehensive as Eddie parked the car in the drive. What if Charlotte regretted her invite now? They'd never got on and just because she helped with Rosa the other night didn't mean they would suddenly become best buddies. She probably should have made some excuse not to accept her invitation.

To her relief, Charlotte was delighted to see her, kissing her on the cheek as soon as she came in. 'I was worried you might change your mind,' she said.

'I thought you might change yours,' Jess replied and they both exchanged a smile. Okay, hostilities had ceased. For now.

Rosa was lying in her cot, gurgling. Jess walked over to her and the baby waved her arms and legs frantically as if she recognised her. Her cheeks were no longer red, and she seemed happy and relaxed. 'The granules worked, then?' Jess asked as she bent over and tickled Rosa's tummy.

'They were marvellous. Rosa actually slept most of the night. It's the most sleep we've had since she was born isn't it, Ross?'

Both Ross and Charlotte looked quite relaxed, Jess noticed. Maybe that's what they needed, a good night's sleep and some adult company. Rosa was gorgeous, but she knew how full on caring for a baby could be. Rosa was now gazing at her with wide eyes, looking so sweet, that she felt an irresistible urge to pick her up. 'Can I hold her?' she asked. 'Or are you hoping she'll fall asleep?' Not that there was much chance of that judging by those bright, sparkling eyes.

Charlotte's face broke into a big smile. 'Yes, of course.'

***

Eddie watched as Jess lifted the baby out of the cot and cuddled her for a moment, then picked up a rattle and squeaky toy, sat down on the sofa and started to play with her. She was such a chameleon, with her pillar-box hair and bright clothes she seemed like the sort of girl who was out for a good time – and yes, she did like to enjoy herself, he thought, remembering how Jess and Libby had worked the floor dancing at the nightclub in Majorca – yet she was kind and caring, too. Here she was, after all the things Carly had said to her, contentedly cuddling Rosa whose christening she hadn't even been invited to. Jess could hold her own, he'd seen that, yet she was quick to forgive and give people another chance. She was warm, caring, and he loved her.

What? The thought had sneaked into his mind unexpectedly. He held it for a moment then pushed it away. He liked Jess. Enjoyed her company. And he was going to miss her when he went back home on Monday, but no, he didn't love her. Love was something he wasn't going to get into ever again.

***

Much later, when Rosa had fallen asleep in Jess's arms and Jess had gently laid her down in the cot, they ordered the take away and were busy tucking into it, washing it down with wine, chatting easily, when Charlotte suddenly put her glass down and looked earnestly at Jess. 'Please come to the christening on Sunday. I want you to be there.'

That took Jess by surprise. Should she accept? Mum would be delighted, she and Phil were going, and Mum had been annoyed that Jess was snubbed, even though Jess had told her she didn't mind. Which she didn't.

'*Please*. I wish I'd asked you to be her godmother now. You're so good with her. She seems really relaxed with you.'

Oh, why not? At least she'd get to see Eddie for an extra day, and she was becoming so fond of Rosa. She really was a cutie. 'Sure,' she nodded. 'I'd love to come along.'

Charlotte beamed. 'That's fantastic.'

The rest of the evening passed in pleasant conversation. Rosa woke for a bottle, which Jess asked to give her, then she handed her to Ross while she went to the loo and found the baby fast asleep again when she returned. Charlotte looked astonished when she walked in with a tray of coffee and saw Rosa snoozing in Ross's arms, with Ross looking every inch the proud dad. He gently put the still-sleeping Rosa in her cot and Charlotte handed him a coffee. As the evening went on they both relaxed so much they even started to flirt with each other.

'I hope Rosa sleeps well tonight, I think those two could do with some couple time,' Eddie said as he and Jess got into a taxi after helping to clear up and promising to come to the house before the christening on Saturday so that they could all go to the church together. 'That's the most relaxed I've seen them. When I arrived a few days ago they were at each other's throats. I seriously thought they were on the verge of splitting up.'

'A new baby can do that to couples, but they usually work their way through it.'

'You're a natural,' Eddie said, putting his arm around her shoulder and pulling her towards him. 'I think you'll be a wonderful mother when you have your own kids.'

'Oh, that won't be for a good few years yet,' she told him.

'Too busy enjoying life?' he teased.

'Yes, and you know, I've been thinking. I need a career change. Mum and Phil, they don't want me living with them – even if it's only for a few weeks a year. They want to buy the home they want, get it how they like, live in it just the two of them.'

'So, you get a flat. You don't need a career change for that.'

'Well yes, I do, otherwise I'll be paying rent on a place I only use once in a while.' She paused. 'Anyway, I'm thirty next year. I can't live in hotel rooms forever. I want a home. So I guess I ought to get a different job.'

'Like what?' They were at his hotel now.

'I don't know.' That was the trouble. She had always been a travel rep. And she loved it. What else could she do?

Eddie's arm snaked around her neck and he pulled her closer to him, and then all she could think of was his kisses, which were getting deeper, and his hands that were wandering lower...

***

'Stay with me again tonight,' Eddie said softly as they lay in each other's arms the next morning. 'We only have two more days together.'

That sounded so final. Jess looked up at him. 'Will you miss me?' She teased. She was going to miss him. More than she cared to admit.

'Yes. Very much.' He kissed her to show her how much. 'This doesn't have to be goodbye, does it? We can keep in touch, can't we? Maybe visit each other now and again.'

Like they'd said they would at Charlotte and Ross's wedding, before it all went wrong. Well that was history now. And yes, she did want to keep in touch. She enjoyed Eddie's company.

'I'd love to, but it'll be a while before I can come to France. Ziggy hates anyone having time off in the holiday season.' She fancied going to France for a weekend though; seeing where Eddie lived, spending some more time with him. 'What about you? Could you come to Majorca again?'

'Not for a while. The restaurant is so busy. I might be able to at the end of May, before the summer season gets too busy. Meanwhile,' he drew her closer. 'Let's not waste the precious time we've got together.'

Chapter Thirty One

'Honestly, Mum, it's fine' Jess said as her mum explained that they had only just decided to sell and was going to talk to Jess about it before she went back to Majorca.

'If you're sure. I don't want you to feel that I'm pushing you out.' Pam hesitated. 'There is one thing I need you to do though, if you don't mind...'

'Let me guess – you want me to clear out my bedroom?' Jess said with a grin.

'Well, yes. You've still got so much of your childhood stuff in there. I don't expect you to get rid of everything, keep the things that are special to you and we'll put them in a box and store them in a cupboard. Then you can put them in the spare room in the new house, to make it feel personal to you.'

'I'll sort it all out before I go back to Majorca and give the stuff I don't want to a charity shop,' Jess promised. 'Now come on, we're supposed to be hat shopping.'

She hated to see her mum look so worried. She shouldn't be apologising for seizing a chance on happiness. Dad had moved on years ago, while Mum had put everything on hold to look after the family. It was about time she put herself first now.

It was a fun morning. They went to all the major stores trying on various bonnets, fascinators, and some hats so outrageous that they both giggled. Finally, Pam decided on a mesh hat with a flower corsage and feather and loop detail almost the same shade of violet as her dress. She had a photo of her dress on her phone so she could be sure.

Jess couldn't find a hat that she was comfortable in. She wasn't a hat person, usually only wearing a sunhat when it was very hot.

'Why don't you try a fascinator, dear?' the assistant suggested, when Jess shook her head once again at her reflection in the mirror.

'I'm not sure... I mean they're a bit fancy, aren't they?' Jess asked doubtfully. The fascinators seemed to be mainly decorated hairbands with flowers and feathers on them. She doubted that they would suit her.

'Not all of them, and they look so much sassier than a hat,' the assistant said. 'Let's try one and see what you think. What colour is your outfit?'

'Dusky blue,' Jess told her, selecting the picture of her dress on her phone. 'This is it.'

The assistant looked at the photo. 'That's gorgeous — pretty but fun. I think I have the very thing.' She walked off, returning a few minutes later with a jaunty flower fascinator disc a shade darker than Jess's dress. She placed it on Jess's head. 'Perfect,' she announced.

Pam clapped her hands. 'It's wonderful, Jess. It's pretty, but a little outrageous and flirty – like you!'

Outrageous and flirty? Jess smiled to herself. She'd have to remember that description and see if Eddie agreed. Mum was right though; the fascinator was perfect for her.

'That's it, wedding shopping finished.' Pam said. 'Now let me treat you to coffee and cake before we go home.'

'That sounds great, Mum. But let me treat you,' Jess replied. 'I don't often get the chance.' She raised her hand as her mum went to protest. 'I insist.'

Jess could see that her mum was uncomfortable with the idea, but she wanted to spoil her for once. 'Please let me. It isn't every day your mum gets married.' She linked her arm through her mum's. 'Come on, let's go to the Daisy Café.'

The elegant café was pricey but worth it. They had a mouth-watering selection of cakes and pastries, and an array of coffees, mochas, lattes, and hot chocolates to choose from, all served on exquisite china crockery. It was the very place for a treat. Jess was delighted to see her mum's eyes light up when she walked in. Mum was so used to watching her pennies that she'd probably never been anywhere like the Daisy Café.

'This is lovely, Jess.' She turned anxiously to Jess. 'Are you sure?'

'Positive. Choose whatever you want.'

They chatted easily as they ate their cake – a strawberry concoction with lots of cream for Pam and a triple chocolate slice for Jess. 'I meant to ask, how did you get on at Charlotte's last night? I still can't believe she asked you and Eddie to come for dinner.'

'It was okay. Quite pleasant, actually.' Jess bit into her cake. 'She's invited me to the christening on Sunday.'

Pam's jaw dropped open, the hand holding the chunk of cake on it suspended in mid-air. 'Really?'

Jess nodded. 'Yep, she seems to genuinely want me there.'

Pam beamed. 'That's made my day,' she said. 'Me and Jean have always wanted you two to get on. Especially as neither of you have sisters.'

'Well let's not get too carried away, it's early days yet and she might go off me again – but for now it's good.' Jess licked the chocolate off her fingers. 'So, any chance of getting a lift with you and my step-dad-to-be tomorrow?'

'We'd love you to come with us.' Pam leant over and patted Jess's hand. 'You do like Phil, don't you? You don't mind me marrying him? I've already asked the boys, and they're fine with it, but what about you? You haven't had much chance to get to know him.'

'He's lovely, Mum. And he makes you happy, that's all that matters. Stop worrying about everyone else.' Jess wiped her hands on her napkin. 'I've just remembered I've got a gift for Rosa, but not a card. I'd better nip to a card shop before we go home.'

***

'Are you and Jess an item, then?' Ross asked when Eddie popped in to see if they needed any last-minute shopping for the christening.

'We're just enjoying each other's company,' Eddie replied casually.

'You like her though, and she likes you.' Carly finished feeding Rosa then propped her over her arm to wind her. 'I can tell. You make a good couple.'

'That's praise coming from you, considering you couldn't stand Jess until a couple of days ago,' Ross pointed out, taking the baby wipes off the table and handing them to her.

'I was wrong.' Carly wiped the milk dripping from Rosa's mouth. 'I never really got to know Jess, we didn't spend much time together. And she was always so...

bubbly and out there with her red hair and hippy clothes. And then there was that business with Simon. I thought she'd set out to steal him but I'm not sure now.'

They'd both misjudged Jess, Eddie thought. And he could see why she and Carly hadn't got on. They were like chalk and cheese, and he knew which one he preferred. Although to be fair Carly was starting to unwind a bit. Jess was nice through and through. Gorgeous, fun, sexy, kind. The whole package.

He was going to miss her. A lot.

***

Thankfully the christening went off without a hitch. Rosa looked gorgeous in the vintage lace gown that had been passed down through Uncle Gerald's family.   Charlotte and Ross looked every inch the proud parents. Aunt Jean and Uncle Gerald were actually nice to her, and Mum and Phil radiated happiness. As for Eddie, he looked amazing in the silver-grey suit he'd worn to the wedding, this time matched with a dark blue waistcoat and dark blue tie.

I wish he wasn't going back to France, she thought. Then again maybe that was a good thing. The more time she spent with him the harder it was going to be to say goodbye. One more night, that's all she had to spend in his bed, in his arms. The thought of sleeping alone once more made her feel strangely bereft.

***

Monday morning came too soon. Jess woke early, enjoying the closeness of Eddie's body spooned against hers, his hand resting lightly on her breast. This was it, the last time she would wake up next to him. She glanced at the clock. Seven o'clock. Three more hours and he'd be leaving for the airport.

She was going to miss him.

A feather light kiss on the back of her neck made her shiver. 'Are you awake, Jess?'

'Yes.' She turned towards him. 'Morning,' she whispered and wrapped her arms around his neck.

Later, when they had made love one last time, Eddie sat up in bed and unfastened the silver chain around his neck. He handed it to Jess. 'I'd like to give you this, to remember me by. Will you accept it?'

His dark brown eyes held hers and she felt herself drowning in their depth. For a moment she felt a frisson of fear – this was a bit heavy, wasn't it? The dog-tag pendant was obviously important to him. If she took it what was she saying?

She swallowed. 'Are you sure? Won't you miss it? You always wear it. I thought maybe... someone special had given it to you.'

'My French grand-mére gave it me for my 18th birthday, so yes it means a lot to me, which is why I want you to have it. I think my grand-mére will be delighted that I've given it to you. But if you feel it's inappropriate?' His eyes clouded over as he closed his hand over the necklace.

She hesitated. She was touched that he wanted to give it to her and it seemed churlish to refuse. For goodness sake, it's a pendant not an engagement ring, she told herself, don't make such a big deal of it. She reached out her hand. 'I'd love to have it. Thank you.' She scooped up her hair with both hands and turned her back to him. 'Would you fasten it for me?'

***

'Come with me to the airport?' Eddie asked as he snapped his case shut. 'You're not due in work until two, are you?'

She nodded, reluctant to say goodbye until she had to.

What was the matter with her? She knew this had only been a fling, a bit of fun only meant to last a few days. That's how she usually liked it. That way there was no time for anyone to get serious. But as she felt Eddie's

298

pendant dangling around her neck, she knew that this was already far more serious than she'd planned.

They both chatted away as Eddie drove to the airport. Light, everyday talk about the christening, her mum's wedding on Saturday, going back to Majorca at the end of the month. Eddie returned the hire car, checked in his baggage, and they had a coffee. Friendly, casual, like friends. Not like the lovers they'd been the last few nights.

Stay a bit longer, Jess wanted to ask, but she didn't. Eddie had his life, she had hers. They lived so far apart. And neither of them had promised more than this. Yet she wanted more. Did Eddie?

If he did, he didn't say so. He smiled and chatted as if they could meet up next week or the week after rather than them probably never seeing each other again because, to be honest, they were both so busy with work. And they weren't in a relationship, were they? Eddie hadn't suggested officially becoming a couple. And if he had, would she want to take that step?

Finally, it was time for Eddie to go to the departure lounge. She stood in front of him, awkward. How did she say goodbye? Why did they melt into each other's arms so easily in bed, yet here, today, they were distant, not touching, not kissing?

'Goodbye, have a safe journey,' she said, leaning over to kiss him on the cheek. Then suddenly his arms were

299

around her and he was hugging her to him, kissing her cheeks, her lips. 'Keep in touch, Jess.' His voice was thick, his words a bit broken.

'I will,' she nodded, swallowing the lump that had suddenly jumped into her throat. 'We'll message, let each other know how we're getting on.'

Eddie's arms were around her, hugging her close. 'You're very special, *ma chérie*.'

She smiled, but stupidly she felt like crying. *Pull yourself together Jess!* 'You're not so bad yourself.' She tapped him lightly on his nose. 'It's been fun.'

Something flitted across his face but was gone before she could put a name to it. 'I must go. I hope your mum's wedding goes well on Saturday. I'll message you soon.'

'You do that,' she said.

One last kiss and a hug and he let her go, turned away. She watched him striding through to the departure lounge, going where she couldn't follow. He paused at the end of the corridor and waved. Then he was gone.

She stood for a moment, half-hoping he would turn and come back out. Say that he couldn't go after all. That he didn't want to leave her. But she knew he wouldn't. His life was in France. He had a home, a business. A life she wasn't a part of.

She had a life, too, and she had to get on with it. Put Eddie out of her mind. She turned and walked away,

300

towards the entrance, every step she took making the lump swell bigger and bigger in her throat until she felt she couldn't breathe. Then the tears she'd been holding back sprang to her eyes and started to roll down her cheeks.

Why the hell was she crying?

Because Eddie had gone, and already she was aching for him.

***

'It's been fun.' Jess's words spun around in Eddie's mind as he walked over to Customs. Fun. Is that how she saw their time together?

All morning he'd been dreading the moment they had to part, had wanted to beg her to come with him, to forget Majorca, tell her that he had contacts who could find her a job in France where they could be together. He didn't want to say goodbye to her. He'd never felt this way about anyone, not even Yvette, and he'd planned a wedding with her! He'd been on the verge of asking Jess to come with him when she'd said those words. *It's been fun.*

Fun. Jess obviously didn't feel about him as he felt about her. He should have known that. She was too free, too outgoing to fall for someone like him. Jess with her unique style, bubbly personality, love of travel. She'd made it clear from the beginning that she didn't want to settle down, that she only wanted a casual relationship, but he'd stupidly thought he was different, that she was falling for him as he had fallen for her.

He was wrong. For Jess it had just been a bit of fun.

Chapter Thirty Two

'Aw, bless you, dear. Have a tissue.' Cath, Jess's mum's best friend, scrambled in her bag for a packet of tissues, pulled one out and handed it to her. 'It's a beautiful ceremony isn't it?' She took a tissue for herself and dabbed first her right eye then her left. 'Mind you, I always cry at weddings. Can't help it.'

Jess carefully dabbed at the unexpected tears, hoping she wasn't smudging her concealer. It had taken her ages to cover the dark circles under her eyes – the result of a restless night thinking of Eddie.

'Hey sis, I didn't have you down as being the soppy sort.' Her brother, Ned, put his arm around her shoulder. 'Good to see Mum so happy, isn't it? About bloody time!'

'I know. That's what's made me blub,' she replied. 'I'm so pleased for her.'

It wasn't just that, though. Seeing Mum and Phil declare their love for each other and the way Phil had kissed Mum so tenderly had made her think of Eddie. And how much she missed him. It had seemed so strange to be back in her own bed in her old childhood room last night. She had longed to feel his arms around her. And today she wished he was with her, like he'd been for the christening.

What was the matter with her? She never cried over a guy.

All this christening and wedding business was making her go soppy. She'd be fine once she was back in Majorca in a couple of weeks. She put the tissue in her bag. 'Come on, it's time for the photos.'

***

Whilst Mum and Phil were on their honeymoon in Cyprus, Jess spent her spare time sorting out her bedroom. Gerri came over and helped her one evening and they giggled as they read through Jess's old school workbooks. So many memories.

'How long have you lived in this house?' Gerri asked as she helped Jess sort everything out into piles – one pile for the charity shop, one pile to dump, and another – very small pile – to keep.

'All my life,' Jess told her.

'Are you sad that your mum's selling up?'

Jess rested back on her heels as she thought about it for a moment. 'Not sad, exactly. I'm glad Mum's moving on. But it's like a new era, isn't it? My childhood home will be gone, Mum has a new husband, a new life.'

'Yeah, it's a big change, isn't it?' Gerri added a torn magazine to the 'dump' pile. 'Do you feel awkward about living with her and Phil?'

Jess fingered the dog-tag pendant, something she'd got into the habit of doing lately. 'Yes. It was different before Mum got married, I was simply going back home. But now I feel like I'll be a guest in her and Phil's new home.' She paused. 'I'm thinking about giving up repping, getting a more settled job and my own flat.'

'Hey, growing up at last!' Gerri grinned. Then she leant forward. 'Where did you get that unusual pendant from? You've been messing with it all evening.'

'It's Eddie's. He gave it to me – a sort of goodbye present to remember him by.'

Gerri looked at Jess thoughtfully. 'So you two aren't going to meet up again?'

'I don't know. We've messaged each other a couple of times since he's gone home, but it's a bit difficult when he lives in France and I'm back off to Majorca next week,' she pointed out.

'Err, not in this day and age. It's the twenty-first century, Jess – Skype and airplanes have actually been invented, you know. Don't let him go if you like him. And you do, I can tell that.'

Like him. She spent most nights lying awake thinking of him. How stupid was that? But she wasn't about to admit that to anyone, not even Gerri. 'Oh, we'll keep in touch,' she said as if she wasn't bothered either way. She reached out and picked up a battered grey donkey wearing a hat. 'Remember this? I bought it that day we went to Blackpool?'

***

Jess stepped out of the plane and into the sun. It was good to be back in Majorca. Now she'd be so busy she wouldn't have time to keep thinking about Eddie and could finally get on with her life. Amazingly, Charlotte had seemed sad to see her go.

'Come over to visit soon, won't you?' she said as she hugged Jess goodbye. 'We'll all miss you.'

'We'll Skype,' Jess promised. 'And remember to send me lots of photos of this little cutie.' She gave Rosa a cuddle. 'I want you to record her first words, first steps. Everything.' And she meant it.

Normally, once she landed in whatever country she was working in, she barely gave her family and friends a second thought, she was too busy working and enjoying herself. Now, as Ned dropped her off at the airport, hugging her goodbye and telling her to keep in touch, it was as if something had changed. Somehow, she'd felt closer to everyone. It was as if Rosa's christening and

Mum and Phil's wedding had made her realise how much she loved her family.

And how much she was going to miss Eddie.

Without him she had an empty feeling in her heart, as if part of her was missing.

Well, now she was back in Majorca she had to forget all about him and get back to normal. She collected her suitcase from the luggage carousel and looked around for Libby. She was arriving from Manchester this morning and as there was only half an hour difference between the flights they'd arranged to meet at the airport and share a taxi home.

'Jess!'

Jess turned around to see her friend hurrying over to her, pulling her suitcase behind her. 'Isn't it great to be back?'

'Brilliant,' Jess agreed. 'Let's grab a taxi then we can catch up on all the news.'

There was a lot of news to catch up on even though they'd only been away a few weeks. Libby told Jess about her sister's engagement, her brother's new girlfriend – a total nightmare apparently – and how her best friend Sara discovered her long-term partner was having an affair. Jess told Libby about Charlotte's change of heart and her mum's wedding – things they'd briefly mentioned in their infrequent messages to each other, but not gone into detail about. It wasn't until they were in the hotel, sipping iced lemonade at the bar while they waited for Ziggy and the others to arrive, that Libby asked the question Jess was sure she'd been dying to ask ever since they'd landed. 'What about Eddie? How fantastic that you bumped into each other again. Are you going to see him again?'

'I don't know. Maybe if we get a chance. We're keeping in touch. He messaged me this morning to wish me a safe journey,' Jess replied casually, as if it was of no importance to her whether she heard from Eddie or not, when in fact the first thing she did every morning was check her phone to see if she had a message from him.

'I thought you'd both started to get close?' She peered at Jess's neck then reached out and touched the silver dog-tag dangling on the chain. 'And isn't that the pendant Eddie used to wear?'

'Yes, he gave it to me as a goodbye present.' Jess flicked her hair back from her face. She'd have to tie it back. It was hot and sticky already. 'Did I tell you Mum was selling the house?' she asked, quickly changing the subject.

Then the other reps started to arrive, and they were caught up in briefings, details of refresher training, given their rotas, and moved into their rooms. Jess was so busy that it was almost midnight before she checked her phone and noticed a message from Eddie. Her heart did the usual ridiculous little flip as she opened it.

Hope you arrived safe. Miss you. Take care. xx

She read it over and over again. Miss you. And there were two kisses.

As usual, it was the sort of text you sent to a friend.

Which is what they were, so why was she so disappointed?

She replied.

All good but mega busy. Keep happy. Xx

As she hit send she imagined him, about to get into bed, like her. Would he think of her as he lay in the dark, remember what it had felt like to have her in his arms, how good they had been together? Like she always did.

***

It had been over a month now since he'd said goodbye to Jess. A month in which he'd hardly been able to concentrate on his work, a month in which she'd invaded his dreams every night, a month in which they'd exchanged frequent friendly messages. He missed her like crazy. He wanted to see her again, hold her in his arms. Did she feel the same? He longed to message and ask her but still those three words haunted him. *It's been fun.* It was obvious that Jess didn't feel as strongly about him as he did about her. Perhaps it might be best if he simply stopped messaging all together, make a clean break.

'Look, Eddie just go and see her,' Charles said in frustration.

'What?' Eddie looked up in surprise.

'Your mind hasn't been on your work since you came back. It's obvious that you've got unfinished business with this Jess. Go and see her. Find out if she feels the same way, then at least you might be able to get her out of your head and we can get some work done.'

Eddie pushed the chair back and got up. He walked over to the window, thrust his hands in his pockets and looked out at the restaurant courtyard. Charles was right, he couldn't go on like this. He had to see Jess and find out if she felt the same way.

'You've got to do it, Ed. Yvette messed up your head enough. I don't want to see another woman do the same.' The chair screeched as Charles pushed it back. Eddie knew he was standing up, was about to join him at the window. He turned to face his business partner.

'Jess and I are just friends.' But they'd been lovers, too – fiery, passionate – and he wanted that again.

'It seems to me that she means more than that to you.'

Eddie turned his gaze back to the window. 'Yes, she does,' he finally admitted. 'I didn't realise it at first. We were only together a few days. I thought it would pass. But it hasn't.' He kept his gaze fixed on the courtyard outside with its colourful plant pots dotted here and there. 'I love her, Charles. I've never felt like this about anyone. Not even Yvette.'

'Does she feel the same?'

That was the question he'd been asking himself. 'I don't think so. When we were saying goodbye she said, 'it's been fun'.'

'She could have been saying that because she didn't know how you felt about her. I can't believe that you left without talking to her about it. Finding out if she wanted more.' Charles picked up the cigarette packet from his desk, flipped it open, took one out. 'Take the weekend off, fly over and see her. I'll keep an eye on the restaurant. Benji can cover for you, he's after more shifts.' He walked over to the door, pausing to look over his shoulder as he opened it. 'Think about it, Eddie. You need to either commit to a relationship with this woman or get her out of your system. And the only way you can decide which choice to make is to talk to her.'

Eddie watched Charles light up the cigarette then sit down on the bench outside, his friend's advice whirling in

311

his mind. Finally, he came to a decision. He would go to Majorca. As Charles said, he needed to find out whether Jess had feelings for him. Feelings like he had for her. If she didn't, at least he could forget her and get on with his life.

And if she did?

Then they'd work something out.

The question was should he message her first and find out if she was working this weekend? He thought about it and decided against it. He wanted to surprise her. Even if she was working she'd have a break, and there would be time to catch up after her evening shift. For once in his life he was going to be impulsive.

***

'I reckon you're in love,' Libby said as Jess sat picking at her breakfast.

Jess looked up, startled. 'What?'

'You haven't been the same since you came back. You're off your food and you've lost your sparkle. Oh, you try to be bright and breezy, but I can see that you're forcing it. You're missing Eddie, aren't you?'

Yes. More than she ever imagined possible. 'I guess he's got under my skin a bit,' Jess admitted, finally giving up any attempt at eating her scrambled egg. 'It's weird. I can't stop thinking about him. I've never felt like this about anyone before.'

'About time! Welcome to the world the rest of us live in.' Libby picked up a slice of toast and bit into it. 'I told you, you're in love,' she said triumphantly.

'I am not. I miss him, that's all.'

'You can't fool me. Does he feel the same way?'

'I doubt it, or he'd be contacting me more, wouldn't he? Maybe phone me instead of sending me a WhatsApp message now and again.' She wished Eddie would phone her. She longed to hear his deep voice with that sexy French accent again, to see him, to hold him, to... She shook off the thoughts. 'I'm going for a swim.'

Thank goodness she wasn't working until this afternoon. She really couldn't face dealing with holidaymakers right now. She had to get her head together.

As she passed through Reception she saw a man standing at the desk. Her heart missed a beat as her eyes rested on the dark hair curling at the nape of his neck, the tall, well-toned figure. It couldn't be.

Then he turned around and their eyes met.

'Eddie?' The words came out in a gasp.

'Jess.' His face lit up. He put his bag down, held out his arms and Jess was running into them, being swung around, kissed and hugged.

'What are you doing here?' she asked when he finally put her down and she could catch her breath.

The warmth in his soft brown eyes made her heart somersault. 'I wanted to see you.'

He wanted to see her.

A whirl of emotions swirled through her. He'd come all the way from France to see her. That meant he missed her as much as she missed him.

'Are you working?' He asked, his arms still around her waist, holding her close. 'Have I come at a bad time? I can meet you later if that is better.'

She shook her head. 'No. No. It's fine. I'm off this morning. Let's go and sit by the pool, catch up.'

'I'd like to take my bag to my room first. Perhaps you could come up with me?'

'Yes of course.' His room would be more private. Give them chance to talk.

He reached for her again, as soon as they were inside his room, kissing her hungrily.

'I'm sorry to arrive out of the blue like this. I *had* to see you. I couldn't wait any longer.' He guided her over to the bed and they both sat down on the edge. 'I miss you, Jess. I can't stop thinking of you. I had to see if you felt the same way. If you don't then I'll go home and never trouble you again.'

She swallowed, licked her lips. Was he saying...?

'What do you mean?' Was that frightened little squeak really her voice?

Eddie lifted his hands and gently cupped her face in them. Dark brown eyes brimming with... What? Desire, yes, but something deeper than that.

'I love you, Jess. I want us to be together. A couple. The question is...' The intensity of his gaze mesmerised her. 'Do you love me?'

Chapter Thirty Three

Jess's breath caught in her throat. Men had told her they loved her before, begged her to carry on seeing them, but she gently let them down. Loving someone, getting serious, it wasn't in her life plan.

Yet she loved Eddie. She couldn't deny it.

'Do you love me?' he repeated, his voice like a whisper on the wind, his gaze still fixed on her face.

She couldn't hurt him by lying and saying no. She nodded. 'Yes. I do. I love you.' His face broke into a huge grin and she was in his arms again, lost in his kisses. Kisses that quickly became caresses, caresses that became more and more heated until they were in bed, naked, flesh against flesh and she was home again.

***

Her phone was ringing. She reached out for it, grabbing it just as the ringing stopped – Libby - Jess did a double take when she saw the time. Oh shit, she was due to work her shift in half an hour. A message pinged in from Libby.

Dunno what ur up to but Ziggy is looking 4 u.

Double shit. Don't say Ziggy changed the rota. Again. Tomorrow was her day off and now that Eddie was here she wanted to keep it that way.

'What is it? Have I made you late?' Eddie sounded concerned.

'No, but I need to have a shower and get dressed quick. I'm on duty in half an hour.' She glanced at him, he'd rolled on his side now and was perched on his elbow, looking at her, his eyes still heavy with desire. 'Okay if I use your shower?'

'Feel free. Do you need help?' he asked suggestively.

'We don't have time, I must get to work.' She wagged a finger at him then kissed him tenderly. 'I'm sorry but it's a ten-hour shift, so I'm working until midnight. I'm off all day tomorrow, though.'

'I'll meet you after work for a drink, then.' He reached out to grab her hand as she pushed back the duvet. 'We can spend the day together tomorrow, yes?'

She nodded. 'How long are you here for?' She had been so delighted to see him she hadn't thought to ask him that earlier.

'I go back Sunday evening.'

That soon. 'You timed that well. I've got Sunday morning off, too.'

He pulled her back towards him, wrapping her in the warmth of his embrace. 'I see that you are still wearing my pendant,' he whispered in her ear.

'I never take it off,' she confessed. She wriggled reluctantly out of his grasp, wishing that she didn't have to go, that she could spend the rest of the afternoon in his bed. 'Tempting as you are, I need to move, or I'll be late.'

She dashed into the bathroom and turned on the shower, reaching for the complimentary shower gel and lathering herself under the cascading water, happiness flowing through her. Eddie loved her and had flown over to tell her so. She felt like she was dreaming. For a few minutes, she enjoyed it, the joy of being loved and of loving back. Then reality kicked in. On Sunday evening Eddie would be going back to France and she would be here in Majorca. They would be hundreds of miles apart. How could this relationship work? Where did they go from here? She shrugged the doubts from her mind. Just enjoy the here and now, Jess, you've the weekend together. Make the most of it.

Thankfully Ziggy wasn't changing her shift, he merely wanted to know if she could take over running the quiz in the lounge this evening as Melanie, the rep who was supposed to be doing it, had laryngitis. Jess readily agreed. That meant Eddie could have a drink in the lounge and they could spend the evening together, even though she was working. She might even persuade him to join in the quiz.

He did, joining a group of five other holidaymakers and turning out to be quite an expert on history, leading his team to victory. It was a fun evening.

And an even better night.

***

'Morning, *ma chérie*. What shall we do today?' Eddie woke her with a kiss on the nose.

She yawned and stretched. 'Do you fancy doing some sightseeing?' She never had time to see that much of the island, and there was one place in particular she'd always wanted to go.

'I'd love to. Do you have anywhere in mind?'

'I've always wanted to go to the Caves of Drach. Do you fancy it? It's really popular with the holidaymakers.'

'The Caves of Drach?' Eddie sat up, reached for his phone and tapped in the name. Immediately the website came up, opening with the iconic image of musicians in a boat rowing across the lake at the bottom of the caves. Jess had been told it was a beautiful experience.

'It looks very romantic. Let's do it.' He reached out and traced her cheek tenderly with his finger. 'Shall we get ready now? We can make a day of it?'

The caves were more beautiful than Jess had ever imagined. Huge stalactites hung down from the roof of the cave, almost meeting the giant stalagmites growing up from the cave floor in some places and forming incredible shapes in others. Strategically placed lights gave it a hauntingly atmospheric glow. It was like stepping back in time. And worth the ridiculously long queue in the stifling afternoon heat to get in.

'According to legend, pirates have hidden treasure in these caves, and dragons have roamed here,' Jess whispered as she and Eddie walked, hand in hand, along the slope and down into the depths of the cave, marvelling at the rock formations and the illuminated pools of water.

'I can believe it. They are *magnifique!*' Eddie paused for a moment to take photos. 'So many centuries of history.'

When they finally reached the last cavern, it was time for the grand finale – the underground concert that Jess had heard so much about. They managed to get a seat in the front row alongside the lake, and Eddie reached for her hand, caressing it in his, as they watched the lights dancing on the dark waters and waited eagerly for the concert to begin. Then there was a hush as the haunting sound of music filled the air and a boat containing a string quartet was rowed across the lake. Jess felt Eddie squeeze her hand as if he, too, was lost in the enchantment of the moment.

'That was wonderful,' Eddie said when they surfaced from the caves again. 'A truly spectacular experience.'

'Magical is the word I'd use,' Jess told him. 'I felt like I'd been transported to another world. An ancient, mystical world. Imagine how awed people must have been when they first discovered those caves hundreds of years ago. They must have thought they'd stepped into the Land of the Gods.'

'It's been a truly wonderful day. I wish I wasn't going back tomorrow. *Tu me manque*s,' he whispered, pulling her close to him.

'Sorry my French is a bit too rusty to translate that,' she admitted. 'But I'm sure it's very romantic.'

'You English translate it as 'I miss you' but actually it means 'you are missing from me'.' He kissed her neck. 'That is how I feel when you aren't with me. That part of me is missing. You are *mon coeur*, my heart.'

You are missing from me. That was the most romantic thing she'd ever heard. And was exactly how she felt when Eddie wasn't with her.

She was getting soft.

He had his hands around her waist now, his face so close they were nose to nose. 'And how about you, *ma chérie*? Am I missing from you when I'm not with you?'

321

'Yes,' she admitted. She reached up to touch his cheek. He hadn't shaved that morning and it felt stubbly.

He seized her wrist and kissed the palm of her hand. 'Today has been so special already, let's carry on the magic by having a meal together.'

He was right, it had been a magical day. She'd missed him. She didn't want to say goodbye to him.
Yet tomorrow she had to. Again.

They dined at a restaurant on the sea front. Steak and salad followed by a delicious pecan crème brulée and accompanied by plenty of rich, deep red merlot. They spent the evening chatting, giggling, finishing each other's sentences, and ended up back in Eddie's hotel room with neither of them actually suggesting it.

'I don't want to say goodbye to you, Jess. I want you to be near me, for us to be able to see each other every day. Come and work in France, please,' he said as they lay cuddled up in his bed much later. 'Live with me.'

Chapter Thirty Four

Live with him?

For a moment Jess thought she'd imagined it.

'What did you say?' She asked, her heart hammering. She must have misheard. Eddie couldn't have asked her to live with him. Could he?

He turned to her, wrapped his arms around her, face to face, eyes meeting. She could see the depth of his love there. He was serious.

'Come and live with me, *ma chérie*,' he said. 'You'll love France. You'll find a job there easily, there's loads of hotels and holiday camps that need people with your experience. And until you do I'll look after you.' He kissed her. 'Please say you'll think about it.'

Why did he have to ask her that now? After such a perfect day? On their last night together?

'You don't like the idea?' She could *feel* the disappointment in his voice. His arms relaxed his hold on her. 'Jess? Speak to me.'

She wriggled out of his arms, sat up, hugged her knees, searched desperately for the right words.

'I can't. I'm sorry. It's too much, too soon.'

'How can it be so when we love each other?' He was sitting up, too. Beside her, but oceans apart. She could feel the distance her words had made. 'You do love me, don't you, Jess?'

'Yes, of course I do.' She turned to him, her eyes imploring him to understand. 'But... living together is massive, Eddie. We barely know each other. I can't give up everything and move to France with you. It wouldn't work.'

'If we love each other we could make it work.'

'But what if it doesn't?' She hated to see the disappointment in his eyes. 'Put it on the other foot. Would you give up everything to move to Majorca with me?'

'I would if things were different, but I have a home and a business in France whereas you live in hotel rooms here – which I couldn't share. And your work is seasonal. You can work anywhere.'

'Right now, my job's here. And my home is in England.' Except she still lived with her mum, didn't she? And her mum was selling the house.

'You said you wanted a home of your own. And a career change,' Eddie reminded her.

'I do but I can't up sticks to France and move in with you just like that.' She could hear the panic in her voice and saw the shadow cross Eddie's face. Reaching out, she touched his cheek in an effort to soothe, reassure. 'There's no rush, is there? Let's take it slowly, get to know each other more. We can Facetime every day, message each other. I'll fly over when I have a weekend off. And you can come here, like you've done today.'

He placed his hand on her cheek, so they were facing each other. His eyes searched hers. What was he looking for? Sincerity? She held his gaze, hoping he could see the love she felt more than the panic. Finally, he nodded. 'You're right. We should take it slower. Don't worry, *mon coeur,* we will work it out.' He pulled her into his arms and held her tight but as they embraced Jess sensed she'd hurt him. He'd been jilted by Yvette, yet still entrusted his heart to her and she was refusing to live with him.

Well what did he expect? If you counted the days they'd spent together it wasn't even a month. Far too soon for a commitment like that.

This was why she'd never wanted a serious relationship. Love was like walking through a minefield and it was a path she hadn't wanted to walk, but despite all her intentions, she'd fallen in love. And now she was trying to keep her head and not hurt Eddie in the process.

Why did love have to be so complicated?

***

So here they were, at the airport again saying goodbye. He'd swore he'd never give his heart to anyone after Yvette had trampled on it, but along came Jess and it seemed that his heart was going to be permanently pierced by the pain of goodbyes.

'*Je t'aime*' he said, holding Jess close, kissing her one more time. 'You are my heartbeat.'

'I love you, too.' She kissed him, hugged him. Tears brimmed in her eyes. 'I'll see you very soon. And I'll speak to you tonight.'

He watched her go, her red hair swinging as she walked. He noticed a couple of men stop, look back at her. She was the kind of woman that men looked at twice, the kind of woman that you were proud to be seen with. *And she loved him.* Yet it was so difficult. Who knew when they would see each other again? But seeing each other now and again was better than not having Jess in his life at all.

***

'We've sold the house.' Jess could hear the excitement in Mum's voice, she'd Facetimed her for a quick chat after work. 'And we've found this lovely little cottage in the Cotswolds. It's so pretty, Jess. You'll love it. It's on the outskirts of a village, so near to facilities, but it backs onto fields. Here's a picture of it.' She held a photo of a chocolate box cottage up to the camera. 'Isn't it pretty?'

'It's gorgeous. Perfect for you both,' said Jess. 'I'm so pleased for you. When do you move?'

'We're aiming for the end of next month. It'll be nice to enjoy the summer there.' She put the picture down and pushed back her glasses – a sure sign that something was bothering her. 'There's two bedrooms so don't worry, there'll be somewhere for you to stay when you come home.'

'Thanks Mum, but actually I'm going to get a flat of my own. I thought that I could buy one and rent it out on a short-term lease while I'm away. It's time I had my own home.' The idea of renting the flat out had only just come to her, but it seemed the perfect solution. Then she wouldn't be a gooseberry in her mum's love nest and she'd have a base if she changed her job.

Suddenly a text pinged across the screen.

Hello, ma chèrie. It was Eddie. *Are you free to talk?*

'I've got to go, Mum. Eddie's trying to call me. I'll talk to you again in the week. And it's fab news about the house. I'm really pleased for you.'

'Okay dear, give Eddie my love.' Pam waved as Jess exited the call and switched to the other screen.

Instinctively her face broke into a wide grin as Eddie's image filled the screen and asked how she was.

'Okay. Missing you. Sorry to keep you waiting, I was speaking to Mum.'

'And *tu me menques aussi*,' Eddie told her. Why did the French accent sound so sexy? Especially the way Eddie said it. Much sexier than the English. *I am missing you, too*.

'I only spoke to you last night,' she told him. They had tried to talk to each other every day in the two weeks since he'd returned home. Eddie often worked at the restaurant until late so they both touched base when they'd finished work.

'It's not the same as seeing you, holding you.' He pulled a mock-doleful face. 'I miss you most at night. You are *mon coeur,* it is difficult to sleep without you.'

'So that's all you want me for?' She teased.

He gazed at her through the screen, his eyes smouldering. She loved him like crazy. How was she going to get by until she could see him again?

They chatted for a while, both of them reluctant to end the call, as usual, declaring their love for each other, trying to work out a time when they could see each other again. It was impossible for Jess to take a couple of days off for the foreseeable future, and Eddie was too busy at the restaurant to come over again. When they finally did say goodbye – both counting to three so they could end the call at the same time – Jess felt a surge of loss. She longed to see Eddie in the flesh again, to talk to him, feel his arms around her and his lips on hers.

She walked over to the fridge, took out a bottle of rosé and poured herself a glass. She couldn't carry on like this. Eddie in France and her in Majorca. She either had to finish with him or find a way to be with him. A long-distance relationship didn't suit her.

She rolled the cold wine around in her mouth before swallowing it.

She didn't want to finish with him.

So she had to find a way to be with him. One that didn't involve living with him as he'd suggested. She was way too independent for that... She took another sip of wine then opened up her laptop and logged on. There could be a simple solution to this.

Chapter Thirty Five

'I'm thinking of leaving.' She told Libby as they limbered up at the pool the next morning. 'Do you think Ziggy will go ape?'

'Leaving? Why?' Libby asked, jogging on the spot. She stopped and stared at Jess. 'You're going to France to be with Eddie, aren't you?'

'I'm going to try to. There's a holiday resort in Marseille, about twenty minutes from where Eddie lives. They're looking for resort staff. Accommodation's provided so I wouldn't need to worry about that. I thought if I moved there me and Eddie could give our relationship a proper go.'

'Relationship! I never thought I'd hear you say the word.' Libby picked up her bottle of water from the nearby table and took a swig. 'Here come our ladies. You'll have to tell me more about it later.'

Jess waved at the group of ladies in assorted swimwear heading towards them. 'Morning, ladies! I hope you're all ready to do some stretching today. Libby and I have some great moves for you.'

'Want to show me them later, babe,' a youth sitting at a table by the side of the pool wise-cracked.

'Sure. Do you want me to try the headlock or the arm breaker?' Jess quipped back. A roar of laughter greeted this, and the lad raised his glass good-humouredly.

It was another ten-hour shift, so she had no chance to speak to Eddie all day, and he was out that evening. They exchanged messages of course, but it wasn't the same as seeing his image on the screen. Which was nowhere as good as seeing him in person, but at least it made her feel closer to him.

'This is crazy,' she said to Libby as they sat having a drink together in Jess's room when they'd finally finished work. 'Eddie and I hardly have time to talk.'

'I don't know if it will be any better if you transfer to a holiday resort in France,' Libby told her. 'The hours will still be as long. Okay you'll see each other on your day off, and the occasional evening, but that's all.'

'I know, but what else can I do? It's the only way I can move there quickly. I'm not trained at anything else.'

'Have you thought of taking up Eddie's offer of moving in with him?'

'No way. We need to know each other a lot more before we get to that stage.'

'Very wise. Men aren't easy to live with. I lived with an ex once and he drove me mad. I moved back out within a month.' Libby said.

Jess got up and fetched her laptop. 'I'll show you the place I was thinking of working at.' She sat down by Libby, opened her laptop and booted it up.

Libby leaned forward, picked up the wine bottle on the table in front of them and refilled their glasses. 'What's it called?'

'*Joyeux Vacances*. I saved it to my favourites.' Jess clicked on the link at the top of the screen and selected the website. It sprang open.

'It looks like a nice place,' Libby said, peering at the screen.

Jess scrolled down. 'Hey, this job has only just been listed. It sounds perfect.' She read out the job description.

Entertainment organiser required at family run hotel. Must have good customer skills, experience at working with the public, able to organise daytrips, arrange entertainment for the guests, experience at working with children necessary. Five day week, eight hour shift, some weekend and evening work.

'What do you think? It's fewer hours than here and it's only a short drive to Eddie's house.'

'You know his address?' Libby asked.

'Yes, I asked for it, said I was planning on going over for a weekend a bit later in the year when we aren't so busy here.'

Libby read the job ad again. 'This looks ideal. And look, you can apply online. Go on, what are you waiting for?' She urged.

Why not? What had she got to lose?

She filled in the application form – getting Libby to check everything over to make sure she hadn't made any typos – attached her CV, then pressed 'send' before she could change her mind.

'I can't believe I've just done that,' she said to Libby as she closed down her laptop.

'I think it's exciting. And dead romantic. Who'd have thought you'd change your job and move to another country to be with a man.'

Who indeed. Was she doing the right thing?

Relax, all she'd done was apply for a job. She might not even get it. And if she did she didn't have to take it.

***

Two days later a reply pinged into Jess's inbox. The manager of the hotel wanted her to come for an interview. Why hadn't she realised that? Of course, they wouldn't offer her a job without an interview. And there was no way Ziggy would give her time off to attend an interview in France. What could she do?

333

'Why don't you ask them if you can do a Skype interview?' Libby suggested when she told her. 'Lots of overseas companies do that nowadays. They know you're working in a resort over here so should understand that you can't take time off to fly to France for a job interview.'

It was worth a try. She pinged an email off to the hotel manager explaining her position and asking if they could interview her by Skype instead. And Libby was right, the hotel agreed. The day after the interview they emailed her to say she'd got the job. Could she start next month? She stared in disbelief at the email for a moment then read it again. And again. She'd actually done it. She'd got herself a job and accommodation in France. If she wanted it.

Did she?

Thankfully she wasn't on duty until later, so she went for a long walk along the beach to think things over. It was a drastic step to quit her job and move to France to be near Eddie. Should she take it?

Her mum always made a list when she had an important decision to make, wrote down the pros and cons. She said it helped her see things clearly. Jess didn't have a notebook and pen on her, so she made the list in her mind as she walked along the seashore, the warm, azure water trickling over her feet.

Pros.

She got to be near Eddie. They could see each other every day if they wanted. Spend weekends together. Go to bed together. Wake up with each other. That was a definite pro. She stood still for a moment, turned and gazed out at the horizon. There should be other pros surely?

She got to spend some time in France, that was a pro. And a job change. The hours here could be exhausting.

It gave her chance to find out if she and Eddie worked.

Okay, now for the Cons.

She and Eddie might not work. Within a few weeks they might be tired of each other, then she'd have given up her job, her friends here, for nothing.

She might not like her new job.

She might not like living in France.

She might be making a complete fool of herself.

'*Hola,* Jessica. You look very thoughtful.'

Jess turned at the sound of Damián's voice. He was standing behind her, hand in hand with Marta.

'Is everything alright?' Marta asked, her eyes clouding with concern.

Jess nodded. She thought of how Damián had given his job up in mainland Spain to be with Marta in Majorca. They were happy, she knew that. It had worked for them.

'I've been offered a job in France,' she told them. 'I'm trying to decide whether to accept it or not.'

The couple exchanged knowing glances.

'Near Eddie?' Damián asked.

Jess nodded.

'I think you must like him very much,' Marta said softly.

'I do. But I wonder if it's enough to give up my job here.'

'Do it, Jess. Take a chance on love,' Damián told her. He squeezed Marta's hand. 'What have you got to lose? You can always get a job repping somewhere else if it doesn't work out.'

'Whereas if you don't go you could lose the love of your life.' Marta smiled into Damián's eyes.

'You're right. Thanks guys. I'd better get back to work now.' As she set off back towards the hotel she thought of Damián's words. *Take a chance on love.*

Yes, she would do that. He was right, she could always get another job if it didn't work out. What was the worst that could happen?

Her heart being broken. That's what. Something that had never happened to her before.

She logged onto her laptop and accepted the job before she could change her mind. Then she went to find Libby.

'OMG, that's amazing!' Libby squealed. She threw her arms around Jess in delight. 'I'm going to miss you, but I'm so pleased for you. Have you told Eddie? I bet he's made up.'

'I haven't mentioned it to him. I want it to be a surprise.'

'Fancy you having such a romantic streak. I'd love to see his face when you turn up with your suitcase and tell him you're living and working twenty minutes' drive from him.'

She couldn't wait either. She missed Eddie so much. He'd begged her to come and live with him again when they were Facetiming yesterday. 'I want to feel my arms around you again, to wake up with you beside me, *mon coeur*,' he said, his eyes soulful. 'It's been so long.'

'I'm due a couple of days off soon. I'll see if I can get a flight over,' she'd promised.

She was longing to be in his arms again, taste his kisses, feel his body against hers.

Not long now.

All she had to do was give notice to Ziggy. A month her contract said, which would time it just right. She would have three days to spend with Eddie before starting her new job. Perfect.

As she'd expected, Ziggy wasn't pleased to learn of her decision. 'France? You're quitting just before the main holiday season to go and work in a hotel in bloody France,' He exploded. 'Why the hell do you want to work there?' Then his eyes narrowed. 'It's that French boyfriend of yours, isn't it? Things getting serious with you two?'

She nodded. 'It's hard being so far apart. He wants me to go and live with him, but I think that's too big a step. This job will give us chance to get to know each other better.' She took a breath. 'I'm sorry if I'm leaving you in the lurch.'

Ziggy thrust his hands in his pockets and studied her for a moment. Then his expression relaxed. 'Okay, if that's what you want to do. I guess I've got time to find someone else before the busy season starts. I need you to work out your notice, mind, and to show your replacement the ropes.' He paused. 'I hope it works out for you, Jess, but if it doesn't... Well... You'll always have a job with me. You're a good worker.'

'Thank you.' She could hardly believe it. He was letting her go without a fight. One month's time and she'd be with Eddie. Happiness flooded through her. She couldn't wait to see his face when she turned up on his doorstep.

Chapter Thirty Six

A month later

Jess looked out of the taxi window as it stopped outside an exquisite cottage, her stomach fluttering with nervousness and excitement. She was actually here, in France, parked outside Eddie's house. She'd checked last night that he'd be home, pretending she wanted to know so she could FaceTime him. She smiled to herself, imagining the delight on his face when he saw her. It had been so hard keeping the secret from him this past month, but she'd managed it.

She paid the taxi driver and wheeled her case up the drive. The curtains were open, and the light was on. Good, Eddie was home. Her face broke into a smile as she imagined his expression when he saw her, and she quickened her step, eager to see him again, to feel his arms around her, his lips on hers. As she got nearer to the window she saw Eddie walk into the room, a mug in his hand. She was wondering whether to knock on the window to attract his attention or to carry on to the front door when a woman sashayed into the room behind him. She was tall, slim, shoulder length dark hair, elegantly dressed, and pretty in a well-groomed sort of way. Jess frowned. Who the hell was she? The woman had a mug in her hand too and looked very much at home.

Jess bit her lip as she watched Eddie sit on the sofa, the woman joined him, they both put their mugs down on the table and faced each other, talking earnestly. It all looked very cosy. Jess felt a surge of anger, was he living with someone? The two-timing rat! How stupid of her to give up her job and fly all the way here, ready to start a new life with a guy she hardly knew.

Don't jump to conclusions. Things might not be how they seem, she reminded herself, thinking of the episodes with Ross, and Sleazy Simon. But when the woman leant forward and kissed Eddie on the cheek it was like a stab through Jess's heart. She blinked back the tears then gasped as she saw Eddie push the woman away and jump up out of his seat. He looked angry, fists clenched at his side. He obviously hadn't wanted that kiss, she realised in relief.

The woman flounced out of the room and Jess stepped away from the window, turning to the front door as it was flung open. The woman stepped out, her face a mask of anger, then her eyes fixed on Jess, flitted down to the suitcase by her side, and her lips curled with disdain. 'So, *this* is the woman you've turned me down for?' She sneered.

Jess folded her arms. 'Who the hell are you? And what are you doing trying to snog Eddie?'

'Jess!' Eddie stood at the doorway, his expression was incredulous. He held out his arms and walked towards her, a beaming smile on his face. '*Mon coeur*, what a lovely surprise. You managed to get a weekend off? Why didn't you tell me you were coming?'

'Because I wanted to surprise you,' Jess told him as he wrapped his arms around her. 'Turned out I was the one who got the surprise.' She glared pointedly at the woman.

'You saw Yvette kiss me?' Eddie's voice was soft. He pulled her closer. 'I am so sorry. She just turned up here unexpectedly saying she wanted to talk. I should never have let her in.'

Yvette? His ex-fiancée? 'You've got a nerve,' Jess told Yvette, trying to keep her voice level and not reveal how angry and upset she was – the depths of her emotions shocked her. 'You dump Eddie at the altar then come back a few years later and try to wreck his new relationship.'

'*Mon Dieu!* Don't be so dramatic! It was just *un petit bisou.*' Yvette said scornfully. 'You're both welcome to each other.' She marched off to a silver car parked on the drive, got in and drove off.

'It is wonderful to see you,' Eddie said softly, lowering his mouth to hers and drawing her into a deep, lingering kiss.

It was good to be in Eddie's arms again, to feel his lips on hers. When they finally came up for air she asked the question that was bugging her. 'So, you had no idea that Yvette was coming?'

'None at all.' He kept his left arm around her waist, grabbing the suitcase handle with his right hand. 'Come inside and we will talk.'

He led her inside, into the lounge. 'First, let me do you a drink, you must need one after travelling here – and the scene you just witnessed,' he squeezed her shoulder tenderly, concern etched on his face as he studied hers.

She hoped he couldn't read her conflicted emotions. She was still trying to come to terms with the fact that she'd actually been jealous of Yvette. Jealousy was a totally new experience for her. 'Actually, I could do with a glass of wine.'

'Of course.' He released her and put the suitcase by the side of the sofa. 'Please, sit down. I will be back in a moment.'

Eddie returned with two glasses of chilled red wine, then sat down beside her on the sofa and explained how Yvette had turned up asking him if they could talk. He'd refused at first. but she'd begged him to hear her out, so he'd let her in and she'd told him how much she'd missed him, how she regretted walking out on him, and wanted him to give her another chance.

'I should never had let her in, but part of me wanted her to apologise and regret her action. Not because I wanted her back...' He explained quickly.

'Because you wanted the chance to turn her down, to get a bit of revenge?' Jess asked gently. She could understand that. She guessed she'd feel the same way if someone had jilted her at the altar.

He nodded, his eyes troubled. 'I didn't expect her to kiss me. I am so sorry that you had to witness that, but I did push her away. Instantly.'

'I know.' She took a deep breath. 'Are you sure you have no feelings for Yvette at all? Not even a pang?' She had to know before they got too involved. While she could still walk away.

'Of course not. I love *you*.' He placed his finger under her chin and gently tilted it up, so he could see her face. 'You believe me, don't you, *mon coeur*?'

She could see the love shining in his eyes and nodded. 'Yes, I do.'

'Good, then let us enjoy our weekend together. I can't believe you are here, I wasn't expecting to see you for another month at least. When did you learn you had the weekend off? You didn't mention it when we spoke the night before last.'

She grinned at him. 'Actually, I'm not here for the weekend. I've given up my job and moved over here to work so we can be together.'

His face lit up. '*C'est merveilleux*! I have missed you so much.' He leaned forward and enveloped her in a tight embrace. 'This is wonderful news. Why didn't you tell me? I would have made plans, got the house ready, but no matter, you wanted to surprise me. And it is a lovely surprise.' His lips found hers and this time the kiss was deeper, longer. Then he caressed her cheek as he gazed at her. 'It won't take long to sort things out. You can have the big wardrobe in my... our room...' He corrected himself with a smile.

Oh no, he was assuming she was moving in. She had to say something quickly. 'I'm not moving in with you, Eddie. I've got a room at the hotel I'm working at.'

Disappointment clouded his face as he drew away. 'You don't want to live with me? But I thought...'

She wrapped her arms around his neck, pulling him back to her. 'I do,' she said softly. 'But not yet. it's too soon. If I stay at the hotel we will both have our own space, it'll give us time to get to know each other. I don't want to rush things. This is too important.'

Time seemed suspended as they gazed into each other's eyes. She saw doubt and confusion on Eddie's face and hoped he could see the love on hers. A wave of relief flooded over her as she saw him relax and nod slowly. 'You are staying here this weekend, though?'

'Yes. And the days I have off. If you want me to.'

He smiled, brown eyes dark with desire. 'Let me show you how much I want you to,' he said softly.

***

Later, as they lay in each other's arms, Eddie hitched himself up on one elbow and looked down at her. 'I still can't believe that you've moved to France to be with me.'

'I can't believe it either,' she admitted.

'Does this mean we're in a proper relationship?'

She thought about that. 'I guess it does,' she agreed.

'And that scares you?' his voice was soft.

'Sort of. I don't do serious. And this is…' She hesitated.

'This is serious,' he finished for her.

She guessed swapping jobs and moving to another country to be with a man was pretty serious. 'I wanted to be with you,' she confessed.

'And I, *mon coeur* want to be with you. Forever.'

Forever. That was even scarier. Jess had never thought she'd commit to one man. What was happening to her?

'Don't look so worried. Let's take it one day at a time,' Eddie told her.

One day at a time. Yes. She could do that.

Chapter Thirty Seven

A few months later.

'It's lovely. I'm so pleased you're settled over here,' Pam said as Jess showed her and Phil around the cottage. They'd flown over for a mid-week visit.

'Your mum's made up that you've finally settled down in a proper relationship and got a permanent home,' Phil told Jess. 'She thought it would never happen.'

'Maybe there might even be a wedding next,' Pam said, with a smile.

'I have proposed, but you know Jess and her fear of committing,' Eddie said, walking in on the tail end of the conversation.

Trust Mum to be talking about weddings as soon as Eddie turned up. He'd worked at the restaurant this morning, deliberately giving them time to catch up before he joined them.

Eddie wrapped his arm around Jess's shoulders, pulled her to him and kissed her on the cheek. 'I'm happy to have Jess living with me. There is no rush for marriage, but I hope that one day she will say yes.' He smiled into Jess's eyes.

He had proposed. Twice. Once was the first night she'd moved in two months ago. At first, she'd stayed over at Eddie's house on the occasional night, but soon she'd been practically living there so it had made sense to move in. Eddie had helped bring her things over, cooked a special meal for them both, then asked her to marry him. The panic she felt must have shown on her face because he had reached over and placed his hand reassuringly on hers. 'I am sorry, *ma chérie*, it is too soon for you, I know. I just wanted you to know how much I love you.'

'I love you, too,' she had whispered back. 'And I'm not saying never but…'

'But you are not ready yet. I understand. As long as it isn't no, not ever. It isn't, is it?'

She had swallowed and shook her head. 'It's no, not now,' she told him, but even as she said the words she wondered if she would ever be able to say yes. Eddie had well and truly snuck into her heart, but the thought of getting married terrified her. Moving in with Eddie was a big enough step for her to take. She was flattered though, that he was prepared to take that step with her after his experience with Yvette. He must really love her. And she loved him.

She couldn't believe how at ease she soon felt, how comfortable it was to share their lives. The feeling of being loved like this was something she'd never experienced before. She loved waking up with him, coming home from work to the home they shared, going to bed entwined together. She couldn't imagine not being with him.

But when he proposed again she panicked once more. Marriage was still a massive step. Too big a step for now, but one that she felt she might be comfortable taking in the not-too-distant future. Footloose and fancy-free Jess was finally settling down, putting down roots. She loved being with Eddie and living in France. She had never known life could be so good.

So she had shook her head slowly and smiled at him. 'I love you, but it's still too soon,' she'd said.

Now, as she stood in the lounge of their cottage with her mum and Phil, she realised that marriage wasn't such a terrifying step after all.

'Ask me next year,' she said.

Eddie's eyes lit up and he kissed her tenderly on the cheek. '*Oui, certainement mon coeur*,' he said, and she could hear the happiness in his voice. Then he turned to Pam and Phil. 'I've booked a table at my restaurant for us all tonight. I hope that you will like that.'

'It sounds delightful,' Pam said. 'We'll look forward to it.'

'You've got a lovely place here,' Phil said. 'I love the beamed ceiling.'

Eddie reached for Jess's hand. 'Thank you. It suits us, doesn't it, Jess?'

'It's perfect,' she agreed. Life was perfect. She couldn't imagine feeling any happier than she was right now.

'Come on, let me show you the garden, it's a mild day so we could have refreshments on the terrace,' Eddie said.

'That sounds lovely,' Pam said with a smile.

As she and Eddie walked hand in hand down the garden path, Eddie pointing out the various plants to Phil, Jess realised that she'd more or less agreed to marry Eddie.

Epilogue

Two years later

'You look amazing.' Libby said as Jess smoothed down her dress. 'That dress is gorgeous – very you. Remember I said you'd have a rainbow wedding dress? You always have to be a little bit different.' She shook her head. 'I still can't believe you're getting married – and before me! I thought you were the eternal bachelor girl.' Libby and her fiancé Connor were getting married later that year, and Libby had already chosen her very traditional white lace wedding dress.

Jess couldn't quite believe it either, but these past two years with Eddie had been so wonderful she knew she was ready to take the step. She looked in the mirror at her fitted white dress with its multi-coloured bottom layer. It was perfect. She'd seen the design on Pinterest and loved it so much that she copied it herself, buying a fairly simple, white wedding gown then paying a local artist to carefully airbrush the colours in a wide border along the bottom of the skirt; vibrant rows of red, orange, yellow, pink and blue all fading into each other. She'd repeated the colours in the flowers of her bouquet and the

353

bridesmaids' dresses. Libby, her maid of honour, was dressed in pink, much to Libby's delight, and the other four bridesmaids were each dressed in one of the other colours. Eddie, Ross, and Phil – who was giving her away – Ned and Jake were all wearing silver grey suits with a different coloured tie. Red for Eddie as he said that reminded him of Jess, and was the predominant of the colours.

Jess studied her hair, swept up in a boho chic half-up, half-down style, adorned with matching coloured flowers. Had she gone overboard with the colours?

'Are you sure I look okay?' she asked, suddenly unsure of herself and conscious that all eyes would be on her today.

'You look bloody gorgeous. Doesn't she, Carly?' Libby asked as the door opened and Carly stepped in, holding the hand of Rosa who looked so cute with her dark curls tied up in deep yellow ribbons that matched her buttercup yellow dress.

Carly nodded approvingly. 'I must admit that when you said you were going to have the hem of your dress dyed I thought you'd lost your senses, but it looks spectacular.' She walked over to Jess and gave her a hug. 'You and Eddie are going to be so happy together.'

Jess returned the hug, thinking again how amazing it was that she and Carly were so close, almost like sisters, so close that she no longer thought of her as 'Charlotte', her snobby cousin. Carly had been delighted when Jess had asked if Rosa could be bridesmaid and had helped her plan the wedding. Ross, of course, was the best man.

The other bridesmaids filed in: Gerri, Mae, and Becky's little daughter Amy, followed by Danni and Mandy. They'd all flown over from England yesterday, with Jess's mum, Phil, Ned and Jake and stopped the night at the chateau where Jess and Eddie were having the ceremony. It had its own chapel and a wonderful reception room.

'Wow! That dress is stunning,' Danni told her. 'Eddie's one lucky guy, but then I've already told him that.'

'Thank you,' Jess said with a smile. 'And thank you everyone for coming over here and making my day so special.' She beamed at them all.

'Don't be daft, how could we miss your wedding?' Becky said. 'None of us thought we'd ever see the day!'

Laughing, they all gathered their colourful bouquets and headed for the small chapel nestling in a leafy corner by the lake.

Jess's mum and Phil were waiting for her outside the chapel, so were Ned and Jake. Her two brothers whistled as Jess swept over to them, Libby and Mae holding the train of her dress.

'I'm so happy for you, darling,' her mum told her, her eyes brimming with tears.

Phil stepped beside her and hooked his arm. 'Shall we?'

'Is Eddie inside?' Jess asked, taking his arm.

'He's been waiting for ages, looks like a cat on hot bricks. I think he's scared you might not show up,' Ned jested.

Ned was only joking, but Jess wondered if Eddie was a bit worried about that. She nodded at Phil. 'Let's go.'

She held her head up and walked slowly down the aisle, her eyes fixed on Eddie standing beside Ross. He turned as she reached him and smiled, his eyes brimming with love.

'You look beautiful,' he whispered as she took her place by his side. *'Je t'aime, ma chérie.'*

'Je t'aime, aussi,' she whispered. 'Forever.'

The End

Acknowledgements

As always, grateful thanks to my husband Dave for the constant supply of refreshments while I work, for being a sounding board to my ideas, and for booking the anniversary trip to Majorca that inspired this book. To Dave and Naomi for their eagle eyes when checking the proofs and to my daughters for their constant inspiration. I love you all.

Thanks also to my fantastic editors at Accent Press; Kate Ellis, Caroline Kirkpatrick and Katrin Lloyd for their expertise and support.

I'm indebted to the many Facebook author friends, in particular members of The Romantic Novelists' Association, who take the time to answer my queries and are always willing to share writing tips, experiences and advice. You are all amazing.

Last, but definitely not least, many, many thanks to all you wonderful readers for buying my books and spurring me on to write even more stories. Without you, I'd be writing in the dark.

About The Author

Karen King is a multi-published author of romantic fiction and children's books. She has published five romantic novels, 120 children's books, two young adult novels, and several short stories for women's magazines.

'The Cornish Hotel by the Sea', published by Accent Press, became an international bestseller, reaching the top hundred in the Kindle charts in both the UK and in Australia, and #2 and #3 in Holiday Reads respectively.

She is member of the Romantic Novelists' Association, the Society of Authors, and the Society of Women Writers and Journalists. Karen now lives in Spain and spends her time writing romances while her husband, Dave, grows vegetables and tends to the zillions of fruit trees on their land – when she isn't sunbathing or swimming in the pool, that is!

Also by Karen King

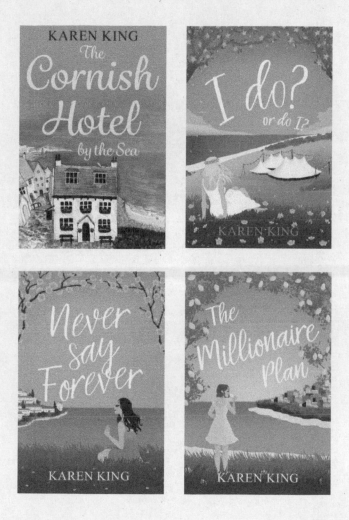

Proudly published by Accent Press

www.accentpress.co.uk